To
Suzanne
Luke
Rachel

Mum and Dad

Chapter 1

I picked up my phone on the second ring. 'We've been watching you and want to talk.'

Another bloody prank call, I thought. We seemed to have been inundated with them recently.

'Who are you?' I asked, irritated that my thought pattern had been broken.

'A higher authority than the one you're currently with.'

Having been employed by MI5 for the past couple of years, I was somewhat sceptical. 'What sort of scam is this?'

'I understand your concern, the head of HR will call and then we can talk again.' The line went dead and I sat gazing at the phone, willing it to ring. After several minutes I was about to report a crank call when the name of the HR manager flashed up on the screen. He asked me to join him immediately for a meeting.

After running up two flights of stairs, I felt a little breathless walking across to his desk. He stood talking to my boss and following a brief handshake we sat down.

'I gather you've already had one call this morning, I do wish these people would follow procedure for this sort of thing. It saves a lot of confusion and distrust. However, you've been selected for a special operation, working with individuals from other national agencies. I'm afraid I don't have any more details at this time, they'll contact you again shortly and no doubt tell all. I'm just here to confirm the legitimacy of the undertaking. Whether you take the role is up to you, but if you decline the offer I can assure you there'll be no effect on your career progression.'

'Who are these people?' I asked.

'I can't say any more, they'll give you the background.'

'Do these operations come up often?' I felt a little bewildered and was trying to make sense of it all.

'Once in a blue moon,' came the terse response.

'It may be a good opportunity,' piped up my boss, 'though I'd be sorry to see you go.'

'You'll be contacted again shortly by the powers that be, good luck.' With that the meeting was over and I wandered back to my work station in somewhat of a confused state. Almost immediately the phone rang again. It sounds as corny as hell but we agreed to meet at Cleopatra's Needle on the Victoria Embankment.

I arrived and, gazing out across the river, heard the same voice behind me.

'Don't turn around, just listen. We work closely with NATO, but we're not part of the FBI, CIA, MI5 or MI6. We are however funded legitimately through government sources from around the world, but nobody would admit to it Surveillance is part of our work, that could mean tracking and interviewing terrorists, working in political hotspots, dealing with the mafia, drug barons, business despots, in fact anyone with a track record of not playing it straight. Our job is to take these people out by fair means or foul, but quietly. If you join us you'll become a wealthy man, but you could also die We lose about five per cent of our manpower in the line of duty. You will continue to be paid through MI5, which should confirm our legitimacy. Are you interested?'

Interested? I was staggered. 'Why me?' I blurted out.

'You're a bright boy. Language skills, athletic an enquiring mind. you have no real ties and the perfect personality profile for this job. Whether you take the job is up to you.'

'How much?'

'One hundred and twenty thousand sterling per year, plus expenses and bonuses. The bonuses will be considerably more if you're successful and paid into a Bahamian bank account, tax free. Not bad for a twenty four year old.'

Nearly four times as much I was earning currently, plus bonuses! This was a dream come true. What did I have to lose?

'Who've you been responsible for taking out?'

'Berlusconi, Mubarak, Morsi, Gaddifi, Malesevic, Asil Nadir, to name but a few. You may have noticed Murdoch's operation is having a difficult time.'

'What about the bankers?'

'We're working on them.'

'How do I know you're for real?'

'You've already spoken to the head of HR and your boss. The deputy head of MI5 will come to see you this afternoon, give you an envelope and wish you luck in Northern Ireland. Hopefully that will suffice.'

'Where do we go from here?'

'Return to your office, tie up any loose ends and say you're off to Northern Ireland on secondment for a few days. Leave quietly at five and go back to your flat. In the envelope you'll find a passport, flight tickets from Heathrow, money and credit cards. Sign the cards with the name on the passport, phone your parents and tell them you'll be out of contact for a few weeks on a training course. Explain it's all hush hush due to the nature of MI5, they'll understand and feel very proud.'

'You've thought of everything.'

'That's our job, that's how we succeed. Are you on board?'

'Why not?'

'Good man. Don't turn around for ten seconds.'

I counted to ten and guess what? There was nobody to be seen.

Chapter 2

I read Italian at Balliol College, Oxford, an obvious choice really. With an Italian mother and an English father I'd been brought up bilingual and languages came easily. By the time I got to Oxford I'd become quite fluent in German and French and had a fair understanding of Spanish and Portuguese. By graduation I'd added Russian and Mandarin to my armoury. I could never work out how but without any real effort I could pick up a language and have a level of fluency within a few weeks.

Work wasn't exactly top of my agenda at university, truth be told. I spent far too much time in the bar or on the football field. I actually got a blue for the sport but, to be fair to myself, I did study as well.

Much to everybody's astonishment I walked off with a first, not top notch, there were a few borderline 2:1 papers. However, I'd done enough to scrape through at the highest level. Then the inevitable question, what do I do next? People kept telling me to study for a doctorate or become a lawyer but I'd had enough of academia and wanted something different.

Then I saw a poster on a London tube posing the question: "Parked? Our work throws up all kinds of questions. It's our job to investigate them. Make it your career." The advert was for MI5.I wasn't naïve enough to think I'd become the next James Bond but the thought of working in intelligence intrigued me. After an initial screening by a recruitment agency, I went through a series of interviews and psychometric tests before facing nearly six months of security vetting. Even my drop-out brother and grandparents in Italy were checked. There was a lot of hilarity in the Tuscan hills when the man who turned up spoke little Italian and my grandparent's English wasn't up to much. I think large quantities of Chianti and Tuscan sausage secured me the job!

They were especially interested in my language ability. Did I speak Arabic or Urdu? Just to prove the point, with a six-week gap between one set of interviews and the next, I set about learning Urdu. I'd become almost as fluent as the assessor by the time we met. He was staggered I'd pulled it off in such a short time. I had a gift but wasn't sure yet how I could use it to my advantage.

So after nearly a year I joined MI5, the United Kingdom's internal counter-intelligence and security agency. The training was pleasant but not exactly taxing. The internal academy covered a wide range of topics, from corporate training, IT, communication skills, leadership and management to more specialist and technical stuff, including investigative and analytical techniques and covert operations.

I bounced around the UK a fair amount which was quite entertaining, Starting out at the national headquarters on Milbank in London I spent time in both Manchester and Northern Ireland. I liked being on attachment as the expenses were more than generous. Living the life of Reilly, I stayed in decent hotels, picking up the local talent in squalid disco bars.

After about eighteen months I started to use my language skills and spent time working in the Language Unit on surveillance. I'd kept up my Urdu and by then was fairly proficient. Just to impress, I'd set about learning Arabic.

It was then that I got the call.

****

I strolled back to the office along the Embankment, passing the Houses of Parliament. *How many people in there know about this organisation?* I pondered. It was starting to drizzle and on this cold February lunchtime I could see the breath of the people walking by. Just ordinary individuals going about their business.

I wanted to scream, 'I've got a job paying a hundred and twenty grand a year, plus bonuses!' To say that I was dazed was an understatement. 'What the hell have I got myself into?' I grinned. Well, I didn't want to become an academic, and the thought of being wealthy had a certain attraction! The thought of dying never seriously entered my head'. I was far too young to think about irrelevances like that.

Back at the office I started to clear my emails, delegating work to all and sundry. Nobody asked too many questions, they were used to me disappearing for weeks at a time. As predicted the deputy head came across, handed me a bulky envelope and wished me luck in Northern Ireland. I'd met him a few times. We might have been a clandestine operation but internally we were quite open.'

One of the girls looked across.

'Mixing with the big boys, I see. Are you leaving us again?'

'Yeah, sorry.'

'That's a shame,' she said, looking slightly embarrassed. 'You always brighten up the place.'

'Thanks' I replied, winking at her. *Who knows,* I thought, *in another life she and I could have...* There was no point thinking about it.

At five, I packed a few personal bits into my briefcase and left the building with a cheery wave.

The tube home was its usual seething mass of smelly and sweaty humanity. *This is one thing I won't miss,* I mused as I thought about my new life. Not that there was much to think about, I didn't know where I was going or what the hell I was getting myself into. It was the most exciting thing that had ever happened to me. I was going on an unknown adventure and earning a ludicrous amount of money for doing what? I didn't have a clue!

I got home and immediately opened the envelope with a kitchen knife. Its contents spilled onto the dining table.

The first thing I saw was a well-worn passport. Opening it revealed my own passport photograph with the name Jonathan Miles. The birth date was seventeen months older than my own and there were stamps and visas for a dozen countries.

An A4 sheet revealed that Jonathan Miles had already checked in online for a British Airways flight to Nairobi. It was leaving the following morning at 10.25 from Heathrow. What's more, I was flying business class.

Also in the pack were three credit and debit cards in the name of Jonathan Miles. I dutifully signed them, astonished that the pin code for each was my normal one. Who were these people? I counted the cash that had been left in a plastic pouch. Three hundred and fifty pounds sterling, five hundred US dollars and fifteen thousand Kenya shillings. Somebody had kindly added an exchange rate, the shillings were worth about one hundred and twenty five quid. Over £800 in cash. I assumed this was for expenses, not a bad start! A note confirmed that I'd had the relevant jabs three months before, having been on holiday to Egypt. How the hell did they know that?

The note went on to say that my rent would be paid up to the end of the lease. Gas, electricity, water and phone would all be settled and the accounts closed. It added I should leave all personal ID such as my own passport, driving licence and bank cards. I was also instructed to leave my mobile and take just an overnight bag as clothes would be provided. All personal possessions were to be put into storage and a taxi would pick me up the following morning at 7.15. Finally, I had to use the name on the passport throughout the training.

I phoned my Mum and gave her the good news.

'Oh it all sounds so exciting,' she said in voluble Italian. 'Your Father and I are so proud.' I said I'd ring again when I had the opportunity.

Having not eaten since breakfast, I opened a packet of long-life tortellini that had been sitting at the back of the fridge for several weeks and a can of mince. By the time I'd thrown in some parmesan cheese, tomato sauce and pesto, it tasted half decent. Knocking back a couple of glasses of Pinot Grigio for good measure, I toasted my success and started thinking about what to pack in the overnight bag.

They said they'd provide clothes so I put together a few toiletries, a couple of t-shirts, spare underwear and a pair of jeans. Given that I was in total darkness about my future, I sure was travelling light!

I looked at my watch and grinned. It was only half past seven, what the hell was I going to do for the rest of the evening? I switched on the TV. The choice was depressing. Having flicked through grotty soaps, nature programmes, second rate sports shows and the news channels, I turned it off in disgust. *That's another thing I won't miss in my new life*, I thought.

I went online and frittered away a couple of hours sharpening my expertise on Kenya and trying to glean some information about my new employer. Wikipedia gave me as much knowledge as I needed on Kenya but I found absolutely nothing on the organisation. Not that I was surprised, they hadn't even given me a name for it.

I emailed a few chums and told them I'd be away for a while and would be in touch on my return. *That should stop anyone pressing the panic button*, I thought.

Having watched a bit of news, I decided on an early night and set the alarm for 6.30 am. Tomorrow would be a new day and a new life. Much to my surprise I slept, the Pinot had done its job and I was woken by the banal chirpiness of the breakfast DJ.

After the usual ablutions, I dressed and grabbed a cup of coffee. I was ready, but for what? I had no real idea. Picking up the overnight bag, I looked around the living room and felt a slight twinge of nostalgia for my previous life. I'd had a few good nights in this place. I smiled and, with a deep breath, headed for the door. It was ten past seven and the taxi was waiting outside.

'Heathrow Terminal 5?' the driver said. I nodded and climbed in. I had no idea whether he was part of this organisation, but the journey passed in silence and the roads out of London were basically clear.

I loathed Heathrow and now even Terminal 5 was beginning to look tired and scruffy. Having the boarding pass enabled me to skip the ludicrous check-in procedures, so I headed straight for security where the Disney ride queuing system snaked for what appeared to be hundreds of yards. After spending thirty minutes making banal conversation with a little fat man from Scunthorpe, I eventually passed through the scanners, stuffed my iPad into the overnight bag and sat down to put my shoes back on. Oh, the joys of international travel!

Wandering aimlessly around the concourse, vaguely looking at the car raffles, clothes shops and fast food restaurants, I had to physically pinch myself to ensure I wasn't dreaming. I kept asking 'What have I got myself into?' I can't say I was scared, apprehensive certainly. It was fear of the unknown. I'd had a very secure and safe life but now I was suddenly well outside my comfort zone.

The flight gate finally appeared on the screen so I made my way along the pier, walking for what seemed like forever along the travelators and across the hard concrete floor. Just an anonymous person hidden between holiday makers and business executives.

At the security gate I handed my boarding pass and passport to a weedy-looking man wearing shades, obviously trying to emulate something out of 'Top Gun'. *What a twat,* I thought as he gave the documents back to me. 'Have a nice flight, Mr Miles.' I looked at him and the penny dropped. *I need to get used to this,* I thought and nodded.

On the plane I found my seat by the window and prayed nobody would come and sit next to me. I needed to try and focus on what I was moving on to, I really wasn't in the mood to have a question and answer session about 'What do you do?' and 'Where are you from?'

Fortunately the flight door closed and no one appeared. There was a guy typing furiously on his laptop across the aisle but he was too far away to start making polite conversation. I breathed a sigh of relief and settled down to eight and a half hours of boredom.

I decided to stay off the booze for the duration of the flight as I needed my wits about me for when I arrived. I also vaguely wondered if they may be watching me to see what sort of character I was. I decided discretion was the better part of valour. On my trips to Northern Ireland, I normally got well tanked up by the time I arrived in Belfast. It's amazing how much you can knock back between check-in and flight arrival, so it seemed rather strange to be ordering coffee when the drinks trolley arrived.

I watched a dull thriller and a couple of old comedy shows, dozed and ate the plastic food. Even in business class it was awful. The stewardesses weren't up to much and certainly weren't on the pick-up, at least not with me. Like most men on flights I had my fantasies but, apart from a one night stand in Belfast, they had always come to naught.

At about eight thirty that evening local time, I could feel the plane beginning to descend. I'd become comatose by then. It was only six thirty according to my body clock but I felt knackered. Probably the stress of what I was putting myself through.

The landing gear came down and the usual announcement, 'Doors to manual'. As always I thought I must check what that actually means, as always I knew I'd forget as soon as I got off the plane.

Just before nine we touched down at Jomo Kenyatta International Airport, fifteen kilometres south-east of Nairobi city centre. At least that's what Wikipedia had told me. We taxied for what seemed like forever before the plane came to an abrupt stop. Dozens of people jumped up and started grabbing bags and coats from the overhead lockers. I remained seated, knowing that I'd be off the plane just as quickly, picking up my bag as I moved up the aisle.

After a couple of minutes of no movement, a few people started to sit down. After five minutes, the rest of them had followed suit. Eventually came the announcement nobody wanted to hear.

'Ladies and Gentlemen, the airport authorities are having a little difficulty manoeuvring the bridge into place. Hopefully they'll have this sorted in a few minutes so that you can disembark. Thank you for flying..........' I felt like screaming 'Shut up, you silly bitch!' as she droned on and on. *Wracked with insincerity*, I thought.

After about fifteen minutes, the door finally opened and we started to trundle off.

As always, the inane pilot wannabes were standing at the front. 'Good night, sir,' they repeated to every passenger. I felt like screaming 'Bog off' just to see their reaction, but thought better of it.

The heat and the humidity hit me straight away. It was pitch black apart from the electric light, darkness having fallen a couple of hours previously. We were bussed into the airport building and shuffled along for three quarters of an hour waiting to get through immigration and passport control.

My employers had organised the visa paperwork so at least I didn't have to mess about filling in long, pointless forms on the plane and handing over $50 in cash. I often wondered what happened to all that money in these third world countries. Sadly, the answer didn't take a lot of working out.

Once through the formalities, I smugly walked straight past those who had been busting to get off the plane as they waited for their luggage. I walked through the sliding security doors and dozens of people were standing outside, shouting, screaming and waving signs with names on them. Most of them were either taxi drivers or porters, all desperately trying to make a crust out of the international traveller. One chap was waving a sign with the name Jonathan Miles emblazoned across it. I acknowledged him and he broke into an enormous smile, his pearly white teeth in such strong contrast to his jet black skin.

'Jambo bwana,' he said. 'Welcome to Kenya, my name is Joshua. Follow me, please.' With that, he grabbed my overnight bag and marched quickly across the concourse. He wasn't in the mood for polite chat and suddenly ushered me through a door marked private, down three flights of stairs and into a big underground car park.

'One of the advantages of working for the Organisation,' he said with a rueful grin on his face. 'We can be out of here quickly.'

'How long before we reach our destination?'

'Not long.' He was giving nothing away.

We climbed into an eight-seater Toyota Previa and before I had time to buckle my seatbelt, we were off. Within minutes the neon lights that made up the airport had vanished and we were driving through the semi-darkness of shanty town after shanty town. Sad, hungry faces looked up, hoping the white man would spare a few shillings.

The road we were following had signs pointing to 'Nanyuki'. I remembered from my research the night before that the British Army and the Kenyan Air Force had bases in that area. I reckoned it would take a couple of hours to get to our destination. I decided to pump Joshua a little.

'Are we going to Nanyuki?'

'You know Nanyuki?'

'No, but I've see it on a map.'

'Oh,' came the response.

We sat in silence for several minutes. The road was in surprisingly good condition for an African country and Joshua really put his foot down. Here was a man in a hurry, and he didn't want to say too much.

An hour and forty five minutes later we arrived in Nanyuki. The dilapidated high street was teeming with people, shanty town bars and tatty market stalls were doing a fine trade. We headed out of the town on a back road and within minutes arrived at what looked like an old British Army base. We could have been on the Salisbury Plain rather than in the middle of Kenya. Joshua spoke to a guard at the barrier who was wearing a quasi-military uniform and the gate was raised. I noticed the guard's finger on the trigger of a rifle confirming these people weren't here to mess about.

Driving past a few Nissan huts, we parked outside a dilapidated three-storey brick building. Electric light blazed out from half a dozen windows but apart from that the whole camp was in darkness. As I climbed out of the Previa, the cold hit me. The car had been pleasantly warm and the difference was staggering. I could feel myself shivering immediately.

Joshua shook my hand. 'Good luck, Mr Miles. I hope to see you again.'

A dapper-looking man in his mid-forties came down the steps from the building.

'Jonathan, welcome to the Organisation. I'm Mark, we only use forenames here.' He was obviously American. I tried to place his accent, probably New England.

'Lesson number one,' I replied. 'Good to meet you.'

'There are eight of you on the training course, four have arrived, and the rest will be here either tonight or tomorrow. School starts the day after.'

'How long is the term?' I enquired.

'All in good time. I'll take you to your room and then you can join the others in the bar.'

I followed him down a couple of musty corridors, at which point he opened a door.

'It's not the Waldorf, but hopefully it'll suffice.'

The room looked as if it hadn't been updated since the 1950s. Heavy, wooden furniture including a big, old mahogany wardrobe and dressing table stared out at me, together with a single mattress on a gun metal bed frame. A neon strip lit the room in a bright, clinical manner, destroying any sense of warmth. I switched it off, leaving a bedside light on to create a little conviviality. There was a fire grate in the corner and I could feel heat coming from an old-fashioned ripple radiator.

'No mosquito net?' I enquired.

'We're too high up to worry about such things. As long as you're onsite, you should be OK. There are roll-on repellents in your bathroom for when you go out. We try to think of everything. Get yourself unpacked and go and have a beer.'

'Thanks,' I said. 'See you later.'

I sat down on the bed and felt totally bemused by the whole thing. They were obviously incredibly efficient and detail conscious, so what could go wrong? I was too excited to shower or change so, after a quick wash, I decided to go and join my new colleagues.

The bar was by the entrance to the building, Mark had pointed to it as we came in. I made my way back and opened the door, feeling like a contestant walking onto the *Big Brother* set.

I felt as if I was walking back into the days of The British Empire. This was obviously the old officer's mess, with rich furniture, a marble floor, fans of the 'punkah wallah' variety together with a grand chandelier as the centrepiece. A fully-stocked bar stood at the far end where a steward was wiping glasses. He was dressed immaculately in a white shirt, bow tie and dark trousers.

Two men and a girl sat at a table in the centre of the room and they looked up in unison as I walked in.

'Hi, I'm Zan,' said a pretty, oriental girl about my age and she got up to shake my hand. *Very nice,* I thought as I introduced myself.

'I'm John,' said one of the men, grabbing my hand and giving a very firm handshake. He was in his mid-thirties and sounded American.

'And I'm Imran,' said the second man, a tall Asian in his mid-twenties.

'I'm Michael, sir,' said the steward, beaming. 'Could I offer you a drink?'

'That sounds incredibly civilized,' I responded, looking at what the others were having. I saw a beer bottle on the table. 'One of those will do nicely.'

'It's good that I've got a fellow drinker,' said the American, laughing.

We all sat down and Michael brought across a bottle of Tusker beer, together with a glass and a bowl of Macadamia nuts.

'Could I get you something to eat, sir?' asked Michael as he poured the beer. He was so formal.

'Have you guys had anything?' I asked.

'Yes, we're good,' responded Zan.

'Just a sandwich, ham or cheese will be fine,' I said. 'And maybe a few chips as well.'

'By chips, I suppose you mean fries,' bellowed John.

'Yes,' I retorted. 'Two countries divided by a common language.'

'Who said that?' inquired Imran.

'George Bernard Shaw,' I responded smugly, 'and he was Irish!'

They all laughed. *Such a merry bunch*, I thought, *for the moment.*

We made small talk, giving nothing away. After about half an hour the door opened and the fifth member of the team walked in. We went through the same formalities. This was Hendrick, looking every inch a Swede, six foot three, blond hair and blue eyes.

He ordered a beer. John and I looked at each other. 'What the hell?' he drawled, 'I'll have another.'

'Make it two,' I said. We grinned at each other like silly schoolboys. I decided I was going to like this guy.

More small talk, and after about half an hour Imran said, 'Well, that's about it for me, I've had a long day. Does anyone know what we're doing tomorrow?'

Michael piped up, 'Breakfast is at nine o'clock, sir.'

We all looked at each other and realised this was a summons. I stood up. 'Goodnight, see you in the morning.' We trooped out of the bar, heading down different corridors to our rooms. John followed me. 'What do you think?' he asked.

'Open mind so far. See you tomorrow.' I felt he wanted a deep conversation but I wasn't going to play that game, not until I knew him better. Apart from anything else, it was half past one in the morning local time and I was bushed.

I bid him goodnight again and went into my room. Everything had been unpacked and hung up together with an array of new clothing. Several shirts, three pairs of trousers, two pairs of shoes, trainers and underwear. All top quality designer labels. Even my t-shirts and jeans had been ironed. I could never make them look like that. I stripped off, threw what I was wearing on the floor and climbed into bed.

Chapter 3

I woke to the sound of someone knocking. Feeling totally disorientated, I blurted out 'Hello,' and the door opened.

'Good morning, Jonathan,' said a pretty, young girl wearing a maid's uniform and holding a tray. 'It's eight o'clock, would you like a cup of tea before breakfast?'

'Thank you, yes,' I said, yawning and rubbing my face. 'What's your name?'

'Theresa,' she responded while putting the tray on the dressing table. 'White, no sugar, I believe,' as she handed me a cup.

They're showing off now, I thought. This attention to detail was getting just a little too much.

'Breakfast will be served in the dining room, which is opposite the bar,' she said as she left the room.

I showered and dressed in a Hugo Boss shirt, a pair of Armani jeans and Ralph Lauren trainers. I felt like the dog's bollocks as I walked down the dingy corridor to the dining room.

'You look nice,' I heard as I came round the corner into the lobby. Zan was standing there wearing a stunning summer dress.

'Second division compared with you.'

'Thanks,' she said. 'It's an Alexander McQueen.'

I nodded knowledgeably, having never heard of him.

'Shall we go in for breakfast?'

She nodded. Opening the dining room door, I noticed two new faces sitting with Imran.

We did the usual introductions. The first was a tall, willowy character in his late twenties. 'I am Alexei, it is very good to meet you.'

'With an accent like that, you must be from Moscow,' I responded in Russian.

He beamed, answering in English. 'You speak good Russian.'

'And I'm Caterina,' a gorgeous latino with sultry brown eyes beamed at me.

'Lovely to meet you,' I said in Spanish.

'How many languages do you speak?' She asked in her native tongue.

'A few,' I responded guardedly, 'Argentina?' I threw at her. I knew her accent wasn't Spanish.

'You ask a lot of questions,' she responded, grinning.

'Shall we have breakfast?' said Imran, killing the drift of the conversation.

We were about to sit down when John walked in.

We went through the introductions again and Michael appeared with orange juice. He took our orders, you could tell the nationalities from these alone. Hot cream of wheat for the Russian, eggs sunny side up for the American, soy bean milk soup for the Chinese girl, toast with dulche de leche (a kind of jam made out of milk) for the Argentinian, steamed rice cakes for the Indian and bread and cheese for the Swede. I ordered a couple of poached eggs.

Nothing fazed Michael as the orders were scribbled down. He'd obviously been playing this game for many years.

'One more to join us I think,' stated Alexei. *Well, at least he can add up*, I thought as I nodded sagely.

Conversation was strained. People were giving nothing away and you can only have so much light-hearted banter. Fortunately, after about ten minutes Mark walked into the room.

'Good morning, team,' he drawled. 'I trust you are all well?'

We looked like a bunch of nodding dogs.

'Good, Mohammed will be joining us later today and school starts tomorrow at ten hundred hours. Enjoy the rest of the day, there's a pleasant enough pool here, walks through the grounds, a play room with a pool table, darts, games, cards et cetera. A buffet lunch will be served in here at thirteen hundred hours, pre-dinner drinks in the bar at nineteen hundred, followed by dinner at nineteen thirty. Apologies, but there will be no communication with the outside world for the next few days so don't bother with your iPads. Stay onsite and have a great day. Any questions?'

'Is there anything we can and cannot say to each other?' asked Zan.

'You can trust each other but I would ask for discretion. I'll be in the front office if you need me. Otherwise, I'll see you this evening.'

With that he turned briskly and exited the room. I saluted as the door closed and Zan burst out laughing.

'Which army was he in?' she asked brightly.

'Fancy a walk?' John asked, looking directly at me.

'Why not? Does anyone else want to join us?'

The nodding dogs appeared again and we all set off into the sunshine. Faded elegance was the best description of the camp. The gardens were tidy, but it was obvious that the work had been done quickly and only recently. Lawns had been mowed, but the grass was all but dead having been cut too short too quickly. It was as if a gardening programme from TV had been given twenty four hours to render the place habitable. We found our way to the pool, which was tatty but serviceable. It was about twenty five yards long with plastic sun beds scattered around grassy banks.

'I think I'll go and change and burn off some energy in there,' I said.

'Good idea,' responded John.

We doubled back to the main building as Zan shouted, 'Wait for me, unless you guys have something to hide!'

'No, I'd prefer to stroll with a beautiful lady than an ugly sod like him,' I quipped.

'Thanks pal,' said John, looking genuinely hurt.

'So gallant,' joked Zan.

'One tries,' I said, grinning. 'One tries.'

She's beautiful, I thought.

Our eyes met and lingered for a split second too long. She turned away, looking somewhat embarrassed.

Ten minutes later I was back at the pool, wearing Bermuda shorts, a t-shirt and flip flops. The management had thought of everything. I threw my towel onto one of the sun beds and dived in. The water was warm and felt good as the temperature was rising quickly that morning.

I swam crawl for about half a dozen lengths to shake off some of the lethargy created by travelling and then stopped, panting just a little.

'You swim well.' Zan was standing in a demure one-piece, but looking fantastic.

'Come in,' I said. She dived from the side and swam underwater right up to me.

'You want to race?' she asked brightly.

I nodded. 'Front crawl, four lengths.'

'OK' she said. 'On your marks, set, go.'

I couldn't believe it. I'm not a bad swimmer but she'd turned for the second length before I'd got halfway. She even had the temerity to wink as she passed. By the time I'd done three lengths, she'd finished. As I arrived at the finish line there was a round of applause.

'Beaten by a woman,' shouted Alexei. 'You should be ashamed.'

'You'd be down the salt mines after a performance like that in his country,' wisecracked John.

'I raise the white flag of surrender,' was the only retort I could think of.

'Does that mean we can have the Malvinas back?' shouted Caterina,

'Bog off,' was my response, much to the hilarity of the assembled team.

We spent the morning having fun around the pool and making many a quip, from which we learned a fair amount about each other. Both Caterina and Zan had a mischievous sense of humour, while John was very dry and sardonic. Hendrick and Imran were more serious, watching and giving little away. Alexei relaxed more as the morning went on and became very much the camp comic, dive-bombing Hendrick and Imran, who were in serious conversation at one end of the pool while the rest of us fooled around at the other.

Michael brought a tray of soft drinks at about noon and reminded us that lunch would be served an hour later. Just after twelve thirty, we all went back to the main building to change.

Lunch consisted of cold meats, cheeses and salads.

'Would you care for a beer, sir?' asked Michael.

'No, thanks,' I responded, even though I could have murdered one. 'Water will be fine.' It was obvious we were being watched and I wanted to put on a good show. I was prepared to play the court jester but I needed all my wits about me. John mouthed the word 'Creep,' so I stuck a finger up at him while smirking.

After lunch I decided to go for a walk with Hendrick and Imran, having spent little time with them that morning. I wanted to get a feel for all these guys as quickly as possible. It was obvious they had already struck up a friendship and I felt a bit like an outsider. However, I listened intently as they discussed the political scene in the Middle East and northern Europe. Not exactly riveting stuff, and by the time we got back to the main building I felt I knew them no more than when we had started.

As we walked in, Theresa and a colleague wearing identical maid's uniforms greeted us.

'Gentlemen, afternoon tea is served in the bar,' announced the colleague.

'And who might you be?' I asked.

'I am Johanna. It's good to meet you, Jonathan.'

My God, these kids are trained well, I thought as I strolled into the bar. Afternoon tea was laid out as if we were in an English country house. Bone china, cucumber sandwiches, Battenberg and Dundee cake. It was too corny for words, but very pleasant.

While helping myself to a cup of tea, I heard John's dulcet tones behind me. 'Is there any coffee in this God damn limey empire?' I turned, pointed at the coffee pot and grinned. 'Yes, we try to look after you colonials.' This time it was his turn to give me the finger.

Yet another new face walked in.

'You must be Mohammed,' piped up Imran, obviously pleased that someone of a similar background had joined the team. Again we went through all the introductions, by now it was beginning to get a bit tedious.

I felt a little frustrated as I couldn't place Mohammed's accent. His English was fluent, yet there was a definite foreign intonation. I suddenly twigged, he was a first-generation Brit of either Indian or Middle Eastern parentage. I began puzzling as to where he had come from, MI5? MI6? the military? I felt a tug on my shirt.

'You seem a long way away, are you OK?' It was Zan.

'Yeah, I'm fine, just taking it all in.'

I'd had enough of pleasant conversation, so I made my apologies and went back to my room. Yet another surprise – a dinner suit and shirt were hanging on the door of the wardrobe, together with a bow tie and silver cufflinks on the dressing table. This stuff wasn't shabby, high street gear either. A note had been placed under the cufflinks.

'Tonight's dinner is formal. Please dress accordingly.'

These people had spent more on clothes than I'd spent in my whole life. Suddenly I wasn't feeling quite so smug. I was beginning to feel a little scared if I'm honest. Again, I asked the question, what had I got myself into?

The phone rang on my bedside table.

'I bet you look dandy in your penguin suit.' It was John.

'How did you get this number?'

'That's what I do,' came his simple response. Obviously some sort of telecommunications expert.

'Are you in touch with the outside world yet?' I asked.

'Nah, I don't wanna piss them off. I thought I'd behave for once in my life.'

I grinned. 'Yeah, I thought you were trouble the moment I saw you.'

'There's a few serious boys here, all trying to play the game. But I reckon they knew my shortfalls before they took me on, so I'm not going to pretend.'

'So can you patch me through to my Mum then?'

He laughed. 'How about meeting at six thirty for a pre-pre-dinner drink, then we can have a chat?'

'Yeah I'd like that. See you in the bar.'

By the time I had got myself ready it was six fifteen, so I strolled to the front lobby and out through the main door. Sitting on a swinging chair in the garden, I watched the sun set. Being in the tropics, it happened quickly and as darkness fell, the temperature dropped rapidly.

'Would you care for a drink sir?' John was putting on a mock English accent.

'You sound like Dick Van Dyke in Mary Poppins.'

He sat down beside me, handing me a bottle.

'Thanks,' I said, savouring the beer. After a couple of seconds, I decided to open up a bit.

'I'm having trouble getting my head around all this. Two days ago I was an ordinary bloke living in London, and now ...' I gesticulated with my right hand.

'You and me both, except I was in Washington.'

'What do you make of it?' I asked.

'Good question, and if I'm honest I really don't know. However, they seem to be for real, the money's good and the perks seem great, so what the hell have we got to lose?'

'I know,' I said, 'and that's what's worrying me.'

Alexei appeared. 'Is this a private party or can anyone join in?'

'Grab a beer and pull up a chair, my friend,' said the ever amiable John.

Alexei sauntered off to the house and Michael opened the door for him. John whispered, 'We will talk,' and with that he patted me on the thigh and squeezed it, just a little too firmly.

Oh, shit, I thought, *don't say he's fucking gay.*

As Alexei ambled back, the door opened once more and Zan appeared, along with Mohammed.

Yet again we stood making polite conversation as Michael emerged with a tray of drinks. 'When you are ready, please join us in the bar.'

'That sounds like another instruction,' piped up John.

'Well, it is nearly seven,' said Alexel, looking at his watch. I noticed it was a Rolex.

'Hey, I didn't get one of those,' I quipped.

'Neither did I, this is a fake!'

We all laughed and strolled back to the house. The rest of the team were already assembled along with Mark.

'Good evening, gentlemen' he said. 'And Zan, may I say you look absolutely stunning?'

I felt guilty for not noticing, but he was right. Both she and Caterina looked amazing. Canapés were served while John organised another round. He was obviously up for it tonight but I decided just to slow things down a little. I looked across at Mark. It looked as if he was sipping on sparkling water, he was obviously a true pro.

We'd effectively formed ourselves into two groups. With me stood Zan, John, Caterina. and Alexei. Imran, Mohammed and Hendrik stood apart. Mark mingled amiably between the two sets of people. At seven thirty on the dot, Michael spoke. 'Ladies and gentlemen, dinner is served.'

We filed into the dining room, in the middle of which stood a large, oval table surrounded by nine chairs. On the table there were name cards; I found my place and had Caterina on one side and Mohammed on the other. I surveyed the other seating positions. John, Hendrik and Zan sat opposite with Alexei, Imran and Mark to my right. It was all rather clever really, they had mixed the two developing groups and split the inner nucleus of our group, i.e. John, Zan and me. *These people miss nothing,* I thought. I looked across at Zan. She was grinning at me, so I winked. She blew a silent kiss.

Life could be worse, I thought.

Mark stood up. 'No long speeches, tonight we enjoy ourselves but from tomorrow, starting at ten hundred hours, we work. Have a great night.'

'I think that's the last lie-in we'll have for a while,' murmured Mohammed.

We had the most incredible meal, giant prawns cooked in garlic and butter, fried Tilapia fish served with cabbage and onions, a Kenyan dish called Kuku Paka which was chicken curry braised in coconut milk, the most succulent papaya I had ever tasted, together with pineapple, passion fruit and banana. The wines were to die for, decent Chablis, superb Burgundy and a wonderful Sauterne with the sweet.

Port was offered with cheese but by then I'd had enough. John was knocking it back like there was no tomorrow, while Hendrik, Alexei and the girls made a good stab at what was on offer. It transpired Mohammed was tee-total and Imran a vegetarian as well as being tee-total. No wonder they were so serious!

I tried to get the inside track on Mohammed but he was giving little away. I found out he was brought up in London and had studied maths at Manchester University. Beyond that, he was charming but deliberately vague. There wasn't much warmth to him and in another environment I would have walked away. Caterina on the other hand was great fun and we flirted constantly throughout the evening. I caught John glaring at us at one point which turned into a wonderful smile as I looked across. *Oh shit,* I thought, *I'm going to have to watch him.*

After the meal we moved back into the bar, where I ordered a beer which I had no intention of drinking. At about ten thirty Mark bid good night to us all, after which the party started to break up. The girls followed him and I said my farewell to the rest of the group. John followed. *Oh shit,* I thought, *here we go.*

He was well pissed, rambling about what a nice guy I was and how I'm the only person he relates to. We got to my room and he grabbed my arm, asking if he could come in for a chat.

'No, John,' I said, 'that is not my scene.'

'Hell, Jonathan, you don't know what you're missing.'

'Yeah, and I'm not going to find out either, now good night.'

'Come on, Jonathan, please,' he turned, grabbing my arms while attempting to kiss me.

I ducked and pushed him against the wall, given his inebriated state, it wasn't exactly difficult.

'John,' I said, forcibly but quietly, 'I'm not gay so don't fucking try it on. You're a nice guy and as a friend I like you, but if you try this again I'll knock you into the middle of next week. Now fuck off and sober up. Tomorrow we'll play Chatham House rules, that is no information about this incident will be revealed. Do I make myself clear?' I eyeballed him and he nodded.

He staggered off, muttering how sorry he was.

I felt sick, sober and wide awake. No way was I going to sleep so I decided to go for a walk. I headed out of the house and down towards the pool. It was dark and I could just about make out the path ahead of me. As I approached the pool I saw the outline of someone sitting on one of the sun beds. I wasn't in the mood for conversation and was about to duck away when the figure turned around.

'Who's there?' It was Zan.

'Hi, it's me, Jonathan.'

'Thank goodness, I thought I may have a problem.'

'I get the feeling that you could handle most situations.'

'Sit down, what are you doing here?'

'I was propositioned and had to get out.'

'How is John?' she asked, laughing.

'Was it that obvious?'

'He's not taken his eyes off you since you arrived.'

I held her hand and she didn't flinch. After a few moments, I said, 'I've only had eyes for one person.' Even in the darkness, I could see she was beautiful. We kissed and became quite passionate. After several minutes she pulled away.

'Now that you have proven your masculinity, do you feel better?'

'No, now that I'm with you I feel better.' We kissed again, but this time she pulled away quickly.

'No Jonathan, not yet, it's too soon. I like you, but we don't know each other, and we may never be able to know each other. Let's take things just a little slowly.'

I was as horny as hell but knew she was right.

'I'll tell you what,' I said, 'I'll escort you back to the house if you do one thing.'

'I'm not sure if I like what's coming,' she responded, giggling.

'Kiss me one more time.'

Chapter 4

The following morning I again woke to the sound of someone knocking on my door. This time it was Johanna.

'Morning, Jonathan, did you have a good night?' she said putting a tray down on the dressing table. 'I thought you may like fresh orange juice as well as tea to help clear the head.'

'Thank you,' I responded. 'What time is it?'

'Eight o'clock. Breakfast is at nine and school starts at ten.'

'Thanks, my love.' As she departed I surveyed her pert bum. *Best not think about it,* I decided.

Considering the mixture of booze I'd had, I felt pretty fresh and full of the joys of spring. I'm not saying it was love, but the thought of Zan made me feel good. The phone rang. *Here we go,* I thought.

'Jonathan, I'm so sorry.' It was John, sounding very sheepish.

'History,' I said. 'Just don't try it on again.' Despite everything, I liked the guy and wanted him on my side.

'Thanks pal, see you at breakfast.' With that the phone went dead.

Breakfast was almost a repeat of the day before, apart from people being much quieter. I put it down to us all getting used to each other and nerves for what lay ahead. My eyes met with Zan's and we smiled at each other. Her smile was a joy to behold. *Thank goodness,* I thought, *I obviously hadn't wrecked anything.*

We all went outside for a breath of air before the start of what promised to be a long day. Zan was standing by herself, so I went up to her.

'Are you alright?' I asked.

'Yes, I'm fine, what about you?' We were being so formal.

'Much better for being with you.'

'Likewise,' she said and beamed. God, I loved her smile.

Caterina and Alexei came over but John was standing by himself, staring into space.

'Come and join us, John,' I said.

He smiled. 'I'd love to.'

'Life's too short,' I said.

'What has happened?' asked Caterina.

'Nothing,' I said. 'Drunken ramblings, that's all.'

'What is the expression?' asked Caterina. 'Boys will be boys.'

'Absolutely,' I responded, chuckling. John burst out laughing as well. I offered him my hand and he shook it vehemently. We were over that hurdle, which I was pleased about because I genuinely liked the guy, but only as a friend.

Just before ten, Michael came across. 'Could I ask you all to follow me to the training room please?' Obediently, we trooped back to the house, up a flight of stairs and into a large room with shutters covering the windows. They were blocking the sun from streaming in and neon strip lights had been switched on, creating a cold and severe atmosphere, so different to the warmth of the garden we had just come from. Three long tables had been set up in the shape of a U with eight chairs around them. The tables were covered with green baize table cloths, on which had been placed eight folders. A drinking glass stood next to each folder, together with water jugs on all three tables.

There was a white board, flip chart and projection screen at the top of the room, together with a small table on which stood a laptop. A projector fixed to the ceiling beamed an image on to the screen. It read 'Welcome to The Organisation.'

This all felt very familiar, just a standard training room, the format used by thousands of companies worldwide. As I looked at the screen, the phrase 'death by PowerPoint' came to mind. There were three seats down each side of the U together with two at the end. I sat on the right hand side at the end of the table. While at college, I'd read this was a position of power within a boardroom environment. It was probably a load of bollocks, but I always tried to stick with the notion.

Alexei sat next to me at the end of the table with Zan to my right. I was pleased she was so close. John placed himself next to Zan with Hendrik at the other end. On the opposite side Caterina sat next to Alexei with Imran in the middle and Mohammed at the far end. I'm sure Freud would have had a field day with the positioning but everybody seemed quite comfortable.

Mark came in and Alexei started to stand.

'No need for that,' Mark said, 'we're quite informal here.' He looked around the room and smiled.

'Well, good morning, team, and welcome to the training phase of your career with The Organisation. I don't have to go through all the usual health and safety presentation because you've been here a while and you'll know where everything is. However, should there be a fire, make your way down the stairs and out into the garden. Any questions at this stage?'

Most of us shook our heads and Mark continued.

'OK, you all have a vague understanding as to what we do. We're the good guys and we're out to get the bad guys. Governments have to be seen to be playing it straight, so sometimes they can't get at the bad guys, and this is where we come in. As far as the world is concerned, we don't exist. If anyone is ever caught in a compromising position, he or she is just seen as a rogue operative from a member state and is dealt with by that member state. That's why it's important you have a second identity, the risk of contagion is reduced. What normally happens is that you would be tried and sentenced by that state and then you'd be spirited away with a new identity. As far as the world is concerned, you are in prison and no one is any the wiser. On the odd occasion when someone asks, that identity dies. It's all very simple and foolproof.

'OK, rule number one, you're not James Bond and you don't have a licence to kill. There could be times, however, when you need to defend yourself and that is a crucial part of this training.

'Rule number two, we will support you as long as you play straight with us. If you get into a mess, we'll do everything in our power to dig you out. Trust us and we'll trust you. But please don't abuse that trust.

'Rule number three, there is no rule number three.' He smiled and went on.

'Training. Like most companies, the best form of training is on the job. However, there are certain things you need to be made aware of before you get involved in a live situation. Over the next few weeks you will be given the following.'

At that point Mark picked up a remote control and the PowerPoint changed page. The word '*Training*' appeared. He pressed a button on the remote and '*Fitness'* appeared under training.

'We think it important that you are fit when doing this job. Not just in terms of handling yourself but also working long hours. The fitter you are the more alert you stay. So at zero-seven-thirty each morning you will have a keep fit class for ninety minutes. Formal classes start at zero-nine-thirty, which will give you half an hour to shower and change. I forgot to mention breakfast is between zero-seven-hundred hours and zero-seven-thirty.

'Formal classes will consist of many of the skills you already possess within this group. We'll be using you to train each other, together with outside support. For example, John will be using his telecommunications skills to teach you the rudiments of his line of work. This guy is one of the leading people in the field and his knowledge is second to none. For information he has already cracked the blanket ban imposed on you with regard to communication with the outside world.'

John looked very pleased with himself and said, 'Ah, so you obviously have a trace on me.'

Mark responded coolly, 'As I said, John, you are one of the leading people, but not the only one.'

'Touché,' responded John.

Mark went on, 'Alexei, you will give us the benefit of your experience with regard to armaments. Alexei will teach us about guns, munitions, ordnance, etc. Those who don't know will learn how to handle weapons and explosives. This doesn't mean to say you will be using them. It could well be that you'll never have to, but forewarned is forearmed.'

Alexei half-nodded and Mark continued, 'Hendrik's skills lie in the world of military intelligence. He'll take us through his approach to collating and analysing information, and assessing that information so that informed decisions can be made.

'Zan has an accountancy and management consultancy background. She'll be teaching us how to analyse a company, its strategy, organisation and performance. You'll be given analytical techniques on to how to read a balance sheet and what to look for in terms of fraudulent activity. She's also a third dan black belt in the Japanese martial art of jujitsu. I'd like you to teach the team the basics of neutralizing the enemy.

'Mohammed's specialisation is cryptography, the practice and study of techniques for secure communication. Applications include ATM, passwords and digital rights management for music, films, books, etc. This is an area that we as an organisation are going to have to get involved with. These industries are losing billions due to illegal free downloads. We don't know the solution yet, but we intend to find one.

'Jonathan has a background in counter-terrorism and espionage. He'll be teaching us the rudiments of this fascinating subject. He also has an extraordinary ability with languages. Hopefully he'll be able to give us a few ideas with regard to picking up the basics of any new language.'

Everybody was looking at me. *No pressure there,* I thought. *What do they think I am, a fucking linguaphone course? Teach yourself half a dozen languages in six weeks?*

Mark read my expression. 'Don't worry, I don't expect you to turn them into multi-linguists. As I said, we're talking rudiments here.'

It all sounded a bit Heath Robinson to me.

Mark continued. 'Caterina's skill is in the world of computing. She'll be showing us how to hack and read data, how to reprogramme systems, how to freeze systems, and how systems can lose data. What use is this? Well, you may remember how the Royal Bank of Scotland suddenly lost customer data a while back. They were getting a bit cocky at the time. Having been instrumental in wrecking the banking industry, they thought they could continue as before. For example, paying stupid bonuses and not lending money into the market. We decided to teach them a lesson. Nobody died but the world economy is now on a much firmer footing. Word spreads quickly.

'Finally Imran, our Middle Eastern expert. In his recent past he's been working with government agencies in areas such as electronic surveillance, physical surveillance and covert operations. He's been involved with the likes of Hezbollah, the Israel defence force, the National Liberation Army in Libya and the Syrian rebel forces. Very much at the sharp end, his information will be invaluable to you all.

'So your first task is to prepare an overview of what you do and how you can help each other. Tomorrow I want to see a presentation from each of you lasting about an hour before questions, on your area of expertise and how you can help your colleagues. The whole idea is to show the depth of knowledge we have in this room. Following on, you will begin to realise how much experience you can draw on from within The Organisation. You're not going to become experts in each other's areas. What you will become is experts at knowing there is a solution and who to call on to find that solution.

'Over the next few weeks, you will meet others from The Organisation who can help you in terms of survival, be it in the corporate jungle of Wall Street, the illicit world of drug trafficking in Columbia or on the streets of Damascus during the shelling and looting of a bloody civil war.

'Any questions?'

Alexei half-raised his hand. 'If I'm going to teach people how to handle weapons, I will need equipment.'

'We have on-base Kalashnikov rifles, Browning Pistols, L86A2 Light Support Weapons, Heckler & Koch rifles, FN Minimi light machine guns, grenade guns, mortars, weapon sights, anti-tank weapons, rocket artillery, satellite tracking systems, etc., etc. I also want to draw on your experience with regard to radar and surveillance. I think that will do for starters.'

I poured some water. My mouth felt very dry. A combination of the booze from last night and the fear of what I was hearing had put me in a bit of a spin. I'd suddenly been catapulted into the big boy's league, and I wasn't at all sure that I could play at this level.

It was as if Mark had again read my thoughts. 'You're probably feeling a bit scared and apprehensive at this point. Don't worry, we've all been there and do understand. We're not superstars here, most of us are just ordinary Joes with a few special skills. You've all been selected carefully to ensure the success of The Organisation.'

Caterina raised her hand. 'Mark, are we allowed to ask you, what is your specialisation?'

Mark looked at her and smiled. 'My specialisation?' He paused. 'The Organisation. Let's go and have a coffee break.'

Chapter 5

So began three months of training. To say we worked hard is a major understatement. The fitness classes were enough to kill anyone off. Mark brought in an evil little Sergeant Major type called Benson to put us through our paces. Every morning we were running, doing press ups, sit ups, squat thrusts and any other grotty exercise Benson could think of to make us throw up. Suddenly we were aware that we were earning our money.

We'd do half-day sessions on our specialist subject which, needless to say, took a lot longer than half a day to prepare. Thus a leisurely evening became something to dream of. It became second nature to strip a Kalashnikov rifle and rebuild it. I learned what to look for in balance sheets and had accountancy ratios reverberating nonstop around my head. I became confident in cracking computer and telecommunication codes and systems. Once I got into the psyche, it all became remarkably simple.

Many of the subjects lead off from one another. For example, we learned that cracking a bank system ensured we could look at an individual's statement. That in itself gave a lot of personal data and we learned how to track an individual's movements accordingly, invaluable in a street war such as that in Syria. We also learned how to track money through the banking system, be it for money laundering, drug trafficking or good old fashioned bribery. I even had a look at my mother's bank account and was confounded to see that she donated thirty pounds a month to a children's home in India. I had no idea, and it made me realize how little I knew of the ones I loved.

Parts of the training were familiar, which gave a bit of respite. On occasion, Zan and I would endeavour to find free time and go for a swim together. Sometimes we just held and caressed each other. To have a full blown romance in this environment was impossible. We were all on top of each other and spent far too much time together as a group. Bearing in mind we were from such varied backgrounds, it was amazing that World War Three didn't break out. However, we held it together and got on with the job in hand. There was many an occasion when I wanted to explode because one person or another was winding me up. Usually it was Mohammed, an opinionated little prig, but using Zan and John as sounding boards I was able to hold myself together.

Zan and I became close, not lovers as such but what we had was very special. John became a firm friend and confidant. We'd parked our little upset and it was never mentioned. His private life was nothing to do with me as long as he kept it that way. The three of us worked well together and helped in terms of presenting our own subjects and ensuring that we made sense to other people, rather than going off into technical jargon or management speak.

Alexei and Caterina worked as a team, more as a convenience than a relationship, but it worked for them. Hendrik, Mohammed and Imran continued as a grouping but the relationship became increasingly fraught. Mohammed tried to dominate and by doing so effectively isolated himself from the other two. Fortunately all the teams were a relatively loose relationship and we would regularly rally round each other, becoming a self-help society.

As time drifted on, I forged good relationships with both Hendrik and Imran, although I thought they were far too serious for their own good. While they would love to talk about the political scene in Central Africa, I occasionally wanted to lighten up and one of the joys I discovered was that Kenyan TV regularly showed English football matches. This is where Alexei and I bonded as he loved his football as much as me. It transpired that he had had a trial with Spartak Moscow, but at the top level wasn't quite good enough. We took great delight in trying to teach John the basics of the round ball game. His love was baseball and trying to explain the offside rule created great hilarity.

Sadly these moments were few and far between, as the workload at times became intolerable. I'd regularly find myself working until three in the morning only to be up again at seven for the fitness class. It's incredible what your body will accept when you really push it to the limit and it was obvious that the physical training was paying off, albeit painfully.

By the end of the third month I was amazed at what I had learned. I was more than proficient at jujitsu and fancied my chances as a management consultant, or maybe a fraudster. I could now clone a bank card, hack a bank account and even transfer funds from one continent to another without anyone suspecting anything. I could also handle any type of weapon you could think of and had a good understanding of street warfare, field communication and computer hacking.

As John said, 'This is the best training school for crooks you could wish for.'

Mohammed put it into perspective. 'You need to know how a crook's mind works in order to beat him.' Irritatingly, he was right.

Towards the end of the third month it became obvious that the course was nearing completion. The pressure became less and we found we had more free time on our hands. Mark even organised a weekend away at the Aberdare National Park and booked for the first night a luxury campsite with en suite tents and four poster beds. We dined under the stars and gorged on the most incredible barbecued steaks. Staying up until three, we sat by a log fire watching animals making their way to a watering hole. Zan and I shared a blanket and snuggled together as it was damned cold that night. I'd never felt so close to a woman in my life.

We were up again two hours later and took a tour of the park in a minibus. The sights we saw were unbelievable, two lions feasting on the carcass of a bison, cheetahs chasing hyena across the African plain, a herd of elephants crossing the road one by one with a baby trotting behind. It was remarkable seeing rhino, zebra, giraffes and many other animals in their natural habitat. I vowed I would never go to a zoo again.

The following night we stayed at Tree Tops, the safari lodge where the then Princess Elizabeth learned that her father had died and she became Queen of England. Again, we feasted well and drank far too much wine, but as Mark said, we deserved it. Very late on I went to bed, Zan followed me and our relationship was finally consummated. I didn't at this stage give a damn about the future. For the first time ever I felt contentment, it was love and life felt good.

We arrived back at the training camp late on Sunday and after fitness training the following morning Mark called Zan and me into his office. My immediate thought was that we were going to get a bollocking for having a relationship.

We chatted amiably about the weekend and then Mark got to the point. 'You've both performed remarkably well on the training course and passed with flying colours. I feel very proud, many, many congratulations.'

We grinned from ear to ear and he shook us both by the hand. He then said, 'I have an assignment that's come up and, although you have no field experience as yet, I feel it is right for you both. I really would be throwing you in at the deep end if you commit and I won't be offended if you think you're not ready for it.'

'Go on,' I said, intrigued to hear what was on offer.

'You may have heard of an Italian company called Orlanda. They started life twenty two years ago as marble and stone exporter based in Bologna, Italy. Over the past seven years they've expanded beyond all recognition. Although marble is still part of their business, they're now into all sorts of operations, a chain of coffee shops across Europe, hotels and casinos in the States and a chain of pubs and hotels in the UK. Their accounts suggest they are cash rich, which doesn't really make sense when you look at the recent growth. You'd expect them to be highly geared.'

Zan nodded. With her accountancy background she was probably way ahead of Mark with her depth of understanding, but she allowed him to continue.

'We want to take a look at this company to find out what they're all about. We've been trying to find an opportunity to get involved and one has just arisen.' Mark threw a copy of the *Slough Observer* across the table, open on the jobs page. Someone had drawn a circle around an advert. It read:

'Billing and Collections Specialist

Orlanda Marble, a successful Italian marble importer, is currently looking for an Italian-speaking Billing and

Collections Specialist for its UK operation based in Slough.

The purpose of this role is to provide administrative and collections support to the credit and receivables team for all products and services. You will be responsible for the collections and cash and sales ledger administration, assisting the Billing Analysts and ensuring that receipts are recorded accurately and on time.

The advert then went into detail about knowledge, skills, experience, education salary etc. I skimmed through the rest as Mark spoke.

'The idea is that you apply for the job. As far as they are concerned, you're currently a trainee auditor in the Civil Service going nowhere fast and you're looking for an opportunity to use your Italian and accountancy skills. This is very deliberately not a high powered position but one that may give you a good vantage point to find out what, if anything, is going on.'

'I'll put my application in straight away,' I said.

'You already have,' replied Mark, smiling. 'Your interview is on Thursday.'

'And where do I fit in?' asked Zan.

'We want a two-pronged attack,' responded Mark. 'You'll be parachuted into KPMG, who are the auditors for the Orlanda Group. We work with them often enough and they have proved to be very cooperative over the years. It helps them with their money laundering credentials. Although Orlanda was originally an Italian company they are now based in Zurich, which in itself begs questions. You will be seconded to the Zurich office of KPMG as part of the audit team for Orlanda. As far as the locals are concerned, you're a bright graduate trainee from Shanghai who is over in Europe as part of your training programme.'

'What about references?' I asked.

'Good question, your application included details of your current position. You'll be pleased to hear that you're currently working for the Department for Environment, Food and Rural Affairs, commonly known as Defra. You're based at their office in Smith Square, London SW1, not a million miles from your recent location.'

I smiled, knowing the area well.

Mark went on, 'You have asked in your application that references are not to be taken unless you are successful and that you are not to be contacted at work. Nothing unusual about that, assuming you are successful the request for a reference will be passed to us and we will respond.'

'When do I go?'

'You're on the British Airways twenty three forty from Nairobi tonight, arriving six twenty at Heathrow tomorrow morning. You'll spend the rest of today being briefed and tomorrow you'll meet a colleague in London who'll help with accommodation, identity, etc.'

'What about me?' asked Zan.

'We want you to spend time in Shanghai to familiarize yourself with the KPMG operation and culture before coming across to Europe. It will add to your credibility. The audit team is due to go into Orlanda in five weeks' time and you'll join them just before they start work. If, therefore, anyone was to check up on you, highly unlikely but we try to think of everything, you will know the Shanghai operation and have contact points. The team in Zurich will suspect nothing, and more importantly nor will the people at Orlanda.'

'So when do I go?' asked Zan.

'You are booked on the fourteen twenty Etihad flight tomorrow, Nairobi to Abu Dhabi. There's a two and a half hour stopover, then a direct flight to Shanghai. You'll arrive at eleven ten on Wednesday morning where you will also be met by a colleague who'll help with accommodation etc.'

Zan and I looked at each other. I wanted to grab her and hold on tight.

'Will we keep this identity?' Zan asked.

'No, you'll have new names, passports, driving licenses, bank accounts, etc. Zan and Jonathan never existed, the important thing is that you do and by changing cover your chances of survival are increased tenfold.'

'Will we be able to communicate?' I asked.

'Yes, that's important, you need to be able to liaise and swap notes on a regular basis. Firstly you'll have the 'O' communication system through which you can phone, email and swap information.'

I thought back to the training. The powers that be had said the 'O' system was impenetrable to an outsider. John and Mohammed spent hours trying to break the codes. They were encouraged to do so and it became an obsession. They couldn't get close and finally had to admit defeat. If it was beyond them it would certainly do the job for me. The mobiles had been christened 'O' phones.

'Secondly, your 'O' phones have central numbers that will automatically transfer calls from one to the other. That way there is no chance of you being linked. All other forms of communication must be kept to a minimum. It's much safer this way.'

'So we won't be able to meet?' said Zan, sounding slightly alarmed.

'Unlikely,' was the response. In other words, no.

After an uncomfortable silence, Mark spoke again. 'I'm going to leave you now guys for ten minutes to discuss this. After all, the two of you will be working very closely, albeit at a distance. You both need to be on board, otherwise the thing collapses. Let me know your thoughts. I'll send Theresa in with some coffee.'

He left the room and we just looked at each other.

'It could never have lasted,' I said. 'The other night when we made love I thought I'd found my soul mate, yet immediately you're taken away from me. To say that I'm fed up is the biggest understatement imaginable.'

'I know,' responded Zan, 'and if it's any consolation I feel exactly the same way. I'll be quite honest, I love you, Jonathan, and want you for evermore. And you know what makes it even worse? I don't even know your real name.'

I grabbed her and we kissed passionately. Somebody fumbled at the door so we broke away. Theresa came in with a tray of coffee and biscuits. She smiled and put the tray down on Mark's desk.

'Thanks, Theresa,' I said.

'Good luck to you both,' she responded with a sad smile as she left the room.

'She's obviously seen this scenario before,' Zan said.

'Many times,' I replied, sighing. 'Look, with what we've learned in recent months it won't be beyond our capabilities to meet up without creating any traces. Zurich and Slough aren't a million miles apart, we can make it work.'

'We'd better, mister, otherwise I'll come and get you.'

'I look forward to that,' I said, grinning ruefully as Mark walked back into the room.

'OK, we'll do it,' said Zan.

'I'm delighted,' responded Mark.

'What do we tell the others?' I asked.

'We'll go and talk to them now, they're having a coffee break.'

We got up and headed for the bar and the rest of the team looked at us as we walked in.

'I have an announcement to make,' Mark said. 'Zan and Jonathan are leaving us shortly as they have been assigned.'

Everyone clapped, knowing what this meant. The course was at an end and they would also be given operational experience in the near future.

'When do you go?' asked John.

'Later tonight,' I responded.

'I'm leaving tomorrow,' said Zan.

'Good luck,' replied Caterina with tears in her eyes. 'It's the end of an era, I'll miss you both.'

'If you'll excuse us, people,' said Mark, 'we have a few things to sort out. I'll meet you all back here at eighteen hundred hours for a farewell drink and dinner. Come on you two, now it's time for some real work.'

Zan and I followed him back to his office.

'OK, here are the consolidated accounts for the Orlanda Group. Zan, tell me what you think.'

Mark handed us both a copy and Zan turned straight to the balance sheet.

'Turnover 11,405 million dollars, up about fifteen per cent on last year.' She was very much in her comfort zone. 'Net profit 2,375 million dollars, up seventeen per cent on last year. Current assets 3,242 million dollars, current liabilities 3,410 million dollars, so they're basically liquid. Gearing ratio …' She paused, working out the maths. 'About 1.8:1, which means borrowings are a little higher than you would hope to see but nothing to be concerned about. So superficially we have a company with good growth, good profitability and a reasonably strong balance sheet.'

'Quite,' said Mark. 'It's all textbook, but it doesn't make sense, bearing in mind they had a turnover of little more than a million ten years ago. We need to get a handle on what this company is all about, and that is your mission.'

'What are your thoughts?' asked Zan.

Mark looked at her. 'I have my suspicions, as do others, but nothing we can hang our hats on. If I'm honest I don't want to jaundice your views, I want you to go in with an open mind. Maybe we are wrong, perhaps this company is just incredibly successful. However, I've never seen growth on this scale without there being something intrinsically rotten. I'm going to leave you now to read up on the company. There are two files here with all the information we have, you've got full internet access to see if you can find anything on the web. Also I would ask you, Zan, to prepare Jonathan for his interview on Thursday. Remember, it's basic book-keeping, not high powered accountancy. I'll see you for dinner.'

'Thanks for giving us this opportunity Mark,' I said as he stood up to leave.

'Not at all,' he responded, 'I know the two of you will bring a lot of added value to The Organisation. Good luck.' With that, he shook us both by the hand and left the room.

Zan and I looked at each other. 'Fancy a quickie?' I said, grinning.

'Don't be so disgusting,' she responded, throwing the set of accounts she was still holding at me. I ducked and they skittled across the floor.

'Having said that,' she said in an alarmed manner, 'I have no idea when I'll see you again.' I could see tears welling up in her eyes. I went over and held her tight.

'Come on, darling,' I said softly. 'We'll find a way.' We kissed for a long time. This was more than sexual, it was real love and we both knew it.

After a while we pulled apart and started looking at the files Mark had left. They went through the various takeovers, press articles from the past seven years, together with credit reports from reference agencies and consolidated accounts for each year confirming the rapid growth. They didn't reveal anything of interest and it soon became apparent that the Organisation had little to go on.

We joined the others for lunch and it transpired that Mark had formally closed the course after leaving us. The others would all be leaving over the next couple of days. No one else had been given an assignment but they had been told they would be involved in projects in the very near future. Everyone was subdued and probably a little scared about what the future held.

Afterwards, Zan grabbed my arm. 'Come with me,' she said curtly. I wondered what the hell I'd done. She took me to her room, pushed me in and kissed me passionately, Within seconds we were on her bed and making love as if there were no tomorrow. She was violent and rampant, fiery and fierce, she was just incredible.

After we'd become completely sated we lay there, holding each other.

'You'll be over in Europe in five weeks' time,' I said. 'Come hell or high water, I'll see you then.'

'Please God, let that be the case, because I love you so much, Jonathan. I've never felt like this about anyone.'

'Likewise,' I said, 'I love you with all my heart and soul.' I'd never said that in my life.

'One thing,' she said. 'When you get back to the UK, pick up a cheap tablet or laptop and we can contact each other from wi-fi hotspots. Set up a Facebook account in the name Michael Cook from London. I'll do similar and we can keep in touch away from the Organisation. As long as we don't use the company's internet access nobody can trace us, it will be foolproof.'

Simple but brilliant, I thought. 'Come on,' she said, 'we'd better get back to work.' I nodded, we dressed and headed to Mark's office.

We spent about an hour doing a mock interview in anticipation of Thursday. Zan really knew her subject and coached me well. When Mark came in we went through our findings, he nodded sagely.

'I think you've found out as much as you can without getting closer to the company. Call it a day, go for a walk and have some fresh air. I'll see you tonight.'

We strolled through the grounds arm in arm, not caring if we were spotted. Given that we probably wouldn't see the rest of the team again, it didn't matter who saw us. As we approached the pool we heard laughter and splashing. John, Caterina and Alexei were there, obviously having a lot of fun.

'Ah, the love birds join us,' shouted Alexei. I stuck two fingers up at him and everybody laughed. Suddenly I felt a push from behind and fell into the water. As I came to the surface, Zan bobbed up beside me. We were both fully clothed and soaked to the skin. John was standing where I had been seconds earlier.

'That'll teach you for leaving us early,' he shouted. We were all in hysterics, it was that end of term feeling and nobody really knew what the future held. As we climbed out of the pool, William appeared with a tray of drinks. I grabbed a beer and yelled, 'To the best bunch of people I've ever known, whoever you are, cheers!' I took a long swig. 'I'm going to miss you guys.' *Especially one of them*, I thought.

We fooled around at the pool for the rest of the afternoon and eventually made our way back to the house. The end was in sight and an eerie silence fell on us.

I returned to my room to find a suitcase packed and a change of clothes. Having showered and dressed, I went back to the bar for the final time. The farewell was going on too long, by now I just wanted to get away. Drinks and dinner were strained and I felt relieved when William came in and said, 'Your taxi has arrived, Jonathan.' The room fell silent and I looked around.

'Well, I guess that's it,' I blurted out. 'Good luck to you all, and thanks for your company.' I shook hands with everybody including Zan, which seemed somewhat surreal. I really wanted to grab her but decorum took over and we kept it formal. Our eyes met and we didn't have to say any more. Joshua, the driver who'd brought me, was waiting by the front door.

'Mr Miles, it's so good to see you again.'

'And you, Joshua, how are you?'

We walked out of the house together and down the steps to where his Toyota Previa was waiting. I looked round and everyone was standing by the door apart from Zan, who was nowhere to be seen. Rather than tears, she'd obviously decided to go back to her room, at least that's what I hoped. I gave a cheery wave and jumped into the car.

Chapter 6

The flight home felt like the end of a holiday and I was totally deflated. This worried me, I knew I was moving on to an important chapter in my life, and yet I couldn't raise any enthusiasm for it. The thought of living and working in a grotty place like Slough depressed me and the thought of being without Zan brought a lump to my throat. I loved her and felt like shit.

Having had a couple of drinks to anaesthetize the flight, I slept most of the way back to Heathrow and woke to the air stewardess holding a breakfast tray. I took it from her, and drank the orange juice while playing with the congealed scrambled egg and dried up bacon. '*How can they get it so wrong*?' I mused.

Much to my surprise we taxied straight up to the pier at Heathrow and were off the plane in a matter of minutes. After a half mile walk we arrived at passport control only to wait twenty five minutes to pass through and a further fifteen minutes for the luggage to arrive. I smiled grimly as I waited. If only they could get this right. Sadly, there's no joined-up thinking, each little department a law unto itself. If one area collapses, the whole thing is brought down.

I collected my suitcase and walked through customs. The double doors opened to the usual throbbing mass of humanity and yet again I saw a man waving a sign with the name Jonathan Miles written on it. I raised a half salute and was beckoned to follow him. No shortcuts this time and I had to carry my own baggage as we made our way to the short-term car park.

He didn't say much and was one of those individuals that I doubt I would recognise if I saw again. I would guess he was about five foot eight, white, mouse-brown short hair, thin rather than fit looking with a pasty face.

'Am I allowed to ask where we're going?' I said, trying to keep up with him as we darted through the crowds at Heathrow.

'You'll hear more later.'

For the next five minutes we didn't speak a word and eventually I saw the flashing lights of a car unlocking as we made our way across the multi-storey car park. It was nothing special, a three year old Ford Focus. He opened the boot and I squeezed the suitcase in.

We drove out of the airport and onto the M4 heading west.

'Straight to Slough?' I asked.

'Not quite,' came the response. 'Aren't you the lucky one?'

I was getting a bit aggrieved with this bloke's approach. We were on the same team supposedly, yet he was giving nothing away. It wasn't as if at some point in the very near future I wouldn't find out. I decided to play him at his own game and sat in silence, listening to the radio. It seemed odd being back in England and hearing the familiar voices and music. Although I'd kept in touch with news and events, I had become incredibly distanced from my former life. Sitting on the M4, it was as if nothing had changed.

We drove past Slough, eventually pulling off the motorway at Reading. Passing the Madejski football stadium, I pondered how such a poor team could have such a splendid facility. We cut behind a motor dealership and parked adjacent to a bland office block.

'Bring your suitcase with you,' he said tersely. I thought back to Joshua, and the words '*Welcome to the real world*,' came to mind.

We caught the lift up to the fifth floor and the door opened to reveal a cavernous space with only a couple of desks and chairs by the window.

'Delightful,' I commented.

'We're just using it for a brief period. Wait here, someone will be with you shortly.'

With that he disappeared back into the lift. I felt I wouldn't be sorry if I didn't have the pleasure of his company again. I wandered over to the window and surveyed the salubrious sights of Reading. After a couple of minutes, a thickset, middle-aged man appeared, clutching a large briefcase and looking a little flustered.

'Sorry I wasn't here to meet you, old boy. I've been waiting for a few bits and pieces with regard to your secondment. Call me Frank, can I offer you a cup of coffee?'

'Lovely, thank you, white without.' I had no idea what he should call me, but thought I'd probably find out in the near future.

'Follow me,' he said, beaming. We walked to the back of the office, down a corridor and into a little kitchen. He switched a kettle on and put a teaspoon of instant coffee into two cups. We made polite conversation about the flight and British weather while he made the drinks, eventually handing me one.

'This way,' he said as we made our way back to one of the desks in the main office. He pulled up a chair, ushering me to sit while grabbing a file from his briefcase. Sitting behind the desk, he theatrically put on reading glasses and opened the file.

'Right,' he said, 'for this little caper you'll be known as Dean Farlow. Here's your passport, birth certificate, national insurance card, debit and credit cards, bank statement and driving licence.' He put them on the desk in front of me one by one. 'That Ford you came in is registered in Dean's name and insured accordingly. I've got the keys somewhere.'

He rifled through the briefcase and then put his hand in his jacket pocket.

'Ah, here they are,' he said, placing them next to the passport. 'There's sat nav in the car and it's programmed to take you to your flat in Slough. The car's documents are in the glove compartment along with the keys to the flat. Dean has lived there for a couple of years and is on the voter's roll.'

'What about neighbours?'

'You're in bedsit land. The flat is one of three in a converted terraced house. The people below have just moved out and the flat above is rented to the council for short-term housing issues. They come and go.' I said nothing so he continued talking. 'This is the watch you'll use from now on, it's a clever little bugger and there's a tracker built in. If ever you're in trouble, press the knob on the right-hand side and you'll see the date change. That tells you the tracker is operational and we can come and find you. The thing is, the baddies would never suspect that an old Seiko watch is anything more than an old Seiko watch.

'Dean has got a 2:2 in Business Studies from the University of Brighton. It's an old poly,' he sneered. 'His family are from Chelmsford and his father is a local government officer in the archive office. His mother does charity work and is second generation English of Italian extraction. She brought Dean up bilingual and he has two younger brothers named Christopher and Glenn. Don't worry if you forget things, the detail is on the "O Cloud", should you need it. Here are your laptop and 'O' phone, which hopefully you've been trained to use.'

We'd spent several hours playing with both pieces of kit during training. They were redesigned Apple affairs with watertight communication. Again, they had all been built on the "O" platform. Without iris recognition and several codes, an outsider could never begin to access the data.

For the next couple of hours we went through Dean's life, covering what seemed like every aspect. I couldn't catch them out, the detail was incredible. With only broken sleep on the plane, by lunchtime I felt punch drunk and knackered.

Frank looked at me. 'I think you've had enough for today. Let's go and have a spot of lunch, then you can go to your flat and sort yourself out. I'd ask that you get back here for ten o'clock tomorrow morning for a resume. Your interview is at four pm with a Mr Jeff Andrews, the Financial Director, and we need to make sure you're ready.'

He took me to a pub a couple of hundred yards away, which was quite busy as we entered.

'They do a wonderful real ale here, can I suggest a pint?' Frank asked.

'Just one, as I'm driving.'

'Absolutely,' he responded. 'And I would recommend the shepherd's pie, it's home-made.' He seemed to be in his element, playing the part of the *bon viveur*.

We chatted over lunch about football, theatre, films and politics, but truth be told said nothing to each other. This guy was a master at being your best chum and you walking away knowing nothing about him. *Obviously a true pro*, I thought.

After lunch, we went back to the office and he handed me the briefcase.

'Take a look through everything, play with the toys and we'll talk again tomorrow. You'll find a safe under a loose floorboard in the bedroom. The carpet is slightly ruffled where you lift it and you'll see a piece of string going across the joint between carpet and floor. Replace the string whenever you lift the carpet. If someone comes snooping around, the string will move, giving an immediate signal. Corny but effective. Your bank pin code will open the safe. There's a bureau in the living room where you'll find all the domestic bills in Dean's name, gas, electric, phone, etc. Should you have any problems, phone the help desk. They'll look after you and if need be I'll come and read you a bedtime story.'

I burst out laughing. 'I'm sure that won't be necessary.'

'Good man,' he said, offering his hand. 'See you in the morning.'

I headed back to the lift and made my way to the car. Sure enough, the sat nav was set to an address in Slough and it pointed me back to the motorway. The keys to the flat were in the glove compartment as promised. As usual, the attention to detail was exemplary. Forty minutes later, I heard the immortal words, 'You have reached your destination.' I could see I was outside number twenty four on a tree-lined avenue of Victorian houses, obviously faded elegance now turned into bedsit land. The address on the screen said number forty four, so I edged up the road until I saw the number on a door of a three-storey house.

I parked the car, grabbed my two cases and walked up the path. There were three doorbells, the centre one had the name Farlow scribbled in felt tip on a name plate, the others were blank.

I had two house keys and put one into the lock. Needless to say, it was the wrong one. 'Good start,' I murmured. As I entered, the odour of decay hit me and took me straight back to the squalor we used to live in as students. I made my way up to the first floor and let myself into the flat. I was pleasantly surprised, it was warm and reasonably well furnished. Not antiques, more flat-pack, but good enough for my needs. I had a bedroom, living room, kitchen, bathroom, TV, hi-fi and, more importantly, internet and landline. 'Luxury,' I said out loud.

As usual, the Organisation had looked after me. The fridge and cupboards were stocked with plenty of food, a few tins of beer along with a dozen bottles of half decent wine.

I unpacked the suitcase quickly, putting clothes in a wardrobe and a chest of drawers adjacent to a made up double bed. *I don't suppose that'll be seeing much action*, I thought sadly, as Zan came to mind.

For a second I wondered where the safe was. I saw the ruffled carpet in the corner of the room with a small piece of string lying across it. The string looked totally innocuous, just a bit of rubbish that had landed on the floor. I pulled the carpet up without too much effort and found a loose floorboard which, with the aid of a coin, I prised open. There lay a small safe with a keyboard on its door. I entered my bank pin code and the door sprung open. All my personal ID had been put in there, my own passport, driving licence, 'O' phone and bank cards together with pay slips from the last three months. I grinned as I realised how much had been paid into my account. Given that I hadn't paid rent, utilities, food and entertainment during that time, I had a sizeable amount saved up.

I decided it was time to go and buy the new laptop to contact Zan so I fished out my old debit card, replacing it with all the new ID that Frank had given me earlier. I'd seen a Tesco superstore on the way to the flat so I closed the safe and replaced the floorboard, carpet and string, remembering Frank's words, *corny but effective*.

I still had three hundred in sterling from the initial expenses I'd been given, and knew that would be more than enough to buy a cheap laptop. My thought was that if I paid by card the purchase could be traced, and I wanted to keep my employer off this particular scent. It felt quite strange driving through Slough and then strolling around the supermarket. My life had changed so dramatically and yet the rest of the world had remained static.

The shop had an array of laptops and tablets. I found a netbook reduced to £149. Its spec included wireless internet connection and a webcam, perfect for my needs. The gigabytes and processor speed were irrelevant so I took it to the checkout, praying they wouldn't ask for ID. I really didn't want to leave any evidence for The Organisation to pick up on. The young girl slid the box across the scanner.

'Do you want a bag?'

I nodded, 'That'll be £149.05' she said, 'Do you have a clubcard?'

'*Why can't they make disposable bags and not charge'* I thought.

'Oh, don't worry about that,' I handed over one hundred and sixty pounds in twenty pound notes. 'You have the points.'

'I can't do that, it's not allowed,' she said, giving me the change and receipt.

'Thanks, sweetheart,' I said, with a smile on my face. She smiled back, looking a little embarrassed

No trail there, I thought as I walked out of the shop with the most important communication tool in my armoury, hidden in a Tesco plastic bag. How many times had we been told in our training that the simple ideas were often the best?

Back at the car I took the dainty little machine out of its box, plugged in its battery and switched it on. Amazingly, there was life in the battery and it whirred into action. Realising I needed internet access to complete the installation, I drove up to a McDonalds I'd seen on the way in. Parked outside, I was able to access their free wi-fi. The McDonalds page appeared on the screen asking for a mobile phone number to send a code for internet access.

Bugger, I thought, *that would leave a trail*. Then another page popped up. 'If you don't have your mobile, you can still have two hours free on the internet.'

Perfect! Within seconds, I was online. Via Google, I accessed Facebook and started setting up an account in the name of Michael Cook. Again I was scuppered as they asked for an email address and there was no way round it. I thought for a second and went into MSN. I clicked on 'Outlook' and the 'Set up a new account' icon.

I answered the questions:

Name - Michael Cook

Birth Date - 29/10/84

Gender - Male

How would you like to sign in? – I entered michaelcook.

Create a password – Jonathan or Zan would be too simple. I typed in mcdonalds01.

Phone Number – I looked at the Tesco bill and pumped in that number

Security question – Mother's place of birth – I typed in Slough

Post Code – Again, the Tesco postcode SL1 IJP

I then had to enter a series of letters to confirm I wasn't a robot and the system announced michaelcook@outlook.com was already taken. I tutted and typed in michaelcook101@outlook.com. I then had to retype the robot letters, by which point I was beginning to lose the will, but hey presto! I had a live email address.

Suddenly the screen went blank, the battery had died.

'Fuck it!' I shouted out loud.

Grabbing the power lead, I went into McDonalds and the acrid smell of stale burgers wafted over me. I ordered a coffee and explained to the pimply youth that I needed a plug to power up my PC. He looked at me blankly and went over to speak to a buxom lady in her mid-twenties. She came across. 'We only have two sets of plugs in the restaurant,' pointing to where they were. Sod was up to his usual tricks, with people sitting at the respective tables.

I placed myself in the centre of the restaurant so that I had a clear vantage point. A woman was sitting at one of the tables with two young kids, and an old couple at the other. The kids were throwing chips around and being generally obnoxious. The mother was getting more stressed as time went on, trying to keep control. I hoped one of them would disgrace himself so that the mother would get up and leave. The elderly couple sat there defiantly, eating one chip at a time. I wanted to scream, 'Will one of you please fuck off?' but I just sat quietly and drank my coffee.

Eventually the old man stood up. *Here we go,* I thought. Sadly, his wife stayed put as he went off to the toilet.

The mother looked across at me. 'Rather you than me,' I said, grinning.

'I'm sorry,' she replied, 'are they annoying you?'

'Not at all,' I said, explaining about the power problem. Immediately, she ushered the kids to another table.

'Thanks ever so,' I said as I sat down and plugged in. With the email account live, I set up the Facebook page in seconds, just as Zan had instructed, in the name of Michael Cook from London.

By now one of the kids was asleep in his mother's arms and the other mopping up the rest of his burger.

I turned and smiled. 'Appreciate your help. I've just moved house and there's no internet connection as yet in the new place.'

'I know the problem,' she said. 'It's taken three weeks to sort mine out.'

'Have you moved far?'

'No,' she hesitated, but went on. 'My husband walked out on me six months ago. I had to sell my house to clear the mortgage. People tell me I was lucky because I'm not in negative equity, but I've ended up in a sordid little flat.'

I looked at her. She was a pretty little thing in her mid-twenties.

'Can I buy you a coffee?' I blurted out. I wasn't trying to pick her up, we were just two lonely souls feeling a bit sorry for ourselves.

'Thanks,' she said. 'White without, if I may.'

'What about the kids?'

'They're OK. With the little one asleep, I may get half an hour's peace.'

I went and got the drinks, along with a colouring sheet and crayons for the elder one.

'I'm Dean,' I said, offering my hand.

'So formal,' she responded, with a lovely warm smile. 'I'm Caroline, this is Jake,' she said, pointing to the kid now happily absorbed in colouring pictures, 'and the little one is Jamie.'

I wasn't sure what the hell I was up to, but there was a real attraction here, despite the two kids. We chatted amiably until the younger one started to stir.

'I'd better go,' she said, 'otherwise there'll be hell to pay with this one.'

'Perhaps we could go out for a drink one night,' I said.

She looked at me directly. 'I dunno, I'm off blokes at the moment.'

'Look,' I retorted, 'I'm not on the pick-up, I wouldn't come to a place like McDonalds for that.' She laughed. 'I do have a girlfriend and we are close, but she's in Shanghai and I'm here. All I'm saying is that if you want a pal to have a drink with or go to the pictures one night, I'm your man.'

'Thanks' she said, 'I appreciate that.' By now Jamie had woken up and was beginning to whimper. She opened her bag and fished out a business card. 'That's me,' she said. 'I'm a bit tied up this week, but if you want to give me a buzz on Monday or Tuesday feel free.'

I looked at the card, *Caroline Shelley, Computer Graphics.*

'Talented lady,' I said.

'Yeah,' came the wistful response. 'At least I can work from home and look after these two. Not that there's much work around the moment, but that's another story.'

'You can tell me all about it next week,' I said brightly.

'I look forward to it.' she hitched Jamie up and grabbed Jake by the hand.

'Come on, you two, it's past your bed time.'

I walked to her car. She strapped in the kids and climbed in. Winding down the window, she said, 'Nice to meet you.'

'And you, see you next week.' With that she drove off.

I felt strangely saddened and a bit confused as I drove back to the flat. That night I primed myself for the interview. I went onto the "O" Cloud and re-read the info I had on Orlanda and Dean Farlow's background. I also prepared answers to the probable questions on book-keeping and accountancy. Finally, I hid my new laptop under the floorboard, pushed up beyond the safe and well out of sight.

By ten o'clock I was absolutely bushed and decided to call it a day. I set the radio alarm by the side of the bed for seven thirty, and slept.

Chapter 7

As the alarm went off, Zan and Caroline were glaring at each other. I opened my eyes and shook my head. Getting up, I checked the work phone and could see a message. It read, 'Good luck today, Zan x'.

I smiled and felt a slight pang of guilt. Why? I hadn't done anything, but I could feel the temptation. I responded, 'Thanks, hope you had a good flight,' deliberately keeping it formal. We could talk later, once we'd sorted out our personal communication system.

I showered, dressed, grabbed some cereal and set off for Reading at eight fifteen. It was far too early, but I didn't want to be late for Frank. The traffic was hideous and came to a grinding halt as I approached the slip road onto the motorway. All the drivers sat looking at each other for half an hour before we started to move at a snail's pace. Two miles on, I drove past an accident with police cars, an ambulance and two fire engines in attendance. After the rubberneckers had stopped looking for blood, I was able to put my foot down and arrived at the office at five past ten.

The lift doors opened and I walked in slightly breathless and somewhat stressed. I needn't have worried, the place was empty. I made myself a cup of coffee and sat down at one of the desks for ten minutes before Frank walked in.

'Ah, you beat me,' he said. 'Traffic worse than ever.' No apology for being late, it wasn't his style.

'Do you want a coffee?' I asked.

'Capital idea.'

I made myself another at the same time. By now I had relaxed and was ready to face the day.

We did a mock interview which lasted nearly two hours. Frank was really putting me through my paces and I was able to answer pretty well everything he threw at me. I thought before that he was a true pro, this convinced me. He knew as much about Orlanda as I did, as well as Dean and the world of accountancy.

Eventually he raised his hand. 'That's wonderful, Dean, you've done a great job. I can't see you failing this afternoon, just don't be too overconfident and I'm sure you'll walk it. Give me a buzz when you've finished and let me know how you got on. I'd take you for lunch but I'm not sure a beer would be a good idea before the interview, we can celebrate when you get the job.'

'That's fine by me,' I said, looking at my Seiko watch. It was approaching one o'clock. 'I think it would make sense to head back to Slough, I don't want to get stuck in traffic again and be late.'

'Indeed, we'll talk later.'

We shook hands and I headed back to the car. After programming the postcode of Orlanda into the sat nav, I set off again for Slough. The journey was uneventful and I was directed into a scruffy 1950s industrial estate. The Orlanda building was far from impressive – the sign had a couple of letters missing, green paint was peeling from the walls, the windows looked as if they hadn't been cleaned for several years and the corrugated roof was rusty. For a successful company, they were spending little on the infrastructure.

This time I was far too early, but felt relaxed as I knew where I was going. I turned the car around and headed to a pub I'd seen on the way in for a bite to eat. I ordered a BLT sandwich and picked up a newspaper that had been left behind. The bar was far from busy and I sat reflecting on the past few weeks. Kenya, Zan, John, Caterina and the rest, it somehow seemed like a distant dream. Yet here I was, in Slough of all places, going for an interview as an accounts clerk, with a false identity, working in the dirty world of industrial espionage. I could have pinched myself.

At half past three I left the pub and made my way to the Orlanda office. I parked the car in one of the bays and walked into reception. A large girl of about nineteen sat behind a glass screen, surveying her nails. She looked up, I couldn't decide whether she smiled or scowled.

'I'm here to see Mr Andrews,' I said. 'My name is Dean Farlow.'

'Is he expecting you?'

'Yes, I have an appointment at four o'clock.'

She grimaced and picked up a phone. 'There's a Dean Farlow to see Jeff at four.' After a couple of seconds, she put the phone down and turned to me. 'Take a seat, he'll come and get you in a few minutes.'

There were four plastic chairs arranged around a coffee table covered in magazines. I sat down and picked up a copy of 'Marble Trend', a glossy affair featuring Turkish marble. I silently groaned. How absolutely uninspiring, I thought. Idly, I flicked through the pages, taking little in. Pictures of marble factories were hardly a turn on.

After about twenty minutes I heard someone coming down the stairs. A slim, balding man in his mid-forties smiled and held out his hand.

'Hi Dean, I'm Jeff Andrews, Financial Director, sorry to keep you waiting.' He offered his hand and I shook it.

'Nice to meet you,' I said.

'Let's go up to my office for a chat.'

I followed him, making small talk about the journey and finding the building. He ushered me to sit down and immediately scrutinised his laptop.

'Excuse me,' he said, typing furiously.

After a couple of minutes I was beginning to get bored, as I stared at him banging away on his keyboard. Eventually he stopped and looked at me.

'OK, so this is part one of the interview process. We'll talk for about forty five minutes, after which I'll hand you across to Mr Grimaldi. He's our HR partner from the divisional head office in Italy. OK?' I nodded.

'Right, what do you know about Orlanda?'

This was an easy enough start. I rattled off as much information as I thought he wanted to hear.

'Very impressive,' was the response. 'And why do you want to join Orlanda?'

I continued with the bullshit. I was thinking this was too easy, sooner or later he'll catch me out with my lack of accountancy knowledge.

'And what is your understanding of the role?'

'Here we go,' I thought, taking a big breath. I started talking about collections and cash sales ledger administration, the recording of receipts, systems etc. In other words, everything the original advert specified.

'You sound competent. What about working as part of a team?'

I breathed a sigh of relief. We were over the technical stuff, so I rattled off the importance of being a team player and likened an office to a football team. He liked that.

His phone rang and although I couldn't hear what the other person was saying, I could tell there was a problem. After a few guarded comments he hung up and said, 'I'm going to have to bring this to a close. I'll tell Mr Grimaldi you're waiting, any questions?'

'How many people are up for the job?'

'We've shortlisted four. You are the third person I've seen and there is one more tomorrow. We'll be in touch soon after. I'll take you back to reception and Mr Grimaldi will come for you when he's ready.' The interview was over.

Back at reception he spoke to the girl behind the glass screen, 'Can you get Mr Farlow a cup of tea or coffee while he waits for Mr Grimaldi?' With that he shook my hand, wished me luck and ran back up the stairs. I wondered what the problem was. The girl grunted, 'What do you want?'

'A cup of tea, white without would be delightful.' She scowled and disappeared through a door.

I sat down and thought through what I had said at the interview. I reckoned I'd handled it pretty well and just hoped I wasn't too overconfident. The tea arrived in a cardboard cup and plonked unceremoniously in front of me with half the contents spilling onto the table.

The receptionist grunted again as I thanked her profusely. To think she was the face of the company for any prospective customer who appeared at the door. I shook my head sadly. *How can businesses get it so wrong?* Maybe with this lot it was a deliberate ploy.

I sat drinking my tea and watched as she got up and put on a coat. It was five o'clock.

'How long is Mr Grimaldi likely to be?' I enquired.

'You never know with him,' she responded and disappeared though the door again. Several other people came through reception and out through the main entrance. It was the five o'clock vacuum as my former boss had put it, all the 'jobsworths' disappearing as soon as they possibly could.

I couldn't be bothered with 'Marble Trend' again, so sat quietly. As time drifted on I got more and more uncomfortable. By six o'clock I was convinced I had been forgotten about. Soon after, a greasy little man in his early fifties came down the stairs.

'Meester Farlow. I am Meester Grimaldi. I so sorry to kip you. Geev me 'alf an 'our please' His Italian accent was virtually impenetrable but I could just about follow him.

'Nessun problema,' I responded in Italian. 'Ci vediamo tra mezz'ora.' *See you in half an hour.*

He beamed and disappeared upstairs.

What a shambles, I thought. If I had really been going for a job I would have walked at this stage. I sat back down and out of sheer boredom picked up 'Marble Trend' again. It hadn't improved.

I sat in a comatose state, thinking of Zan. I really wanted to speak to her and hoped we could touch base that night.

An hour later Grimaldi appeared again, he deserved to be slapped. 'Come zis way,' he said. I followed him up the stairs to another office, surprised at the amount of activity still going on. They weren't all jobsworths.

'Now, why you want to join Orlanda?'

I repeated what I had said to Jeff Andrews, but this time in Italian. Much to my delight, Grimaldi responded in the same language. I put this down as a moral victory. We talked about my accountancy experience. Given that he knew less about bookkeeping than me, I was able to sound quite knowledgeable. After about half an hour he raised his hand.

'That's' fine,' he said in Italian. 'I have all the information I need, we'll be in touch very shortly.'

With that he stood up and shook my hand. I followed him out of the office and he shook it again in reception.

'Buona notte,' I said 'Sono ansioso di sentire da voi.' *Good night, I look forward to hearing from you.*

It was dark outside and cold. As I got into the car I noticed a fleet of lorries next to the warehouse area waiting to unload. There was a real hive of activity with fork lift trucks lifting pallets from low loaders and taking them into the building.

As I drove home, I reflected on the interview. My honest feelings were that I had acquitted myself quite well, but I didn't feel any great sense of satisfaction. I think I was just tired.

When I got in, I rang Frank and gave him a recap of the day's activities. He sounded genuinely pleased.

'What do I do tomorrow?' I asked. 'Shall I come into Reading?'

'Not much point, old boy, we've vacated that place, all in the interests of security. The marvellous thing about this job is that you do get free time. Having said that, at other times it is twenty four hours a day. Take the weekend off and enjoy yourself. Just let me know if you hear from Orlanda.'

As I hung up there was a knock at the door. A rather large, black lady in her early thirties smiled as I opened it.

'Hi, I'm Jasmine, I've just moved in upstairs.'

'Hello, I'm Dean,' I replied, stumbling over the name and nearly forgetting my cover.

'Sorry to trouble you, but I'm having trouble with my internet connection. I don't suppose you know anything about computers do you?'

Bloody hell, I thought, *all I want to do is sit down and have a glass of wine*. I smiled. 'Like most people, I get by. Would you like me to look at it?'

'Do you mind? Thank you so much.'

I grabbed my keys and followed her upstairs. 'I've been put in here by the local authority until they can find me something bigger,' she said, opening the door. 'If I can't get the laptop going, my kids will go berserk.'

'How many have you got?

'Three. Daniel is thirteen, Nelson ten, and little Erica, who is three.'

'A tight squeeze,' I said.

'We'll try and keep the noise down.'

She ushered me into the flat and I saw the wireless router sitting on a cardboard box flashing at me. I could hear a TV blaring from the living room. Homer Simpson sounded in good form.

'Where's your laptop, Jasmine?'

She took me into the kitchen. Given that four of them were living in cramped conditions, the place looked remarkably tidy.

'When did you move in?' I asked.

'Monday. I thought at first no one lived beneath me.'

'I've been away,' I said airily. 'Now let's have a look.' The laptop was a vintage Toshiba, it was switched on and the message on the screen read 'Internet Explorer cannot display the webpage.' I smiled, remembering I had a similar problem a while back.

On the side of the laptop there was a switch, which I pressed.

'Have you got a piece of paper and a pen?' I asked.

'Of course.'

I noted down the wireless password printed on top of the router, fed it into the laptop, and within seconds I was a latter day hero!

Jasmine gave me a huge hug. 'I need a man,' she said, her dark brown eyes flashing.

'I'll see if I can find you one,' I quipped.

'You'll do,' she responded, laughing. 'You must have a glass of wine with me.'

'That would be nice.'

As she opened the fridge door I had a brainwave and stuffed the bit of paper with the wireless password into my pocket.

I was then introduced to the kids, the surly teenager, the cheerful ten year old and the delightful, sweet-natured little girl. I made polite conversation for about ten minutes and then made my excuses. I had things to do.

Back at the flat I fished out the notepad from under the floorboard and fed in Jasmine's wireless password. Within seconds I was live on the internet, using an access point that would never be detected. My own brilliance astounded me!

I'd set Internet Explorer to open on my Outlook page, and there was the email I wanted to see: 'China Sam San wants to be friends on Facebook'. I looked at my watch. It was nearly ten o'clock, six in the morning Shanghai time, too early, I thought. I sent an email.

'When you get up, if possible, can we Skype?'

The response was almost immediate. 'Ready when you are.'

I went onto Skype and typed 'China Sam San' into the search engine. There was only one. She'd done her homework. I pressed the call icon and Zan appeared, smiling at me onscreen. I could have cried, God, I loved that girl. All thoughts of Caroline evaporated.

Tears started streaming down my face. 'Hi,' was all I could say.

'Are you OK?' I heard her wonderful, sultry voice coming through the speakers.

'Now I'm looking at you, everything is fine.'

'Technology does have its uses,' she said.

'I thought Facebook was banned in China,'

'With the training we've had, it wasn't the biggest obstacle to overcome. I set up a domain and off we went. Free wi-fi in the hotel too, so no trace.'

'Clever girl.'

I told her about the interview, my internet piracy, the flat, and we talked and talked for nearly two hours. She wasn't going to KPMG until the following Monday and so, like me, had a free weekend.

We agreed to Skype again the following morning, later in the day in her case, and she blew a kiss as the screen went blank. Seeing her had revitalised me and suddenly life felt very good. I went to bed happy and slept.

Chapter 8

The following morning I woke naturally at about eight am and put on the radio to hear the news. Considering I'd been away from the UK for over three months, little had changed. The banks were in turmoil again, inflation and unemployment were up and the problems in the Middle East were escalating. I turned it off and went and had a long shower.

Realising I hadn't eaten since lunchtime the previous day, I cooked bacon, eggs, mushrooms and toast, together with a steaming pot of coffee. I was feeling lazy and slobbed in front of the TV eating my fine feast.

The company phone rang, it was Zan touching base through official channels. What a game we were playing. She briefly repeated parts of our conversation from the night before, ensuring I understood that she was covering our tracks. I curtailed the conversation, saying that I wanted to keep the line free for Orlanda. As I hung up, I switched on the laptop and went straight into Skype. I pressed the icon and there she was in front of me again. Now we had a much more relaxed conversation but agreed to talk every morning through official channels.

When we had finished I felt at a bit of a loss and wondered what to do. I phoned Mum and Dad and had a long conversation about nothing in particular. We agreed I should visit them the following day.

Realising I needed to keep fit, I looked up fitness clubs in Slough on Google and found one that had a decent pool and gym, together with a trial membership period of three months. I said a silent prayer that I wouldn't need to extend it.

I drove down to the club and spent several hours working out. It felt good to be back in a fitness regime and I could feel my body tingling as I changed to go back to the flat. There was a message waiting for me on the phone.

'Hi Dean, Jeff Andrews from Orlanda. Could you phone me when you have five minutes?'

I immediately phoned the number and he picked up straight away.

'Dean, thanks for coming back to me. How do you think yesterday went?'

'OK, I think,' I responded, stepping straight into character.

'You did very well and we'd like to offer you a position if you're still interested.'

I grinned. This espionage game was too easy. 'That's fantastic,' I replied.

He went on. 'Now as per the advert your salary will be £23,000 plus benefits, and if you're agreeable I'll put an offer letter in the post to you today.'

'Fine, once I've got that I'll resign from my current job.'

'Will they make you work a month's notice? We could do with you here asap.'

'I've got a couple of weeks' holiday owing to me, so with a bit of luck I'll be able to start with you in two weeks' time. I'd agreed this with Frank to add a level of credibility while at the same time getting the show on the road as quickly as possible.

'That would be good, see what you can do, and welcome to Orlanda.'

We bid our farewells and I immediately rang Frank to give him the news.

'Splendid, old boy. Let's hope the offer comes by Monday and then we can do the necessaries.'

I agreed to touch base with him as soon as I received the letter. I was about to phone Zan when I realised it was the middle of the night, so I sent her a text instead. I then realised I had nothing to do and nobody to talk to. I'd been used to my own company in the past, but for three months I'd had people around me all the time and now I felt very alone.

The phone rang, breaking my solitude.

'And how's the master spy getting on?' an American accent drawled. I burst out laughing. It was John.

'Took you long enough to find me,' I joked.

'I am now officially your communications manager,' he replied, sounding a little pompous.

'Somehow I don't think I could be in better hands,' I responded seriously.

We talked about the adventure so far, with John being a little reticent about his role. He was evasive every time I asked a question and wouldn't tell me where he was based, how many people he was working with or what other responsibilities he had. I got a bit fed up with his approach and told him so.

'All in good time, my friend,' was his response. He said he was the third link after Zan and Frank, and gave me a short code to contact him if I was in trouble. He also confirmed that if I used the Seiko watch tracker the signal would go directly to him. I found this somewhat comforting, knowing there would be someone who cares to help bail me out.

The following morning the offer letter arrived from Orlanda. I contacted Frank and we agreed that I should phone Jeff Andrews on Monday and tell him I could start in two weeks' time.

'Take a holiday,' said Frank. 'With what you're going into, best to have a break while you can. You don't know when the next opportunity will be. China seems a nice place to head for. Use your own passport to avoid contagion.'

Yet again these guys had missed nothing. However, I was being given official sanction to go and see Zan. It was an opportunity too good to miss.

I immediately went online but Zan wasn't around. *Sod it*, I thought, and phoned her on the company 'O' phone. I repeated what Frank and said and could hear her giggling down the line.

'Here's me starting a new job and I've got you to contend with,' she said.

'Life's a bitch,' I retorted. 'I'm hanging up now to try and find a flight.'

'Don't forget you'll need a visa.'

I immediately went onto the website of the Chinese embassy to work out how to get one. It looked quite easy. I downloaded the visa application and made an appointment for the following Tuesday at ten thirty am. That was the earliest they could see me. The theory was that if I could pick up the visa later in the day I could fly out on either Wednesday or Thursday. Virgin Atlantic had a lunchtime flight on both days for £750 return. I smiled at how things had changed. A few weeks ago I would have panicked at the cost, now it was irrelevant.

The following morning I went down to see Mum and Dad. The prodigal son was incredibly well received, with the fatted calf being brought out. Nobody asked any questions about what I was doing. They knew it was 'hush hush' and that was enough. My mother decided I was looking a little 'peaky' and was determined to build me up within a twenty four hour stay. The amount of food that appeared was astonishing. My father wanted a drinking partner and spent the day plying me with booze. I felt more relaxed than I had been for many a month, being back in the bosom of my family.

I left on Sunday afternoon after an incredible five course lunch and drove back to the flat. I felt isolated from the world and thought about contacting a couple of old university pals but decided against it. We'd actually been trained in Kenya on how to react if we bumped into someone we knew when undercover. Although I was keeping the two lives separate, I wasn't in the mood for crossover.

This 'downtime' was getting irksome. Having always had structure in my life, I was finding my current situation difficult at best. I realised that if this was to be a long-term scenario, I would have to become more proactive in life and learn how to fill the empty spaces. I reminded myself that I was new to the roll and needed to give the thing a chance. I'd had such a roller coaster ride over the last few months and felt a little lost at that moment.

On Monday morning I confirmed to Jeff Andrews that I'd be able to start at Orlanda in two weeks. He seemed pleased but preoccupied and hung up quickly. I went down to the fitness centre and worked out again for several hours. The place was quiet apart from a few overweight middle-aged housewives. I kept my distance, not wanting to get involved in that scenario.

The following day I caught the train to London and arrived at the Chinese embassy at ten fifteen. I was seen ten minutes later by an aggressive little man in his thirties, but when I spoke to him in Mandarin his approach softened somewhat. He obviously wasn't used to English people speaking his language and after several minutes of stamping forms and barking questions about the purpose of my visit, how long I was going to stay and where, he instructed me to come back at three thirty.

With several hours to kill, I caught the tube to Trafalgar Square and had a look around the National Gallery. I wasn't heavily into art but it seemed like an obvious place to kill time on a cold rainy London day. I arrived back at the embassy just before three thirty and much to my delight my passport was waiting with the visa stamp in place. I felt thrilled and the frustrations of the last few days disappeared. Suddenly I had purpose in my life again. The visa was dated for the next day so I headed back to the flat and booked a flight with Virgin Atlantic. By now the price had gone up to £895, but what the hell? Zan was worth every penny and a darned sight more. I booked cattle class, still watching the pennies even though I could easily have afforded the 'Upper Class' service. *Old habits die hard*, I mused.

It was then that I thought of Caroline. I didn't want to lose touch because I genuinely liked the girl, but at the same time I didn't want to two-time Zan. *What a stupid position to be in*, I thought, grinning to myself. With that, I phoned her.

'Fancy a Big Mac?'

'You know how to flatter a girl.'

'How are you?'

'I'm OK,' she said, sounding anything but.

'What about dinner tonight?'

'I dunno, I'll have to find a babysitter.'

'Just dinner and a chat,' I said, 'Nothing more, I promise.'

'I've never heard that one before.'

I used the silent sell. After a couple of seconds, she sighed. 'Why not? I've got nothing else on.'

'Any likes or dislikes?'

'No, you choose.'

I agreed to pick her up at seven thirty and booked a table at an Italian restaurant I'd seen which looked half decent.

I knocked on the door of her flat and she seemed very tense as she opened it. As we walked to the car, conversation was difficult and I wondered what the hell I'd got myself into. Once we'd climbed in I said, 'What's the matter?'

'What do you mean?' came the terse reply.

'Caroline, I don't know you well but you seem troubled. Can I help?'

'Let's go and have dinner.'

We made small talk on the way to the restaurant and fortunately were seated in a little alcove away from listening ears.

She ordered a vodka and tonic and the waiter asked if she wanted a large or small one. I took charge. 'I think the lady needs a large one tonight.'

For the first time she smiled, and when she did she looked ravishing.

'Thanks, and I'm sorry. I'm not really a fun person to be with at the moment.'

'A problem shared is a problem halved,' I responded. 'Talk to me.'

'Oh, Christ,' she said. 'Let's order food first.'

With the orders taken, I spoke. 'Let's look at the positives. One, you've got two lovely kids. Two, you've got a nice flat. Three, you're bright and good looking. Four, or maybe that's five, we're in a nice restaurant, life could be a hell of a lot worse.'

She smiled again. 'You know you have this habit of making me feel good. I think you're a nice guy.'

'Steady, tiger,' I quipped.

She went on. 'Since Mike walked out, life has hardly been a barrel of laughs. If I'm honest, Dean, I'm in the shit financially, work isn't coming in as quickly as I need, and if it carries on like this I'll lose the flat within six months, and then what?' She looked genuinely scared.

'OK, let's look at the blackest scenario, you lose your flat.' I told her about Jasmine in the flat upstairs. 'The authorities won't let you walk the streets, they'd find you something, especially a single woman with two young kids. It may not be Buckingham Palace but at least you'd have a roof over your head. Also, in six months something may happen workwise. One way or another, you'll survive. Time is a great healer, just give yourself a chance.'

She grabbed me by the arm. 'Thanks. I needed someone to talk sense to me.'

I held her gaze, probably for too long. 'Look,' I said, 'I've got to go away for a few days. I'm changing jobs and I need to tie up a few loose ends before I move on.' I didn't want to tell her I was going to see Zan, in her current state that really would be rubbing her nose in it. 'I'll be back next week and we can talk again then.'

'Thanks, I'd like that.'

By now the mood had lightened and we spent the rest of the evening chatting amiably. I must admit I felt a little nervous as I drove her home.

I parked outside her flat and killed the engine. Gently taking her hands I said, 'You're a lovely girl and things will work out for you, I promise. Now get out of the car before I do something I might regret!'

She laughed and put her arms around me. 'Thanks Dean, I look forward to seeing you next week.'

She kissed me on the cheek and her lips felt soft and warm. It was a beautiful experience and I held her for far too long. Eventually pulling away, I said, 'I'll phone.'

'I hope so,' she responded, and with that opened the car door and got out. I watched her walk up the drive and before going into the building she turned and waved. I asked the same question again, 'What the hell am I getting myself into?'

I went home and ordered a taxi for seven thirty the following morning. Packing quickly, I felt uptight and confused. I'd gone for years without a girl I really liked and now I had two. I knocked back a couple of glasses of Pinot Grigio for support and hit the sack. *Only I could get myself into a position like this,* I thought as I drifted off to sleep.

Chapter 9

The following morning the taxi arrived ten minutes late, which immediately put me in a bad mood. Fortunately the traffic up to Heathrow was relatively light and I arrived thirty five minutes later with time on my side. Yet again I had to go through the usual garbage check-in procedures and eventually made my way through security with an hour to wait before take-off. I grabbed a newspaper and a couple of magazines for the journey and walked up the pier to the departure point. There were few people around which meant the flight would be quiet. I breathed a sigh of relief, hoping I could find a seat by myself.

On the plane I again settled down to eleven and a half hours of boredom. I felt confused, unsure whether I was looking forward to seeing Zan. Caroline had thrown a real spanner in the works.

I spent hours on the plane trying to make sense of it all, Zan, Caroline, the Organisation, Orlanda and I couldn't make sense of anything. Eventually I decided to take my own advice, 'Time is a great healer, just give yourself a chance.'

The plane touched down at Shanghai Pudong International Airport just after six o'clock in the morning local time. We taxied to the terminal and for once disembarked almost as soon as the plane had stopped. Surprisingly I passed through passport and customs within a matter of minutes. Talking to the officials in their own language helped and I found myself walking through the sliding doors into the main concourse just over half an hour after touch down. I was actually impressed with an airport for once.

As Zan was working that day, we'd arranged that I would catch the train into the city centre and meet her later. I began looking for the Maglev Line when somebody put their arm around my waist. I turned, a little startled, and there was Zan, smiling as only she could.

'I thought you were at work,' I blurted out.

'I am, but I don't have to be there until nine.'

Grabbing her, we kissed hard and passionately. She pulled away. 'It's frowned upon in public over here.'

'Sod that,' I responded and kissed her again.

We had the most incredible week together. While Zan worked I did the tourist bit, travelling on a double decker bus, visiting historical landmarks such as the Bund, the City God Temple and the Yuyuan Garden. Together we discovered Lujiazui with its incredible skyline and did a river cruise down the Huangpu. More importantly, we were together. We couldn't keep away from each other and held hands constantly.

We ate at some of the most incredible restaurants, feasting on such delights as hairy crab, oysters, eel, suckling pig, deep fried squid and wagyu beef, washed down with Shaoxing yellow wine.

At night we held each other tight, making love until early morning when we slept, never wanting to be parted.

All good things come to an end and we knew it would be several weeks before we could see each other again. However we also knew we had a job to do and, if I'm honest, Zan was more focused on it than me. Neither of us had a clue how things would pan out, but the pincer movement made sense. She was looking at the company from an empirical accountancy viewpoint and I was the nuts and bolts man, on the shop floor so to speak.

She'd been well received at KPMG and was settling in nicely. Nothing fazed her, she was well ahead of the majority of people she'd met and felt very comfortable being back in an accountancy environment.

Her programme had been put together with the efficiency we'd come to expect from the Organisation. She was spending one or two days in various teams, learning procedures, looking at the industries and companies they worked with and the services offered. The clever thing about her secondment was that she spent enough time with people for them to recognize her, but they would know little about her.

As I flew home I was able to put things in place. Although I had a soft spot for Caroline, I knew Zan was my first love. I felt happy about joining Orlanda because I could see I wasn't joining as a clerk, I was on a mission and playing a character was part of that mission. I felt very pumped up and ready to go, tingling with excitement. The week away had done me the world of good and put everything in perspective. The great thing was that Zan would be in Zurich in two weeks so we would be able to at least spend our weekends together. Money had suddenly become irrelevant, my world was changing quickly.

I got back to Slough on Friday and immediately touched base with Frank.

'Had a good time, old boy?' he asked.

'Yeah, terrific thanks, and now I'm ready for action.'

'Good man, give yourself a couple of days to settle in and then phone me with an update. Obviously if anything happens in the meantime, you'll let me know.'

I thought about going to Mum and Dad's that weekend or possibly seeing old friends but, realising I wanted to be on the ball on Monday, I decided to cleanse the system by going to the gym, eating sensibly and staying off the booze. By Sunday evening my body was tired, having exercised hard, but I knew it would hold me in good stead for what lay ahead.

Monday morning came and I got up at six thirty to go for a run. I was determined to keep my fitness levels up. After the pain in Kenya I didn't want to lose what I had achieved. After a shower I changed into one of the suits provided – just a high street job, after all this wasn't a Saville Road exercise.

As I left the flat, Jasmine was coming down the stairs with her kids.

'Hi, Jasmine,' I said. 'How's the internet?'

'It is working perfectly, you are a genius. You must come up for something to eat one night.'

'Thank you, I'd love that. I can't stop, I'm starting a new job this morning.'

With that, I waved and exited the house. I could hear the kids squabbling as I climbed into the car and drove off.

I'd been asked to report to Jeff Andrews at nine am so, arriving at the Orlanda building at eight forty five, I sat listening to the radio for a few minutes, composing myself for the day's activities. I felt somewhat tense, which was probably to be expected. I smiled at the scenario. Here I was, sitting outside a dilapidated building in Slough of all places, about to start my career in industrial espionage.

Life's a funny thing, I thought and climbed out of the car.

As I entered reception, the charm school student was plonking herself down behind the screen. She glared at me.

'Hello,' I said with a big toothy grin, 'I'm Dean Farlow, starting work with Jeff Andrews today.'

'You got the job then,' she said in her disinterested manner.

'Yes, looking forward to working with you. What's your name?'

'Chantelle,' she said, scowling.

That'd be right, I thought.

She picked up the phone and mumbled into it.

'Jeff'll be down in a couple of minutes, take a seat.'

'Another chance to read Marble Trend,' I quipped.

She glared at me again and I realised that we would never become bosom buddies. Jeff appeared five minutes later.

'Hi Dean, welcome to Orlanda! Glad you're here.'

'So am I, looking forward to the challenge.'

'I'll take you up to the accounts office and introduce you to Julie Mc Dermott, my right-hand girl. She'll show you the ropes.'

I followed him upstairs into a large open office with half a dozen desks and two people sitting there.

Julie was a woman in her mid-forties, I estimated, and appeared to have a friendly demeanour. Jeff introduced me and she asked me to sit next to her.

'You can shadow me for a couple of days and then I'll watch you, so hopefully by Friday you'll be able to have a go by yourself.'

'You're hopeful,' I said.

'You'll be okay, it's not complicated.'

She was right as well, it was pretty basic stuff. The first job involved inputting payments that had come through that morning onto the computer system. This was followed by issuing secondary invoices for those who hadn't paid after thirty days. Julie then chased payments due at sixty days on the phone, inputting comments on the system as she spoke to people. She obviously had a good rapport with her customers.

It transpired that she had been with the company for fourteen years and was well versed in the culture. I realised that she would be somebody who could give me a lot of inside information without realising it.

The system was surprisingly basic, with a fair amount of manual inputting. It should have been automated years ago. I mentioned this to Julie and she was quite acidic in her response.

'It works for us.'

In other words, don't get smart, you've only been here five minutes. I suppose she was right and, truth be told, it was an irrelevance to the job in hand. In many ways it made things easier, as an older system would be easier to hack into.

The other girl in the office was a sweet kid, straight out of school, called Amy. Her main task appeared to be inputting orders which were fed down to the Head Office in Bologna. Later that morning she was on the phone, having great difficulty trying to make herself understood. A typical Brit, she was shouting as if that would make a difference. I leaned over to her.

'I speak Italian, can I help?'

She was almost in tears as she spoke.

'They've sent the wrong order and the customer is having a fit. Nobody will listen to me.'

'Shall I speak to them?'

'Please.'

I took the phone. 'Buongiorno, parlo italiano, posso aiutare?'

'Thank goodness, someone with a little sense instead of a silly girl,' came the response in voluble Italian.

'What seems to be the problem?' I asked.

'The problem is that Amy inputted the wrong order and that is what has been supplied.'

I translated, being as diplomatic as possible.

'Amy, they are saying the order they supplied is the one that was inputted.'

'Rubbish,' came the response. 'Look, the order clearly states Bologna Honed Marble, they've sent Bologna Polished Marble.'

I translated, there was a silence at the other end.

'Now we see the problem,' came the eventual response. 'We will send the correct order with tonight's delivery, you will have it by Thursday.

I gave the news to Amy who rolled her eyes. 'Dickheads,' she said.

'Is that okay?' I asked.

'It'll have to be. I'll tell the customer, no doubt he'll go ape. Ask them about offering a discount to show willing.'

I liked this kid, she was thinking forward and trying to resolve problems before they happened.

I asked the question.

'Tell him we'll offer ten per cent.'

'And what will you go up to if need be?' I surprised myself, I was really getting into this.

'Fifteen if need be.'

'OK, I'll pass the news on.'

Amy was waving at me. 'Tell them to confirm by email, I can't do anything unless it's in writing.'

'We'll send it immediately,' was the response. 'Addio.'

Amy smiled. 'Thanks ever so. I think you could be quite useful around here.'

'Happy to oblige,' I said, knowing that I'd created an ally. With her knowledge of the company, I decided she could be quite useful to me as well.

The rest of the day passed off uneventfully but I was quite surprised at the number of customers who hadn't bothered paying. Bad debt seemed quite an issue.

'That's why you're here,' said Julie. 'I've been doing the debt collecting as well as my own job and it's too much for one person, so I'm rather relieved to have you. It's only me who seems worried about the situation. I've been saying for nearly twelve months that I need a bit of support.'

Amy piped up, 'I've agreed twelve and a half per cent discount with the customer, he thinks I'm a marvel.'

'Good girl,' I responded 'that's a real win-win.'

She beamed. I wondered how and when she'd be able to help me.

By the end of the day I felt as if I'd cracked debt collection. Julie was happy with the way I handled customers, so I took charge of the job.

I got home that night feeling quite happy with life. I'd established my cover and been accepted by my colleagues as just another employee. I touched base with Frank, who sounded more than pleased.

'Excellent, my man,' he said. 'Don't try moving too quickly, just ease your way into the company and see what comes up over the next few weeks. Softly, softly is the approach, if you try to move too soon you'll miss something. So don't do anything without discussing it with me first.'

For the first time I saw the man of steel that Frank obviously was. I realised he wasn't someone to trifle with.

I phoned Caroline straight after.

'I thought I'd frightened you off,' she said.

'No way, how are things?'

'A little better. I've got a bit of work, thank goodness, which has kept me busy for the last few days. It's only a short-term project but it'll keep the wolf from the door for a few weeks.'

We arranged to meet for dinner on Thursday. I knew now that Caroline would be no more than a friend. I loved Zan with all my heart and would never cheat on her, but I did like Caroline. I'd decided that she was good company and I needed someone outside of my work environment just to be a friend and have a bit of fun with.

Chapter 10

That week I got on with the job at Orlanda. A lot of the work was quite mundane but that was to be expected. I actually enjoyed the debt collection side of things as it gave me the opportunity to learn about the company from a customer perspective.

There were several things I discovered. Ordering was a complete shambles. My little translation exercise for Amy on the first day was not a one-off. I found myself having similar conversations on a daily basis. There was no control in Italy and no one took ownership. It was as if nobody cared and discounts were given for incompetence as the norm.

The bad debt situation was worse than I had first suspected. Again, apart from Julie nobody seemed concerned. I mentioned this to Jeff after a few days and he brushed it aside, telling me not to worry but to get on with the job.

The third problem was quality control. Much of Amy's time was spent sorting out orders where the marble arrived in a sub-standard state. I began to realise that this company couldn't last in its current form.

Towards the end of the week I found myself getting quite frustrated with the debt collection process. The problem I had was getting hold of people. Quite a few of the debtors were small builders who were never in when I phoned the landline and wouldn't return my call if I left a message on their mobile.

I had an idea which I bounced off Frank on the Thursday evening.

'What I'd like to suggest is that I spend a couple of evenings trying to contact these people. It's not that I'm bothered about the bad debt but I've noticed that for whatever reason many of our deliveries from Italy seem to come in the evening, which strikes me as a bit odd. Also trucks are back out on the road very early in the morning making deliveries. Now, you could argue that by the time the trucks have driven from Italy it's almost inevitable they will arrive late in the day. I realise it's efficient to turn them around quickly and get the stock delivered asap, but the company isn't that efficient and there's little or no communication between the office staff and the warehouse. It's as if they live in parallel universes. The warehouse is a ghost town during the day and a hive of activity at night. I may be wrong but it just seems a bit odd. If I work late at night I may be able to have a little snoop around.'

'I like your thought pattern,' responded Frank, 'but it's just a little too early in the day to start snooping around. The saying *slowly, slowly, catchee monkey* comes to mind. Just keep watching for the time being. I think you are probably onto something and we may well use your plan in a few weeks' time. But I want to build a bigger picture if possible before we go wading in. We're not in a desperate panic to solve this one and we want to cover all the angles. Is that okay old boy?'

I felt a little frustrated but could see the logic in what Frank was saying.

That night I took Caroline to an Indian restaurant which, after a few days of bad debt collection, felt like a welcome relief. She was much happier than on our previous encounter and more relaxed. I was a little preoccupied and had to apologise a couple of times. I explained that with the new job I had a lot on my mind. The truth was I felt a little uncomfortable being with her as I wanted to be with Zan. I dropped her off on good terms but wasn't sure where this relationship was going. It was all very well saying we could be friends but in my heart I knew that was a none starter. I wasn't being fair to either of the girls and it just wasn't my style.

Later that evening Zan called. She immediately put me in a good mood by saying she was flying over to Zurich the following Wednesday. There was a preliminary audit meeting for the team working on the Orlanda account and she had been invited to join them. I was thrilled, it meant I could see her that weekend. I immediately booked a flight leaving at ten past seven on the Friday evening coming back at nine o'clock on Sunday. I shook my head. One minute I was an accounts clerk and the next a jet setter. Life was strange!

The following morning as I was logging in to the Orlanda system, I noticed something that had been bugging me for a couple of days.

'Julie, what's Orlanda Imports?' I asked.

'What do you mean?'

'Well, when I log in there's an icon for Orlanda Imports, but if I click on it I'm asked for a password and domain and it won't accept me.'

Julie came across and had a look at my screen.

'No idea,' she said. 'It's probably something the boffins added in case we set up a new company or something like that.'

'Oh,' I said, trying to sound a little disinterested. *That's one I'll have to talk through with Frank*, I thought. *Who knows what I'll find in there?*

'How've you found your first week?' she asked.

'Not bad, I've enjoyed helping Amy with the Italians and the debt collection can be quite interesting. It's just a bit frustrating when you can't get hold of people.'

'Don't worry too much, as long as the powers that be are happy.'

There weren't too many payments to post that morning so I said to Julie, 'How come the warehouse is so quiet during the day and yet it's busy at night?'

She looked at me. 'You ask a lot of questions.'

'I'm new to the job, just interested that's all.'

'You'll learn that the Italians work in mysterious ways. Their culture is very different. Give it a couple of years and you'll get used to it.'

'I wait with bated breath,' I retorted.

She giggled. For a forty five year old she was quite good looking and had a pleasing laugh.

That night I rang Frank and told him about the "Orlanda Imports" icon. 'It's probably nothing,' I said, 'but definitely worth checking out.'

Frank laughed. 'Oh, the impatience of youth,' he boomed. 'Remember, slowly, slowly. You're doing a superb job, believe it or not. After only five days you've discovered a hell of a lot, none of which ties up. When we're ready we'll start rocking the boat, but not before. Hear me, Dean, I know you want a quick result but you have to accept that time is the thing that brings success. Let's see what you've got so far, the possibility of a dodgy company hidden in the system, strange goings-on at night, a supposed successful company not interested in quality control, bad debt out of control. Not bad for a week's work, my boy, stick at it please.'

'Thanks, Frank.'

'Have a lovely weekend, you deserve it.'

I'd decided to spend the weekend quietly again and talked to Zan on Skype until about two am. If I'm honest, I didn't really need human interaction beyond that and spent most of Saturday at the gym. The place was full of neanderthals with big muscles, shaved heads and tattoos. It summed up modern life in Britain and didn't inspire me. I got back to the flat at about six and as I was walking up the stairs Jasmine cornered me.

'Dean, have you eaten?'

'No,' I replied.

'Well, you must join me. I have jerk chicken on the menu.'

'Sounds irresistible, what time?'

'Shall we say seven o'clock?' She was grinning from ear to ear, her pearly white teeth glistening.

'Perfect, see you then.'

Closing my door, I breathed out slowly. 'God, I hope she's not going to try anything on.'

I'd decided not to shower with the intelligentsia at the club so I luxuriated in the bath for half an hour and then dressed, smart casual as they say. Grabbing a bottle of Prosecco from the fridge, I made my way upstairs to Jasmine's flat just after seven.

She opened the door and I was immediately concerned. Dressed in a tight cocktail dress showing far too much cleavage, she was made up to the nines. In another life I would have been delighted at the prospect but today felt trapped, wondering how the hell I was going to get out of this one.

'Where are the kids?' I asked, fearing I already knew the answer.

'They are staying with their grandmother tonight.'

Oh bugger, I thought. 'Lovely. Shall we have a drink?' I said, handing her the bottle. Given the current situation, I needed one.

'Champagne,' she exclaimed. 'How wonderful, would you like to open it?'

'It's not actually champagne.' I was somewhat flustered removing the cork. 'It's an Italian wine, but very pleasant.'

'As long as it's got bubbles, I don't care where it comes from,' she said laughing.

I poured two large glasses and toasted the evening while thinking, *Help!*

She opened the oven door and pulled out what looked like half a dozen mini pasties.

'These are lamb patties,' she said. 'They are very hot, I hope you like them.'

They were hot in both senses of the word, straight out of the oven and filled with chillies and ginger.

'Delicious,' I said, choking on a chilli and taking a large gulp of wine to cool my mouth. 'How do you make them?'

Jasmine went into a long explanation on the art of Jamaican cooking. It was really quite boring but I let her ramble on just to kill time.

The table was laid for dinner in the living room and, by the time we sat down to eat, the Prosecco had nearly all gone. She opened a bottle of Chardonnay, not my favourite, but in a situation like this anything sufficed.

She'd gone to a lot of trouble and I felt guilty for not being more receptive. Candles were lit on the table and she served prawns wrapped in bacon. They were absolutely delicious and I told her so.

'I thought I was coming up for a bit of jerk chicken.'

'That's your next course, but I like to entertain properly.' Her deep brown eyes bore into mine as she said it. This was the come-on of all come-ons and I had no idea how to handle the situation. The Organisation hadn't trained us on this one!

'So where have you been?' she said. 'We'd only just met and you were off again.'

This was my opportunity.

'I was in-between jobs so I decided to go and see my girlfriend. She's been working in Shanghai for a while.'

'Oh,' said Jasmine. The mood changed somewhat. The comment had the desired effect. 'I'll go and get the main course.'

The chicken was superb. The girl had gone to so much trouble on the off chance that I would be around. She was knocking back the Chardonnay like there was no tomorrow, reminding me of John back in Kenya.

'You must try my rum cake,' she said, leaning over the table, her face only inches from mine.

'That would be very nice,' I replied, trying to cool her ardour.

At that point she kissed me hard. I was somewhat taken aback and found myself responding for more than a few seconds. She was all over me and, hard as it was, I eventually pulled away.

'Jasmine, I can't,' I said huskily. 'I have a girlfriend and she means the world to me.'

'Nobody needs to know,' came the response. 'This could be our guilty secret.'

God, I was tempted. I was half pissed and as randy as hell.

I stood up and walked to the other side of the room.

'I'm sorry,' I said.

'She's a lucky girl.' Tears started welling in her eyes. 'Don't think badly of me.'

'I don't think badly of you, I think you're a wonderful person. At another time things may have been very different.'

'I hope there is another time.'

I went over and held her. 'You'll find someone.' I said. 'You're a lovely girl.'

She kissed me again and I could feel myself succumbing to her charms.

Eventually I pulled away and said, 'I'm going now. Thanks for a terrific evening. Let's be friends. If things change with my girlfriend, you'll be the first to know.'

'I'll have to get a voodoo charm,' she said smiling sadly.

At that I wished her goodnight and went down the stairs. Letting myself in, I breathed a sigh of relief. I actually felt quite proud of myself for pulling away when I did. I really must have been in love.

I rang Zan and obviously woke her. 'Sorry,' I said. 'I needed to talk to you.'

'Why?' she said sleepily. Hearing her voice made me want to hold her. I described the night's proceedings. Zan laughed. 'Poor girl, she must be very lonely.'

'Thanks,' I responded.

'No, I didn't mean it like that, but I'm glad you told me.'

'I'm a very different person because of you.'

'I love you, Jonathan Miles, or whatever your name is. Now let me get some sleep.'

'Night night, my darling. I love you too, with all my heart and all my soul.'

The following morning I bought a bouquet of flowers from a local filling station and took them up to Jasmine. As she opened the door I could tell she'd been crying.

'Thanks for a great evening.'

'I'm sorry,' she said. 'I think I embarrassed you.'

'Don't be silly. As I said, you're a lovely person and your prince will come.'

She smiled. 'Thanks, Dean. Will I see you again?'

'Damn right you will, I want some more of that jerk chicken. Perhaps you can invite me round again one night.'

'I'd like that.'

'See you then.' I kissed her on the cheek and went back downstairs.

Chapter 11

On Monday I arrived at Orlanda just before nine and Amy was grinning as I walked in.

'Must have been a good weekend,' I said, laughing.

'No,' she said. 'Something's up, and I haven't quite fathomed what it is yet.'

'Why, what's happened?'

'Well, I came in about ten minutes ago and Jeff was having a real go at Julie. He was saying things like, "I need your support on this one," and Julie was almost in tears. When I arrived, Jeff demanded they go to his office. Sounds like fun!'

'Wow,' I retorted, trying to make sense of it all.

I sat down and started doing the morning postings on the system. By now I was fairly conversant with it all and didn't need much help. After about half an hour Julie walked in.

She looked at me. 'We've got a problem.'

At first I thought my cover had been blown and suddenly felt rather scared.

'What's wrong?' I asked, trying to sound innocent.

'You're probably aware that we took over a pub chain last year. Well, it transpires that rather a lot of money has gone missing. I've been asked to go and help sort things out from an accountancy perspective. As if I know anything about running pubs.'

'Yeah, but accountancy practices are the same in all industries.'

'I know, but I've never seen myself in that sort of environment. I'm just happy doing what I do here.' She was almost in tears. 'They've already got rid of staff at six pubs including The Crown in Slough, it's a complete mess. They've now got to recruit and train a load of new people asap to get the places open. Could you handle things at this end for the next few weeks without me?'

'Probably, I feel reasonably comfortable with what I'm doing. As long as I can contact you when I have any issues then it shouldn't be a problem.'

'Thanks, Dean, that helps me greatly.'

'When are you off?' I asked.

'Now. If we're not careful this could bring the whole company tumbling down.'

'Oh Christ,' I said, and for good measure added, 'Maybe I should have stayed in the soft world of the civil service.'

'Sorry,' came the response, 'but if you can continue to help Amy it would be appreciated.'

'No problem.'

'Here's my mobile number if you need me,' she said, scribbling on a piece of paper. With that she turned to leave the room.

'Good luck,' shouted Amy.

'I'll need it,' came the response as the door closed.

Amy and I looked at each other.

'Does that make you my boss?' she asked.

'Well, if it does you can make the coffee,' I quipped.

She threw a pencil at me, giggling. 'White without?'

I nodded as she also disappeared.

I had another brain wave and, as there was nobody about, phoned Frank. Updating him with what had happened, I suggested that we needed to put somebody in one of the pubs quickly to see what was happening.

'You're right, old boy, but it'll take me a few days to source someone.'

This is where the brainwave came in. 'That could be too late.' I told him about Caroline, how she was on her uppers and needed an income. I suggested she could be our eyes and ears if she could get a job at The Crown.

'Make it worth her while. Pay her two thousand pounds per week with a minimum ten grand. She'd be in quickly and who knows what she might find?'

'But she's had no training,' Frank protested in rather an alarmed manner.

'No, but she's not stupid and we're not asking that she should put her life in danger. Just report on what she sees.'

'We'd have to security vet her.'

'Surely you could fast track that.' I was really warming to this idea and I could tell Frank wasn't dismissing it out of hand. At that moment Amy walked back in holding two cups of coffee.

'I've got to go,' I said. 'I'll text her details.'

'OK, old boy, phone me when you can.' I put the phone down and thanked Amy for the coffee.

'Do you think our jobs will be OK?' Amy asked. She was obviously concerned and was thinking about that rather than anything she might have heard me say to Frank.

'I don't know,' I replied, being as honest as I could. 'I think all we can do for the time being is keep our heads down and get on with the job in hand.' She was a nice kid and deserved better than this.

There was the usual trauma with the Italians that morning which lightened the mood and I had some reasonable success debt collecting. At lunchtime I dived out of the office and drove past The Crown. It was an old town pub working on volume, offering cheap booze and two meals for a tenner. There was a sign on the door saying, 'Closed due to staff shortages.' I parked and rang Frank again.

'She checks out fine,' said Frank, 'and I could authorise it, but I don't even know this woman.'

'Frank,' I said, 'speed is of the essence here. I know I'm the new kid on the block but let me run with this. Trust me, please.'

He paused and then said, 'OK, old boy, but on your head be it.' We talked about how I would present things to Caroline. Finally I said, 'Thanks, Frank.'

'Don't let me down.'

I immediately phoned Caroline. 'Can you talk?' I asked.

'Oh yes,' she said, sounding incredibly stressed. 'I'm sitting at home with all the time in the world. That contract I was telling you about has blown up in my face and I am totally fucked. Excuse my language but I'm distraught. I really don't know what to do.'

I hesitated slightly, working out how to phrase what I wanted to say. 'I think I may be able to help you. If I'm honest, I haven't been totally straight as to who I am.'

'Here we go,' she responded. 'What is it, wife and two kids?'

'No, nothing like that, but before you put the phone down, how does ten grand sound for five weeks work?'

There was a slight pause. 'I don't do prostitution.'

'And I'm not asking you to. All I want you to do is work in a pub and report anything you might find which is a bit odd.'

'Like what?'

'I don't know, that's why I'm asking you go in there.'

'Who are you?' she asked.

'I work for a government agency which is looking closely at this company. There are some strange goings on and we're trying to figure it out. Phone MI5 in London and ask to speak to Frank Cummings, he'll substantiate everything I've said. I could give you the number but as a form of verification I would prefer you to get it from directory enquiries. You'll be paid on a self-employed basis through the civil service, again to verify our credibility.'

There was a long silence, followed by, 'This is surreal. Where is the pub?'

'It's The Crown in Slough, they are part of the Central pub chain.'

'So what do you want me to do?'

'Go down this afternoon, there's a sign outside saying they are closed due to staff shortages. Knock on the door, say you are desperate for work, that you saw the sign and can you apply for a job? Have you worked in a pub before?'

'Yes on and off for three years when I was at university.'

'There you are then, it'll be like falling off a log. What about babysitters?'

'That won't be a problem. I've used a child minder when I've been working away in the past. Plus my Mum can help out if need be.'

'We'll cover the cost of the child minder,' I said. 'If that helps.'

'I can't believe this.'

'Phone Frank now, he's expecting your call, and get down to the pub as soon as you can. I'll talk to you at about six.'

'Dean?'

'Yeah.'

'Thanks. I can't tell you how much I appreciate this, it sounds like manna from heaven.'

'It's also what's known as a win-win situation.'

I went back to the office and arrived just an hour after I had left.

'Did you have a nice lunch break?' asked Amy.

'Not really,' I replied. 'I had to get down to town to do a bit of banking and buy some new shoes.'

She laughed. 'You live an exciting life.'

'Yes, so true,' I said, smiling. 'I'll get the coffee this time, I can grab a sandwich from the machine at the same time. I didn't have time to buy lunch.'

'I think you're going to be a nice boss,' quipped Amy.

Not for long, I hoped. That night I phoned Caroline. 'How did you get on?'

'Well, I rang Frank and had quite a long chat about how to handle the interview, assuming I got that far. He also gave me a couple of names and addresses for references. He seems very much on the ball. I then went down to the pub and knocked on the door as you said. After a couple of minutes a rather smart looking man in his early fifties opened it and I told him I was looking for work. He let me in and we sat down in the bar area where he asked all about me and my experience of working in a pub. I was basically honest and told him my business was on the verge of closing and I needed an income quickly. I also told him about my marriage situation and that I was living with my mum, who could look after the kids. A slight lie, but I thought it would add credibility.'

'Good girl,' I interjected.

'He then asked me to pour a pint of beer, so I said, "Which beer would you like, sir?" At that point he smiled and said I could start on a trial basis tomorrow morning. I asked him what had happened and he said several people had been caught with their fingers in the till and had been summarily dismissed. I thought it wise not to press him further. I then filled out an application form and that was it. I start at ten am tomorrow.'

'Who is this chap?'

'He's the area manager, but he'll be running the pub until they find a new manager. He also asked if I knew of anyone else looking for work.'

'What did you say?'

'That I'd ask around.'

'Incredible,' I said. 'Well done.'

'I don't know how to thank you,' she responded .

'Just by turning up at the pub watching and listening, and don't try to do anything brave. We employ people to do that sort of thing.'

I then had a conversation with Frank. He seemed quite happy at the turn of events and confirmed that I was not to do anything stupid. He also said I should keep away from the pub to avoid contagion. He stated that he would be popping in at some point to have a look and to ensure he knew who Caroline was.

Things were beginning to move but I felt very frustrated. I really wanted to hack into the computer system and have a snoop around the warehouse. Without Frank's authority that could prove difficult, so I knew I'd have to work on him. I then realized there was something I could do without breaking any of Frank's rules.

I drove up to the industrial estate and parked on a slip road close to the Orlanda building so that I could watch the lorry movements. Much to my amazement, thirty trucks came and went within four hours. This was far more than the level of orders that Orlanda were processing and it became very obvious there was a secondary business going on. As I drove home, I began to formulate a plan. The following morning before I went to work I phoned Frank again.

'Now I've got the perfect excuse,' I said. 'The boss has left me to my own devices so I can say I thought I should catch up on some defaulters by contacting them in the evening. As far as they're concerned, I'm showing initiative as I want to get on in the company, nobody could fault that. I'll work for a few evenings doing nothing stupid apart from going to the coffee machine so that people will get used to me being around. We've got nothing to lose.'

I could hear Frank chortling down the line. 'OK, old boy, you're wearing me down. Carry on, but keep in touch.'

Chapter 12

I worked hard that day building a list of people to contact in the evening. By close of play I had fifty names.

'Are you ready to go home?' asked Amy. She was a real five o'clock merchant.

'I'm going to stick around and try and get hold of a few people I've missed during the day. A bit of an experiment really.'

'Sounds as if you're crawling to the bosses,' she joked.

'Not really,' I said. 'I need the job and if what Julie said is right we really need to bring this debt problem under control quickly.'

'Is it really that bad?' She sounded quite alarmed.

'I really don't know, but if I can find a way to help the situation then it's no bad thing.'

'Well, good luck.'

'Thanks.'

There wasn't much point in phoning people before six, I thought I'd give them time to get home. So I spent an hour reading the newspaper and catching up on Facebook. I wasn't much of a fan but it was a way of killing time. I also tried to phone Zan but there was no reply. Thinking of the weekend that lay ahead, I decided I didn't have to move too quickly at Orlanda. There were so many good things happening in my life, why spoil it?

I worked through until nine o'clock and was astonished at my success. So many of the people I contacted were amazed I was phoning in the evening and were agreeable enough to make immediate payment by debit card. I smiled to myself. Given a few months, I could knock this company into shape.

At one point I got so into debt collection I all but forgot the real purpose of my venture. So at seven thirty I made my way down to the canteen. There were eight people hanging around, most of whom looked like long distance lorry drivers. A couple were seated by the door talking about football in Italian, two sat at a table eating what looked like packed lunches, two were standing by the coffee machine, and a couple of warehouse men sat at the far end.

I put a fifty pence coin in the slot and pressed the button for an 'Americano'.

'These coffee ees crap,' I heard as I bent down to pick up the cup. The two guys standing close by were smiling at me. They looked like Laurel and Hardy, one was rather large and the other like a rake.

'I agree,' I replied in Italian, 'but it's better than nothing.'

'You speak good Italian,' said the larger one.

'My mother is from Tuscany.'

'You follow football?' said the smaller man.

'Fiorentina in Italy, although God knows why, the last time they won anything was the Coppa Italia in 2001.'

They laughed. 'Cin cin,' I said, holding up my coffee. Making my way back to the office, I realized what Frank was saying. By building rapport with these guys, I knew I'd find out much more than by myself. Slowly, slowly, I was beginning to learn.

I went home feeling reasonably content with the day's proceedings. That night I touched base with Caroline first. I could tell from the timbre of her voice that she was in much better spirits than earlier in the day.

'I feel so elated,' she said. 'It's such a relief to know that I've got money coming in.'

'Don't forget, you'll also be getting paid by the pub. That'll be another grand a month.'

'We really should be celebrating!'

'Not tonight, you're starting a new job and you'll need a clear head. I'll talk to you tomorrow, but phone me any time if you need help.'

I spoke to Zan briefly. She had just finished packing and was ready to go to the airport. 'Roll on, Friday,' I said.

Over the next three days I worked until about nine each night. The results with regard to bad debt were astonishing but more importantly I was getting to know a few of the evening staff. They were a pretty strange lot. The drivers were fine but the people actually employed in the warehouse were aggressive and edgy to a man. Where there was banter with the drivers, the warehouse men didn't want to know.

On the Thursday night one of them came up to me.

'I've seen you hanging around here for a few days now, who are you?' His manner was hostile and threatening in the extreme.

'Hi, I'm Dean Farlow from accounts.'

'So what are you doing here at this time of night?' His face was inches from mine. To make matters worse, his breath stank.

'I'm debt collecting. It's the best time of day to get hold of some of our customers.'

He just glared at me and walked off. I felt extremely uncomfortable and went straight back to my office. I was shaking. There was no need for his approach, they had to be hiding something.

Meanwhile, Caroline had started working at the pub. On her first morning six other people had joined, having been sent from the job centre. By lunch time three of them had walked, obviously afraid of hard work. Because of her experience she quickly became the leader and trainer, which strengthened her position considerably.

The pub reopened on her second day and a further three people arrived from the job centre. Somehow they managed to get through the midday rush with one disaster following the next. People were undercharged and overcharged, incorrect change was given, incorrect drinks were served and food was dropped with great regularity. Tables were left unclean and dirty glasses were used to pour drinks into. By three o'clock Caroline was shattered and wondered what on earth she had let herself in for.

However, during the afternoon lull she was able to spend more time with each of the trainees and by the following day the pub was starting to operate in a reasonable manner. The one saving grace was that the chef had stayed on so, despite incorrect orders being given, they were able to serve food which was acceptable.

Caroline was amazed that the area manager hid himself away. She thought it would be all hands on deck, but he was locked in his office most of the time.

'Apart from that,' she said to me on the phone soon after close of play on the second day, 'I haven't seen anything that is particularly odd. But we're in such a muddle I wouldn't have noticed if a London bus had driven in through the front door.'

By the third day service levels were picking up and complaints were becoming less of an issue. A new manager arrived and Caroline could tell within minutes he had little or no experience of running a pub.

One of the team asked him to change a barrel and he snarled, 'That's not my fuckin' job, you do it.'

Everyone was a bit shocked. They had developed a real Dunkirk, spirit in the last few days with people pulling together. In one fell swoop the new man had destroyed much of what they had achieved together.

'We were better off without him,' said Caroline. 'I could cry.'

'Hang on,' I replied, 'you've got to remember this is not a proper job. You are there to watch and report, don't forget that.'

'I know and you're right, it's just that they're not a bad bunch of kids and I don't want an imbecile wrecking the hard work we've put in.'

'It's not relevant,' I said. 'The fact they've put someone like that in situ tells us this is not a normal operation. You're already achieving, well done.'

'Thanks, Dean, I needed someone to make sense of it all for me.'

I packed for Zurich and swept the flat to make sure I'd left no incriminating evidence with regard to my identity. One of the key training points in Kenya was to ensure no trace was ever left, be it in a hotel, office or place of residence. Everything was tucked away in the safe apart from my passport, credit cards and flight ticket. I then put the carpet and piece of string back in place.

On the Friday Julie phoned to see how things were. I told her about my debt collection exercise and she seemed genuinely pleased. 'I knew if we could get the right person in to focus on the issue we could bring things under control. Well done, Dean, I should go away more often.'

'How are you getting on?' I enquired casually.

'It's weird,' she said. 'So far we've been through the books of two pubs and everything ties up. The banking and till receipts are as near as damn it matching. Stock levels are right, the pay roll is in order and we haven't found anything which is out of the ordinary. Turnover is actually up on last year so I've no idea what all the fuss is about. We've had to take on new staff for each pub and they don't know one end of a pint pot from the other. Inevitably mistakes are being made which will be costing the company more than the supposed losses they've recently incurred.'

'How long are you going to be away for?' I asked.

'Difficult to say, I would have thought another week or so. We're working through the weekend to try and get a grip on things as quickly as possible.'

'Think of the overtime,' I quipped.

If I'm honest, I felt a bit tired that day. I'd been working long hours at Orlanda, together with organizing Caroline. I also think the strain of being undercover most of the time was beginning to show. It was taking it out of me and I was looking forward to jumping on the plane to Zurich that night.

'Got anything planned for the weekend?' asked Amy.

'Not really,' I replied. 'Just a quiet one, what about you?' I wasn't really interested but wanted to deflect the conversation.

'My boyfriend and I going for a Chinese tonight and I'm meeting a few of the girls tomorrow night.'

'Well, you behave yourself,' I said, sounding like my father.

'Certainly not,' she responded, laughing.

I drifted through the day and realized that if I continued to bring the bad debt levels down at the speed I had achieved that week I would be doing myself out of a job. I made a mental note to slow down a little.

At lunchtime I went down to the canteen to buy a sandwich. My warehouse buddy was sitting at a table with a couple of similar types. He glared at me so I raised my hand in friendly acknowledgment. He turned and said something to one of his colleagues. None of them looked, but I could tell I was being watched. I remembered Frank's words, slowly, slowly.

I left sharply at five. There were two reasons – one, I had a flight to catch, and two, I wanted to cool down the interest that had been shown in me at lunchtime. The good thing was that I had the perfect alibi. My results from the evening work spoke for themselves.

Driving straight to the airport, I parked in the long term. It was damned cold waiting for the bus to the terminal and, as there was nobody about, I rang Caroline. She had nothing new to report apart from one of the team being sacked by the moron she was now working for. Apparently he turned to the boss and said he didn't like the way he was being spoken to. The boss looked at him and said, 'Well fuck off then, you're fired.' The guy walked straight out of the pub.

What I found interesting was that the manager had a similar mentality to the charm school student from the warehouse. I now had several bits of the jigsaw, but none of them were as yet tying together. I knew it was only a matter of time. With that, the bus came and took me to terminal five.

While on the bus, Zan phoned. She sounded awful, her voice croaking.

'Would you mind if I didn't meet you at the airport?'

'Not at all,' I responded. 'Are you OK?'

'I feel awful, if I'm honest. I think it's a cross between stress, jetlag and picking something up on the plane. You know what it's like, all the germs being constantly recycled around a tube for fifteen hours. I just need a few hours' sleep and I'll be fine.'

'Would you prefer me not to come? We could postpone it until next week.'

'No, no, that's the last thing I want. But maybe we could just take things easy and have a relaxing weekend?'

'That sounds great,' I said. 'All this bouncing around is getting to both of us. Have a sleep and I'll see you in a few hours.'

'Thanks, Jonathan. I love you.'

'One question.'

'Yes?'

'Where are you staying? It would be useful to know.'

She giggled and sounded a little more like her old self.

'The Sheraton Zürich Neues Schloss Hotel. It's in the city centre, room 5102, on the fifth floor.'

'I'll get a cab. See you soon.'

Terminal five was heaving with people and seemed more unbearable than usual. Fortunately, with only hand luggage, I scanned my reference number into a machine and a boarding pass spewed out.

My heart sank when I arrived at security. The queue seemed to trail forever. By now it was six twenty and I had visions of the plane leaving without me. Thirty five minutes later I was putting my shoes back on and legged it to the plane.

Arriving somewhat breathless, the stewardess said, 'No panic, sir, take off has been delayed by ten minutes.' I couldn't decide whether to be relieved or annoyed.

Sitting down on the plane I felt absolutely knackered. I knew precisely what Zan was going through, the international jet setting life wasn't all it was cracked up to be. I closed my eyes virtually as soon as I had strapped myself in and the next thing I knew the wheels were touching down on the runway. I'd slept for nearly two hours and the man sitting next to me glared as I stretched and looked around. I'd obviously upset him. *Life's a bitch*, I thought.

Grabbing a couple of hundred pounds worth of Swiss Francs from a cashpoint, I made my way to the taxi rank.

'Sheraton Zürich Neues Schloss Hotel, bitte.'

The taxi driver responded with an impenetrable Swiss German accent. He probably spoke perfectly acceptable German but, as he wanted to be an arse, I decided to reduce his tip.

Twenty minutes later we arrived at the hotel. I paid him off and said, 'Thanks a lot,' in English.

'Oh sorry,' came the response, 'I thought you were German.' I smiled. The Second World War was still alive and well in Zurich!

Making my way straight to the lift, I was amazed how small it was. Squeezing out on to the fifth floor, I walked down the corridor and knocked on Zan's door. After a few seconds I heard some movement and she opened it. Her hair was all tousled and she was wearing a T-shirt. I'd obviously woken her.

She grabbed me and held tight. It felt good, but she was burning up and covered in sweat.

'You're not well, are you?'

'Come in.'

'I was hoping you'd say that.' She smiled as she led me into the room.

'I didn't know if you'd eaten so I've ordered some food.' On a table stood some sandwiches, cheese, fruit and a bottle of white wine.

'Thank you, darling. Have you taken anything?'

'A couple of aspirin, I'll take some more now.'

We sat on a sofa and I poured the wine.

'Not for me, I'll just have water.'

As I ate, we chatted about Orlanda, the pub chain, and Caroline, at which point she said, 'Is there anything going on between you two?' She was almost in tears as she spoke.

'A few months ago there might have been, just as there could have been a one night stand with Jasmine, but not now. I don't need that, I've got you. To use the old expression, why have a takeaway burger when I've got steak back home?'

She held me tight. 'I've been worried,' she said.

'You don't have to be,' I replied. 'I don't want anybody or anything but you.'

We went to bed and just held each other all night. It was a beautiful expression of our love.

I woke at about eight o'clock Zurich time, seven body time. Zan was staring at me. She'd cooled down overnight and was looking better.

'How are you feeling?' I asked.

'I'm OK, but tired.'

'A day of leisure, I feel, maybe a gentle walk and a spot of luncheon.'

We kissed gently.

'Go and have a shower,' she said. 'And clean your teeth, your breath smells horrible.'

'Love you too,' I responded as I got up.

That weekend was rather like the calm before the storm. Both of us were aware that things were beginning to hot up at Orlanda. Zan was concerned that I had put myself in a dangerous position and, if I'm honest, having seen the people working at the warehouse I felt somewhat anxious myself.

I felt she would be safe. Working in the head office environment for KPMG she should be cocooned from any trouble. She told me she was going to spend a week with the team at the Zurich office of Orlanda and then move on to the divisional headquarters in Bologna.

'I've been thinking,' she said. 'It may be safer for me to access the hidden Orlanda systems once I'm in their offices.'

'I don't want you putting yourself in danger,' I said.

'I don't see how I will be. Even if I'm caught red-handed, what can they say or do in a head office environment? I'll only try to access the system when there are plenty of people around me. Apart from anything else, you're probably being watched now, whereas I'll be seen as just another bean counter. We're a team, Jonathan, and you can't do all this by yourself.'

She was right of course, but I still worried.

'Let me bounce it off Frank,' I said. 'It's important we keep him involved.'

That afternoon we strolled down to the Arboretum, a small park on Lake Zurich. Although it was cold, the sun shone and we felt very close. Trees had been planted from all over the world and above them we could just about make out the Alps looking down on the city. We watched boats bobbing up and down on the lake as we sat eating bratwurst sausages while drinking cold Swiss beer. This was one of those Kodak moments. Everything we did felt wonderful but tinged with anxiety for what lay ahead.

In the evening we watched a production of *Cosi Fan Tutte* at the Zurich Opera House. I'm not a great opera fan but just being together was the important thing.

The following day we spent most of the morning in bed and by then Zan was back to full fitness. I rang Caroline, who was on her way to work. Things were settling down nicely and she had no real traumas to report. The manager was 'a complete twat' but she could live with that. Like the area manager, he spent most of his time locked away in his office. She said one thing of interest – apparently a package arrived each day delivered by a security company. They all had strict instructions to deliver it straight to the manager. She'd made a joke when handing it to him.

'What's this, the crown jewels?' she'd quipped.

'It's got fuck all to do with you,' and with that the door had been slammed in her face.

'That's interesting,' I said. 'Now don't go trying to find out what it is, we'll find another way.'

'We need someone with experience in there,' said Zan. 'Listening to what's going on, things aren't right. You know who'd be perfect?'

'Go on.'

'Caterina. She could play the part of a student needing some money.'

'By God, you're right. Why didn't I think of that?'

'Because you're not a smart Chinese girl.'

'So true,' I said, grabbing her.

'Get off,' she said. 'And phone Frank, we don't want to put that girl into any more danger.'

I grabbed my 'O' phone. 'Sorry to trouble you on a Sunday, Frank.'

'Never a problem, dear boy.'

I told him about Caroline's revelation and Zan's plan. He was silent for a few seconds.

'Let me make a couple of calls, I'll come back to you.'

We were both on tenterhooks awaiting Frank's response and ordered lunch from room service. We didn't want to be in the middle of a restaurant when the call came through. Two hours later the phone rang.

'Firstly, I want to say how delighted I am with progress so far.' It was Frank. 'The two of you are obviously working well together and in a very short time we have come a long way.'

'Get on with it,' I mouthed to Zan.

'Caterina is catching a plane to London in two hours. I'll have her picked up and arrange cover, documentation and accommodation. I'll bring her up to speed and, Dean, I'd like you to update her tomorrow night. Not face to face, again we need to keep contagion to an absolute minimum. The "O" phone will suffice.'

'All these woman, can't you work with men?' quipped Zan.

'There's always John,' I replied, laughing.

Chapter 13

Back at work the following morning I was on a high, having spent a lovely weekend with Zan.

'You seem full of the joys of spring,' said Amy.

'And why not?' I replied.

Jeff Andrews came in and asked how I was getting on. I showed him my results and he was absolutely delighted.

'Well done, Dean, this is fantastic news. Keep up the good work, but pace yourself. I don't want you burning out.'

As he left Amy said, 'Apple for the teacher?'

'Now, now,' I responded, feeling rather pleased with myself. Given that I had a director on my side, it made dealing with the warehouse man just that little bit easier.

That night I worked late and again went down to the canteen at seven thirty. Laurel and Hardy were sitting at a table and they beckoned me over. The warehouse man was on the other side of the room, glaring as usual.

'How's our little English friend?' Laurel asked in Italian.

'I'm fine,' I responded.

'It's good to have someone to talk to,' said Hardy. 'The people here are so unfriendly.'

'I know, I have never known anywhere like it. What's wrong with them?' I asked, trying to sound as innocent as possible.

'Who knows?' replied Hardy. 'Maybe it's the drugs they're on.'

At that Laurel's face hardened and Hardy paled, as if realizing what he had said.

'Whatever. It's nice to meet you two guys,' I said, trying to lighten the tone.

I left them soon after and cleared my desk to go home. As I got into the car I looked up to see the warehouse man staring at me. He was making it clear, I was being watched.

I got back to the flat and phoned Caterina. She was in great form and excited about the challenge that lay ahead. I brought her up to speed and she told me she intended going to the pub the following lunchtime to try and get a job. We agreed she should approach Caroline first, who was not going to be brought into the loop at this stage as we didn't want to put too much pressure on her.

The following morning I was printing off some default figures when the copier ran out of paper.

'I'll go and get some in a minute,' shouted Amy, sounding rather stressed. She was on the phone to Bologna and waiting for a response.

'Just tell me where it's stored.'

She directed me to the end of the corridor and the final door on the left. I'd never been down to this end of the building before and was stunned when I walked through the door. There was a window looking down onto the warehouse. Being daytime there was very little activity, but it was a clear vantage point which I knew I would have to use at some point in the near future.

Later in the day I gave Frank the news. 'OK, old boy, but before you make any further moves I want to see Josephina in place.' It was as if Caterina was dead, that name was now history.

I spoke to her a few minutes later. 'How did you get on?'

'Well, I went to the pub just before twelve and recognized Caroline from your description. I said I was a student looking for part-time bar work, explaining I was over here for nine months and had bar experience in Spain. I'm on a Spanish passport to avoid work permit problems.'

'Frank thinks of everything,' I said.

'Caroline disappeared for a couple of minutes and then asked me when I could start. I said immediately and she told me to fill in an application form. I was given a trial over lunchtime and passed. I now have a job!'

'Good girl,' I said. 'Although I'm a bit surprised Caroline can make that decision.'

'It transpired that the manager was busy in his office and told her that if I was any good I should be given a trial.'

'I'd love to know what he's doing in that office,' I said.

'I'll find out soon enough.'

'Take care, give yourself a few days to settle in before you make any moves.'

I then phoned Caroline. She told me basically the same story, what a great find Josephina was and how she hoped she could hang onto her.

'Are you in charge now?' I asked.

'Not officially but there's no one else, the manager isn't interested.'

'How do you feel?'

'I'm tired but fine, I keep saying to myself think of the money. The first tranche was paid into my bank account today, which made me feel a whole lot better.'

'You're doing a great job,' I said.

The following morning Jeff called me into his office. I wondered if the warehouse man had been talking.

'Dean, I've been looking at the bad debt figures and I have to say I'm very impressed with what you've been doing. Can you talk me through the process?'

I outlined my approach and after a couple of minutes he raised his hand.

'You're obviously a natural. Look, if you think we've got problems, you should see the Italian operation. They've got bad debt coming out of their ears with no apparent control. How would you feel about going over to Bologna for a few days to set up a programme to help them? We'll pay you a bonus of two thousand pounds to show willing.'

Hardly believing what I was hearing, I said, 'I'd be delighted, but with Julie away won't that make things difficult here?'

'She'll be back tomorrow so you can hand everything over to her.'

'When do you want me to go?'

'What about Wednesday? You can come back late on Friday and maybe go back for a few days next week.'

'Sounds like fun.' Thinking on my feet, I said, 'I'd like to stay over the weekend if I may. I haven't been to Bologna for many years and maybe I could combine a bit of work with sightseeing.'

'Good idea. We appreciate your help.'

I walked out of his office slightly bemused. Questions surged through my mind. Was this genuine? Were they really in a mess in Bologna? Were they trying to get me away from Slough? I discounted that, I hadn't been there long enough. Were they trying to get their house in order before KPMG looked at the books? That seemed likely. Maybe the warehouse man had got at him. If that was the case, they'd just get rid of me.

At lunchtime I phoned Frank and gave him an update.

'Interesting, old boy, a fascinating development and I must say I haven't got a problem. Let's just roll with it and see where we end up. If I were a betting man I'd say they were they trying to get their house in order before KPMG look at the books. They want to be seen as a straight, successful and clean operation by the outside world. Bad debt would not help that cause.'

Later that afternoon Jeff sent me an email confirming I was booked on the eight forty from Heathrow to Bologna on Wednesday. He told me to report to Mr Grimaldi on arrival and that he'd reserved a room at the Sheraton adjacent to the airport. He said some external auditors from KPMG would be staying there next week so I would have a bit of company. Seeing the funny side, I flicked up the hotel on trip advisor. They'd given it four stars. *Not bad for an accounts clerk*, I thought.

'What are you so cheerful about?' asked Amy. I told her about my trip.

'It's alright for some,' she said. 'Who's going to be my boss now?' I told her Julie would be back in the morning.

'Oh,' she said, 'I liked you.'

'Well, I'm not dead, and I can still talk to the Italians on your behalf, but face to face.'

That night I worked late again. As usual I had a fair degree of success and at seven thirty made my way down to the canteen. Laurel and Hardy greeted me like an old friend and seemed genuinely thrilled that I was going out to Bologna. They introduced themselves. Laurel was Gustavo and Hardy was Fabio. They told me they drove to Slough weekly, splitting the driving to overcome EU regulations. That way the truck could be on the road for eighteen hours a day rather than nine. One slept while the other drove. Apparently they were stuck in Slough for a couple of days waiting for a return load. I wondered why it was so essential to move marble so quickly and what the return load was, but decided those questions were for another time. Laurel gave me his phone number and said I must contact him while in Bologna.

I phoned Zan when I got home. 'Guess where I'm going on Wednesday?'

'Go on.'

'Bologna.'

I heard her giggle as I told her about the day's proceedings. God, I loved that laugh.

'Tell them to book you on a flight Friday evening so that you can go sightseeing.'

'We shouldn't be seen together.'

'Then we'll have to lock ourselves in a hotel bedroom all weekend'.

I also touched base with Caroline and Josephina. Things had settled down and they were now working in what could only be described as a comfortable rut. Frank had already given them instructions.

'Do nothing, just watch and listen.'

Chapter 14

On Wednesday morning the taxi arrived at six forty and, armed with Dean's passport, I set off yet again for Heathrow. A level of paranoia was beginning to set in as I tried to remember who I was at any one time. With three different identities in a matter of weeks, I was frightened of mixing things up and arriving at Heathrow with the wrong passport.

Check-in was relatively smooth for once and I had an uneventful flight across to Italy. We touched down two hours after take-off and once through immigration I grabbed a taxi to the Bologna head office. The driver said sixty five euros in broken English. In my best Italian I said, 'Il mio amico. No it's not, try again, my friend.'

We looked at each other and it was rather like a Mexican standoff. Given that we had travelled all of two miles there was no way I was going to pay sixty five euros. We agreed on twenty five and he looked most concerned when I asked for a receipt.

'Don't take the piss out of your own people,' I said.

'I thought you were English,' he replied as he took his foot off the clutch and sped off.

The building was even more dilapidated than the Slough office and walking into the reception I half expected to see Chantelle sitting behind the screen. It could easily have been her cousin, as the woman scowled when I asked to see Mr Grimaldi.

'He's at lunch,' she barked.

Here we go again, I thought.

'When will he be back?' She shrugged her shoulders.

I was pissed off in the extreme and thought, *How would I react if this was a proper job?*

I knew the answer. I phoned Jeff Andrews on his direct line.

'Sorry to trouble you, Jeff, I've arrived in Bologna and Grimaldi is nowhere to be seen. Is there anybody else I should ask for?' I tried to sound as innocent as possible. I was really saying, '*I was up at the crack of dawn and I'm pissed off that the wanker Grimaldi has fucked off somewhere and left me sitting here.*'

Jeff took the bait. 'Sorry, Dean, this is just not good enough, especially when you're trying to help them. Leave it with me.'

Three minutes later Grimaldi hurtled through the door, full of apologies. It made me realise that Jeff Andrews was obviously in a position of power with regard to this company. Another piece of the jigsaw but still, as yet, none of it was fitting together.

I was immediately taken to the Ufficio Appalti, the procurement office, and introduced to two women. One in her late twenties named Gina. She was dumpy, with more than a trace of a moustache. The other was a battleaxe in her fifties called Florentina. Grimaldi told them I was an accounts and collection expert from London,

'He is here to help us with our bad debt problem. I'll leave you with these two ladies and talk to you later.'

With that he left the office, *probably to continue his siesta*, I thought.

'Ciao signore.' *Hi ladies.*

'Signore Farlow.'

'How long have you two been here?'

'I have been here three months and Florentina six months.' *A real couple of experts*, I mused, as if I was any better.

'Well, I have had a fair amount of success in England,' I said, making myself sound important. 'Contacting customers in the evening to arrange payment of their invoices. How do you think people will react to that approach in Italy?'

The two of them shrugged their shoulders, showing total indifference. This was going to be difficult.

'Perhaps we could start with you showing me the current bad debt position.'

'What do you mean?' responded the younger one.

'Let me show you.' I sat down at a spare work station. Fortunately my UK access got me straight onto the system. It was a clone of the one used in Slough so I soon picked up exactly what was going on. Or should I say what wasn't going on. To say I was appalled was an understatement. I estimated the problem was about ten times that of the UK on a book of a similar size.

'Who does the collection work?' I enquired. Again the two shrugged their shoulders. 'Is it your responsibility?'

'No, we have our own jobs.'

'And what do you do?'

'We log the orders and send out the invoices.'

'And who posts payments onto the system?'

'Accounts.'

'But nobody chases for non-payment?' The two of them looked at me blankly. 'Not your fault, ladies, but there appears to be a glaring omission in the company's procedures. I need to talk to the accounts department, can you tell me where they are?'

I walked down the corridor into another office where half a dozen people were seated in front of screens. They were all typing furiously. A pretty young girl looked up and smiled. I explained who I was and asked if I could speak to the head of the department.

'You'll have to make an appointment.'

'I've come from London to help sort this problem.'

'I'm sorry but it's policy.'

'And when can I see this person?'

'Mr Boninsegna is free at three thirty tomorrow.'

'Not before?' I asked, glaring at the person I assumed to be Boninsegna. 'Okay.' I said in a resigned manner and walked out of the office trying to show as much disdain as possible.

Back with Gina and Florentina, I sat down and sent an email to Jeff Andrews.

'Hi, Jeff, initial findings. The bad debt position is at least ten times worse than the UK. Frighteningly, there is no collection activity at all. If a customer doesn't pay there is no follow through. Nobody appears to have ownership. Tried to speak to Boninsegna but I had to make an appointment for tomorrow afternoon!'

'Would you like a coffee?' asked Gina.

'That would be kind, thank you, no sugar.' I didn't ask for milk as I was trying to show Italian credentials. Milk in coffee would have been a giveaway. The two of them got up and left me in the office alone. To say they were laid back was an understatement.

Boninsegna walked in, holding a piece of paper.

'You sent this email to London,' he said, glaring at me.

'Sorry, you are?'

'I am Signore Boninsegna.'

'Good to meet you,' I said, standing up and putting my hand out.

'Why did you send this email without talking to me?'

'With the greatest of respect, I work for Jeff Andrews and he's asked me to do a job. Until thirty seconds ago I had no idea who you were. I did come to see you but had to make an appointment for tomorrow afternoon. Jeff required a report today.'

I glared at him as if to say, '*Don't try taking the piss out of me again.*'

He looked away. *One to me,* I thought.

'You have no idea of the problems here and yet you write an email like this.'

'Well it's a pity you couldn't see me until tomorrow. Perhaps you could enlighten me now.'

For the next couple of minutes he rambled on about the problems of the procurement system, the procedures in place, the lack of trained staff and the decline of the Italian economy. It didn't take long for me to realize this was a man way out of his depth.

Gina and Florentina reappeared with three cups of coffee and Boninsegna suggested we should continue our meeting in a private office. I followed him into a meeting room.

'You need to put three people on this immediately, two of them working evenings to bring about a degree of control.'

'And where am I going to get three people?'

'Prioritise.' We glared at each other again.

'Give me the three people in the morning together with an office and work stations. I will then train them.' I was amazed at my self-assurance.

The following morning Boninsegna was waiting for me as I entered the building.

'Come with me,' he said curtly.

I followed him to the procurement office. 'You can use this room for training. The people I have allocated are Gina from procurement together with Giuseppe and Luca from accounts.

'Have you told them?' He nodded. 'Fine, we'll need to offer an incentive. I would suggest a thousand euros for the first month, subject to hitting certain targets.'

I could see him paling. I loved the feeling of control.

'They will be with you in ten minutes,' he said, scowling as he walked out of the room. '*Not a happy man,*' I thought. '*Tough*'.

My three intrepid heroes turned up a few minutes later. The two boys were just that, young lads probably no more than eighteen. You could cut the atmosphere with a knife. They were obviously not happy about being part of this project.

'Mattina buona squadra.' *Good morning team,* I said, trying to sound as cheerful as possible. 'Let's sit down and get to know one another.'

I went through my experiences of debt collection, both at Orlanda and Defra to confirm my credibility. By the time I had finished I almost believed the story myself. I asked each of them to tell me a little about themselves and got very guarded responses. I then asked if they knew about the incentive on offer. Luca shook his head, the other two just stared at me.

'Well, if we're successful and can bring the bad debt position down by thirty per cent, you will each get a bonus of one thousand euros in your salary next month.'

It was as if the light had been switched on. The three of them grinned from ear to ear. Money was the catalyst needed to grab their attention.

'So are you up for it?' I asked. The nodding dog syndrome appeared.

From there on in the training became very easy. The kids were bright enough and willing to learn. After a couple of hours they were more than ready to have a go with live customers.

'Are you guys happy to work tonight?' Again the three nodded furiously. They'd become so keen, it was a remarkable transformation. 'OK, why don't you take the afternoon off and come back at about four thirty? We can then start talking to a few people.'

They were amazed. 'I thought we were going to have to do this on top of our normal job,' piped up Gina, who had become quite a personality girl over the course of the morning.

'This is far more important than your normal job,' I said solemnly. 'Have a good afternoon. I'll see you later on.' I smiled to myself. I was beginning to sound like Mark, the trainer in Kenya.

After they left I rifled off an email to Jeff Andrews, bringing him up to speed. His response was almost immediate. 'Excellent, keep up the good work, let me have a daily report.'

There's a man under pressure, I thought.

I'd agreed with Frank that while I was in Italy I should leave the day to day running of Josephina and Caroline to him. That was fine by me, I had enough on my plate and as Frank said, 'We're all in this together, no brownie points for heroes.'

That afternoon my three charges came back to the office and started calling customers. I was amazed. Italians were obviously not used to being phoned like this and the results were even more dramatic than in the UK.

Gina hit on something very early on. She found that by talking to the wives the results were more effective than talking to the husband. It was obvious who was in control in Italian households. We were all on a high as we left the building and I felt a slight pang of guilt. I wasn't really part of their world and I might bring the company down in the not too distant future.

The wagons were rolling in and out that night and I decided it was as good an opportunity to have a bit of a snoop. My credibility had been well established and I had a good reason to go into the warehouse.

I strolled round to the back of the office where there was a sea of activity. A dozen large trucks were being loaded by fork lifts and the work rate was quite impressive. Men were standing around with clipboards. This was obviously a very well-run and efficient operation.

It wasn't long before I heard the words, 'Hey what do you want?'

I turned round to see a large, aggressive man striding purposefully towards me.

'Hi,' I said confidently, my heart beating at twice its normal rate. 'I'm Dean Farlow, from the Slough operation in England. I've been seconded over here to do some training. Your drivers Gustavo and Fabio told me to come and see them when I came across.'

'Well, you don't just walk in here unannounced.'

'You don't seem to understand,' I said, deliberately playing the daft laddie, 'I work here, I've been training your people for the past couple of days.'

We glared at each other and at that point I heard a familiar voice. 'Dino, Dino, Dino. How are you?' Fabio was running towards us.

'I'm good, my friend, it's great to see you.' He kissed me on both cheeks like an old chum.

'Come with me,' he said, turning away from his hostile colleague.

'He should get a job in Slough,' I quipped.

'We're not all like that.'

'I know.'

'I'll find Gustavo and we'll go and have a drink.'

'What about your families?'

'Nessun problema,' he replied, grinning.

I was taken into what was obviously a rest room with a few tables and chairs and had a similar greeting from Gustavo. They introduced me to half a dozen people, all drivers who shook my hand and made me feel extremely welcome.

I saw Signore Aggressor standing outside scowling and staring at me. Within seconds I was whisked outside and into an old Fiat Punto. While walking through the warehouse I saw a pile of large plastic envelopes about two feet long and eighteen inches wide filled with white powder. We moved too quickly for me to make sense of them and I very deliberately didn't stare. It was at that moment the first piece of the jigsaw slotted into place. *This has to be drugs,* I thought. I remembered Frank's words, 'Slowly, slowly,' and with that I was taken to a wonderful trattoria in Bologna where we ate an amazing pork shank and drank far too much red wine.

Nothing was given away that evening and I deliberately didn't try to push. I had made one startling revelation and that was enough for now. By the time they deposited me back at the hotel I was too pissed to talk to Frank, so I went to bed and phoned him the following morning.

'The things my liver is doing for The Organisation,' I croaked, feeling like death warmed up.

'I know the feeling, old boy, but if it's any consolation, you'll get your reward in heaven, I'm sure.'

I told him what I'd seen the night before. He was silent for a while.

'Dean, I think you've cracked it, but this is really where we have to go slowly to tie up all the loose ends. If we go thundering in now we'll find a few envelopes of drugs and that's it. We need to build a complete picture so that we can trace the supply chain and shut the whole thing down. You have done a fantastic job but for the next few days just watch and listen, nothing else, do you understand?'

This was a very definite command and Frank had made things crystal clear. If I'm honest, with Zan coming that night I wasn't in the mood for industrial espionage, I was happy just to let events unfold slowly for the time being. I rang Zan, concerned she may get upset that I was working late. I tried to be as diplomatic as possible.

'Don't be silly, Jonathan, this is what we're here for. I've got to fly via Munich in any case so I won't arrive in Bologna until twenty past ten. With a bit of luck I'll see you at about eleven. I'll come to your room to avoid contagion.'

'Is that what we're calling it now?'

She giggled as I gave her my room number.

I got into the office at about ten and my head was still spinning. Florentina appeared with a cup of coffee and almost smiled. Obviously word was getting around that I was one of the good guys.

'You know my cousin Gustavo.'

'He's a bad man,' I quipped, 'forcing large quantities of Chianti down my throat last night.'

She laughed. 'Men will be men.'

Maybe she could become another ally, I thought.

The team arrived just before one and immediately set about contacting customers. Again a cultural difference was discovered between the British and the Italians. In so many of the small family-run companies, the wives were the book-keepers, so the need for evening work was less paramount. They could make payment during the day and were happy enough to do so if pressed. We put a rota together, two people working during the day and one in the evening.

'This is an easy bonus,' quipped Luca.

'Don't get too cocky,' I responded, 'it may get more difficult.'

Just before I left at nine that night I sent a report to Jeff Andrews confirming the results from the first two days. We'd already brought the bad debt down by nearly five per cent, so it was very much a good news story. As I walked out of the building, I saw from the corner of my eye Signore Aggressor staring at me again. Frank's words came back to me, 'Slowly, slowly.'

Chapter 15

I got back to the hotel and looked at the room service menu. Most of it was pretty unappealing but I ended up ordering a bottle of Prosecco along with a couple of wraps and a chicken caesar salad. We were hardly tripping the light fantastic, but having had a heavy meal late the night before I wasn't in the mood for much, and I doubted Zan would be looking for a five course gourmet meal.

While waiting for her, I grabbed a beer from the fridge and idly went through the events of the last few months. From sitting in an office in London to the training camp in Kenya, on to Slough and now Italy. Not forgetting the people I had met on the way, especially Zan. I was dozing as I heard a knock on the door. I opened my eyes, shook my head and crossed the room to open it.

There she was, smiling as only Zan could smile. I grabbed her and we held each other tight. I felt as if I hadn't seen her for months and yet it had only been five days.

'Do you want something to eat?' I asked.

'No, I just want you,' and with that she pushed me onto the bed and kissed me passionately. We never did eat that night. Later, much later, we both went into a deep, satisfied sleep, not waking until about ten o'clock the following morning.

We ordered breakfast from room service and sat on the bed sharing eggs, croissants, and fruit while drinking vast quantities of dark Italian coffee. It was so nice just to talk about anything and everything rather than work, which rarely raised its head. We were in our own little utopia and the rest of the world didn't exist. I wanted this forever and the thought of losing Zan terrified me.

She was concerned about us being seen together so I hired a car for the weekend to get away. She caught a cab into town and I arranged to meet her outside the trattoria I had eaten at with Fabio and Gustavo. A smart, yellow Fiat 500 was delivered at lunchtime and I drove straight into the centre. She was wearing a woolly hat and sun glasses and even I hardly recognized her. We laughed as we trundled out of town in a car not exactly built for speed. We headed for Bellaria on the Riviera Romagnola coastline, which would have taken about an hour with a decent map. However the hire car company had given us a dismal photocopy, which Zan tried to decipher as I drove. This was the first time we had an argument.

'With your training I'd have thought you could learn to read a bloody map,' I hollered.

'Well, you read it,' she screamed, throwing it at me.

I pulled in. She was glaring as I took her hand. 'Come on,' I said, 'it's not the biggest issue. Let's book a hotel and go straight there.'

She half smiled as I picked up my phone and typed in Hotels.com. Within a couple of minutes I'd found quite a nice looking place on the seafront called the Blu Suite. It was all of eighty five quid for a night and trip advisor gave it four and a half stars.

'Perfect,' said Zan. I booked immediately.

We were living a life of paradox, the weekends and time spent together were sublime. Everything we did was joyous, but we knew that life in The Organisation wasn't really what we were looking for.

Bellaria was a charming little place. We walked for a couple of hours on the beach and watched the sunset. As darkness fell we made our way back to the hotel, changed and found a charming restaurant that suited our mood perfectly. We felt like a couple of lost souls living in a twilight zone with no escape. We knew we had to find another way, but not yet.

The following day we meandered around the back streets, looked at a couple of churches and a museum before heading back to Bologna. I dropped Zan near the railway station. By then it was dark so we were unlikely to be seen together but contagion was always at the forefront of our minds. She caught a taxi back to the hotel while I found a pizza parlour and had a bite to eat. I then sat in the car and rang Josephina, Caroline and John.

I could tell both Josephina and Caroline were bored. There was little happening apart from the manager either being locked in his room with the mysterious packages every day or disappearing for hours on end without explanation.

'Think of the money,' I joked to Caroline.

'That's the only reason I'm here,' she responded tartly. 'It's not for being chatted up by spotty little kids.'

'It's when you stop being chatted up you should worry.'

John wasn't in a better mood.

'Can you guys create some action? I need something to keep me sane. The hours of silence are beginning to get to me.'

I felt as frustrated as the rest of them so I phoned Frank hoping for a bit of guidance.

'We need something,' I said, 'before we all go mad.'

'I know exactly where you're coming from, old boy, and I'm afraid this is something you'll all have to deal with to make a success of your tenure with The Organisation. Stick with it and something will break, I promise.'

I drove back to the hotel and parked the car. As I got out I saw a shadow dart behind a Portakabin. Even in the dark I could see it was Signore Aggressor. I was being watched and they were making it very obvious. Maybe that something I was asking for was about to happen.

As I handed the keys in to reception, I could see Zan sitting with several men in the bar having a drink. She'd obviously met up with her colleagues from KPMG. I felt a pang of jealousy as I realised I would probably have to spend the evening by myself. I went up to my room and lay on the bed. Zan knocked on my door at about ten thirty. I felt a bit grumpy and she chastised me.

'Look, we're spending a lot more time together than we anticipated so let's just enjoy the moment.'

She was right, of course, and I threw her onto the bed and enjoyed much more than just a moment. The following morning she disappeared at about five thirty and I lay there for an hour before I went for a jog. The air was still cool and it felt good to build up a sweat before the day's activities commenced.

I got into the office at about seven forty five and checked my emails before Luca and Florentina arrived. They set about debt collection straight away and the results were almost immediate. My job was done here, and with Signore Aggressor sniffing around I knew it was time to get out. I emailed Jeff Andrews and suggested I should return to Slough the following day. He responded asking me to stay until Wednesday as he wanted me to brief KPMG on my activities. That comment confirmed why I had been sent here. It was to show KPMG they had discovered a problem but were dealing with it. They wanted to show the credentials of a professional company.

Surreal, I thought, *I'll probably end up briefing Zan and it'll be a question of who's bullshitting who.*

I just drifted through the day doing a bit of collection work and helping Luca and Florentina with objectionable customers. They had really got to grips with the job and problems were few and far between. At lunchtime I went to the canteen and again saw Zan with her colleagues. I was desperate to go over and kiss her on the neck but I just sat down with Luca and made polite conversation about Italian football.

I stayed with Giuseppe until about seven thirty, by which time I'd had enough. I ordered a taxi and went down to reception. As I walked out of the building I heard a voice in the shadows.

'Hey, signore, come here.'

I looked round but could see nothing. Someone grabbed my arm and twisted it up my back.

'Come with me,' said the voice in Italian.

I thought of fighting but discretion got the better of me. If I laid him out I would probably learn nothing. He pushed me towards the back of the building. There were two others waiting, and one was instantly recognizable – Signore Aggressor.

'Who are you?' he said.

'You know who I am, Dean Farlow from the Slough office in England. Now what the fuck is this all about?'

'Si, we know who you say you are, but who are you working for?'

'Jeff Andrews,' I said, trying to play it as straight as my twisted arm would allow me.

'We are watching, and we don't like you.'

With that my arm was released and the three of them sauntered off. I was shaking like a leaf and phoned Frank for guidance.

'Play the daft laddie, phone Jeff Andrews and say you want out.'

I phoned Jeff immediately. 'I don't know what's going on,' I said indignantly, 'but I didn't come here to be assaulted so I want to come home, now.'

'Dean, I'm so sorry,' was the response. 'There's not much I can do tonight, but you'll be on the first plane possible tomorrow.'

I tried to phone Zan but there was no answer. I sent her a text outlining what had happened, copying in John. He phoned immediately

'At last, some action. Are you OK?'

'No probs, but I think things are finally hotting up.'

'What can I do?'

'Nothing at the moment, but before I disappear I want to have a look at the warehouse in Slough from a vantage point I found.'

'Watch yourself, pal.'

I phoned again for a taxi to hear from the irate controller that the previous one had been sent away with no payment. I apologised and explained that was nothing to do with me. He said that all taxi drivers were banned from picking up passengers from Orlanda in future. To say I was getting pissed off was an understatement.

'How about if I pay for two taxis?' I asked in desperation.

'We will be with you in five minutes.' In any language, money talks. As the taxi arrived, Zan phoned and we agreed to meet in my room in half an hour.

When she arrived I could see the concern on her face. This was the first time any of us had been close to real danger and it was a bit of an eye opener. I asked about her findings through KPMG.

'If I'm honest, we've found nothing untoward. The Zurich-based operation appears to be very efficient. All the information requested is on hand and there are some pretty bright people working for them. Things are very different in Bologna. The info requested is difficult to get hold of and Boninsegna is proving impossible. He's on his guard all the time and doing everything in his power to make things awkward for us. It's as if he's trying to hide something but we don't know what. My boss has had enough so I think we'll have more access to info by the time he has spoken to Zurich tomorrow morning. That will give me the opportunity to have a look at Orlanda Imports and what's been hidden behind the icon you found.'

'Go careful.'

'What can they do?' was the response. 'Assuming I can find something, I'll download it onto the "O" platform. If I'm caught, I'll plead the fifth amendment.' She laughed, but I could tell she was a bit scared.

The following morning Jeff Andrews phoned at eight o'clock.

'How are you?' he asked.

'I'm fine, just a bit pissed off.'

'Again, I'm so sorry, and there will be repercussions in Italy, have no fear of that. I've booked you on the one fifteen to Heathrow, so I'll see you tomorrow morning. Can the collection team cope without you?'

'Put Gina in charge, she'll respond well.'

'Could I ask two favours – can you go into the office speak to Gina and set her up so that she's seen as the head of the operation, and then speak to one of the KPMG team about what you've done?'

'No probs,' I said. 'Is there somebody I should ask for?'

'I'll come back to you with a name.'

As the cab left the hotel I received a text, 'The KPMG contact is Miss Fang Hua Li.'

'No prizes for guessing who that is then!' I burst out laughing. *This is getting weirder and weirder*, I thought.

Gina and Luca were in the office so I asked to have a word with Gina in a private room. I told her that I was leaving today and, because of her good work, she'd be taking charge. She was thrilled and immediately came up with a couple of ideas to enhance the operation. *That's the sign of a good manager,* I thought. My fear was that in the not too distant future the whole thing would collapse and she'd be out of work.

As we were walking back to the office I got a text, 'Hello, my name is Fang Hua Li from KPMG, I believe we are meeting this morning.'

I immediately phoned the number. 'Hi, this is Dean Farlow. I am leaving the office at eleven thirty, so I'm happy to meet any time before then.'

'How about in thirty minutes?'

'No probs, do you know where to find me?'

'The procurement office, I've seen it.'

'I'll buy you a coffee.'

'Look forward to it.'

With that the phone went dead. *Weirder and weirder,* I thought again.

Half an hour later Zan walked into the office. We shook hands formally and there was no glint of recognition on her face. I tried to emulate her but to say it was difficult was an understatement.

I went through the systems, the bad debt position as it was and what had been achieved. I showed that within three weeks the situation should be well under control. Zan demonstrated an aloofness which I found fascinating. Her professionalism was something to behold and her questioning showed a deep level of understanding. I half smiled, the last time we had talked about this we were lying naked in bed together and, truth be told, she knew all the answers before she asked the questions. However it was essential we played this straight. Whether people understood us speaking in English was irrelevant, we had to ensure our cover wasn't compromised.

After twenty minutes or so I showed her back to the office where the KPMG team had camped. I was introduced to each of the team members, who all looked incredibly serious. I felt rather pleased I hadn't bothered socialising with them.

There was little more for me to do so I said my goodbyes to the team and got a cab to the airport, feeling relieved to be out of that environment. I really didn't want another altercation with Signore Aggressor, but I felt somewhat concerned about Zan still being involved.

Chapter 16

I got back to the flat in Slough at just after four pm UK time and as I walked up the stairs Jasmine was coming down, looking scared.

'Are you OK?' I asked.

'Am I glad to see you, I've been worried sick.'

'Why, what's happened?'

'Last night I heard some banging in your flat. I crept downstairs and saw two men coming out. They looked very rough, not the sort of people I would expect you to be with. I was frightened as I haven't seen you.'

'What were they like?'

'They were white, well sort of, Mediterranean looking.'

'Italian perhaps?'

'Yes or Arabic, something like that. What's happened, Dean?'

'I don't know,' I said, thinking on my feet. 'There are some strange things going on at the company I'm working for. I was threatened last night in Italy and now this.'

'Go carefully, my friend.'

'Thanks, sweetheart. I'd better see what damage they've done.'

I opened the door and the place was a mess. The bureau had been ransacked, books had been thrown on the floor, together with clothes from the wardrobe in the bedroom. Interestingly, the piece of string hadn't moved.

'What absolute scum,' cried Jasmine. 'You should get the police.'

'Jasmine, I need to focus and try and work out what's been taken, then I'll phone the police. Would it be very rude of me to ask you to leave?'

'Not at all, I'm just so relieved that you are okay. When you've sorted yourself out come and have a glass of wine with me.'

I looked at her and smiled quizzically.

'Don't worry, the kids are upstairs, they will be your chaperone.'

'Thanks, I'll see you later.'

As Jasmine left, I phoned Frank and told him the news. As usual he went silent for a few seconds as he thought things through.

'They're on to us, old boy. I think it may be time to pull the operation.'

'One more day,' I said. 'I've got to have a look at that warehouse, and then I'm out.'

'One more day,' agreed Frank, 'but no longer, I don't like funerals. Keep playing the game for the time being. A normal citizen in this situation would phone the police so do just that.'

I dialled 999 and half an hour later a police officer arrived. I showed him around and after a few minutes he said, 'Druggies looking for money, it's happening all the time.'

'How did they get in?'

'Picked the lock, it's easy if you know how.'

'Is that it?' I asked incredulously.

'Not much we can do. I'll try for prints but I can guarantee there won't be any.' He was right of course, these guys knew what they were doing.

I spent the next half hour tidying up. It was obvious nothing had been taken, this was more of a warning than anything else, Frank was right, it was time to get out. I was scared and not afraid to admit it.

I had a missed call from Zan so I phoned her back. Frank had already been on to her. They'd agreed that she was to try and access the Orlanda Imports system the following day and then disappear. At last things were beginning to move.

I went and had a glass of wine with Jasmine and told her about the police.

'It's not fair,' she cried. 'How can honest citizens get on with their lives with all this crime?'

I had a deep feeling of guilt. Thanks to my actions I was putting too many other people at risk. Who knows what those thugs might have done to Jasmine the night before, had they seen her.

The following morning I arrived at the Slough office at about eight forty five. I walked straight up to the accounts department, where Julie was already sitting at her work station.

'Hi,' she said, 'the return of the prodigal son.'

'We're both back,' I responded. 'How did you get on?'

'It was very strange, we didn't find anything out of order. A load of fuss over nothing if you ask me. I'm just glad to be back home if I'm honest. Jeff said that you had a problem.'

I told her about Signore Aggressor and his chums.

'Oh, how horrible. Nobody deserves that when you're trying to help people.'

'And to top it all, my flat was broken into while I was away.' Julie looked appalled but I wanted it to get around that I was an innocent party.

Amy walked in. 'Ah, the team's back in place,' she said. 'I'm glad about that.'

Not for long, I thought. I spent the morning getting back into the swing of things. Nothing much had happened on the bad debt front since my sabbatical, so Julie asked that I carry on where I had left off. Jeff called me into his office and debriefed me on the activities in Italy.

'So why do you think you were attacked?' he asked casually. I was ready for this.

'I think I may have upset a few relatives by demanding money. It strikes me there may have been something going on in terms of not charging for the marble and then it being sold on for profit.'

I knew this was absolute rubbish but I wanted to keep Jeff off the scent.

'Fraud, you mean?'

I nodded. 'Maybe I've spoiled their little scam by demanding payment.'

Jeff nodded sagely. 'Interesting thought. Again, apologies for what happened. I hope it doesn't put you off Orlanda.'

'I'll be fine,' I said, and with that the meeting was over so I went back to the accounts office.

As I sat down, my 'O' phone rang. It was Zan.

'I've just walked out with a complete copy of the Orlanda Imports file.'

'OK,' I said guardedly.

'You can't talk obviously but I can. I couldn't believe how easy the system was to hack into. You were so right, there's a complete company hidden with a lot of money flying around. We are talking tens of millions. I haven't begun to analyse the info yet but it's now all on the "O" Cloud, safe and secure. I think we've got them.'

'Where are you?' I asked.

'Once I got into the system and started cloning, I ordered a taxi. I told them I was going into a meeting which may take anything from five minutes to an hour. My instructions were for the taxi to wait for me and be paid accordingly. The cloning took twenty minutes so I just picked up my bag walked down to reception and into the cab. It was as easy as that. I then went to the railway station where I changed in the toilet, I doubt anybody would recognise me now. I'm a punk student. I caught the bus to the airport. That's where I am now and hopefully the trail is lost.'

'I'll speak to you at lunchtime,' I said. 'Bye.'

I had to be abrupt because I didn't want anyone to pick up on the conversation. I was finding it very difficult to focus on the everyday activities of Orlanda. I knew my time was nearly at an end but I still had one last job to do. I drifted through the morning and at lunchtime couldn't wait to get out.

'Are you going into town?' asked Amy brightly.

'Yeah, having been away there are a few things I need to sort out. Do you want a lift?' I asked in the hope of the conversation sounding normal while praying she would say no.

'I'm just going to have a sandwich at my desk and have a smooch around Facebook, but thanks for the thought.'

I breathed a sigh of relief as I made my way to the car. Driving a couple of miles I parked just by Kennedy Park.

Firstly, I rang Zan. 'Are you OK?'

'I'm fine, don't worry, I'm now just a student.'

'Then what?'

'I'm on my way to England. Frank wants me to brief him once I've analysed the info we have on Orlanda Imports.'

'Nice to be included,' I said sulkily.

'Don't be like that, my darling. Frank's just a bit concerned about contagion, that's all.'

'I'll feel happier once you're out of Italy.'

'I'm booked on the one thirty five to Heathrow.'

'Take care, I'll phone later.'

I couldn't get hold of either Caroline or Caterina, so I left messages with both of them to phone. I drove back to the office feeling very apprehensive. The end game was in sight but I had no idea where it would lead. I was far from focused that afternoon and Amy even made a quip about it.

'What's wrong Dean? Have you fallen in love or something, you don't seem your normal self?'

'Sorry,' I responded, 'I think the last few days have taken it out of me, I'm a bit tired that's all.'

Caroline rang at about three o'clock and was clearly distressed. Amy was sitting at her desk which made conversation a little difficult.

'Can you talk?' she said.

'No, but you can.'

'I'm fed up,' she said. 'Josephina has walked.'

I sat in stunned silence.

'This lunchtime she was working away and doing very well. The package arrived at about one o'clock and she signed for it. The manager had gone out so I asked her to take it up to his office. He came into the bar a few minutes later and for once was almost pleasant. He asked me how things were going, I told him the bar staff were doing a great job and that Josephina was settling in well. He then asked where she was and I told him she'd taken the daily delivery, as we had come to call it, upstairs to his office. With that he scowled and walked out of the bar. The next thing I heard was an almighty scream and a crash. I ran across to see what had happened and the manager was lying at the bottom of the stairs. Josephina was half way up looking visibly distressed. She said she was coming out of the office when he grabbed her forcibly and asked what was she doing. He was obviously very angry and started to threaten her unless she told him the truth. Apparently he raised his hand to strike her and she pushed him down the stairs. He was OK but obviously shaken up. She was crying as he got up and shouted, "Get out of this fucking pub," and she just ran. The rest of us carried on but if I'm honest I don't want to do this for much longer, money or no money.'

'Do me a favour,' I said, 'carry on to the end of your shift and we'll talk again then.'

'OK, no problem, but this can't carry on. The man's an animal and someone is going to end up getting hurt. I'm scared Dean, this is all a bit beyond me.'

'Hang on in there.'

I could tell Amy was listening. 'A slight family crisis,' I said. 'I'm just going to make a couple of calls in my car.'

'You can stay here,' she said, obviously wanting to hear the gossip.

'No, it's not fair on you, I'll only be ten minutes.'

I ran down to the car, phoning Caterina on the way. 'Are you OK?' I asked.

'Oh, I'm fine,' she said, laughing. 'A silly little man like that couldn't hurt me if he tried. With our training, he's lucky to be alive, and that's only because it would have made a mess of your operation had I killed him.'

'That's for sure,' I responded. 'So what happened?'

'Frank told me about Zan and that things were beginning to move. He said I would probably not be needed over here after this week. I therefore decided to make a positive contribution. The opportunity arrived with the arrival of the package at lunchtime. I took it up to the boss' office. Once there, I hacked into his system and copied everything I could find. As I was shutting down the PC, I could hear him coming up the stairs. I had to play for time to ensure the computer had shut down properly before he came into the room. As I walked out he was nearly at the top of the stairs and he screamed at me, "What the fuck do you think you are doing?"

'I responded sweetly, "I've just brought up the package and left it on your desk."

'"You're a liar," he bellowed, as he tried to slap me across the face. That was enough, I screamed for the sake of authenticity. He seized my wrist and started to threaten me. I kicked him where no man likes to be kicked and he fell down the stairs. I put on the tears while he screamed at me to get out. It seemed like the perfect opportunity to exit, never to be seen again.'

'What have you found?' I asked.

'I've no idea, I'll have a look and get back to you.'

The afternoon drifted on interminably and I couldn't focus on anything. As Amy got up to leave she said, 'I hope you feel better tomorrow.'

'Sorry I haven't been my normal self,' I responded. 'Have a good night.'

To try and regain focus I tried doing a bit of debt collection, but my heart wasn't in it. One defaulter started having a real go at me. 'Who do you think you are phoning up like this?'

'What would you do if your customers refused to pay?' I retorted.

'I'd go and sort them out,' he responded, laughing.

'So it's alright for you to do that, but not for me to phone you.'

'Oh, fuck off,' he shouted and put the phone down.

I went and got a cup of coffee from the canteen. I was hoping to see Gustavo and Fabio for a bit of light relief but realised it was the wrong day for their appearance. The warehouse man was sitting at a table by himself, glaring at me. I couldn't be bothered to even acknowledge him and went back to the accounts office, cup in hand.

Nobody was around so I emptied the copier of A4 paper and, together with a ream of paper stored next to the machine, hid them in one of the empty desk drawers.

I rang John. Speaking quietly, I said 'I'm going to leave the "O" phone video camera on for the next few minutes so you can see what's going on. It'll be in my top pocket so the pictures may judder a bit. If something should happen, kill the call from your end and any trace of it.'

'Take care, my friend.'

'I intend to.'

I then went down to the store cupboard. As I opened the door my heart was beating at about twice its normal rate. The first thing I did was grab a ream of paper to give me some form of cover. I then looked out at the warehouse through the window.

It was a hive of activity. Three wagons were being unloaded using fork lift trucks. They were picking up several large slabs of marble at a time which were then taken over to a corner of the room where men were smashing them into pieces. The second piece of the jigsaw fell into place. Plastic bags were being removed from the rubble with what looked like white powder in them. I ensured John had clear shots of the activity. I turned around to depart as the door opened.

'Well, well, well, what have we got here?' It was the warehouse man.

'I'm sorry?'

'Seems like you've been caught red-handed,' he snarled.

'What are you talking about?' I asked innocently.

'Oh, I think you know. It's known as spying or snooping.'

'Or coming down to the store room to get a ream of paper.' I tried to keep calm but I could feel myself shaking. For a split second I thought about the situation. If I was innocent I'd still be shaking given the circumstances.

'Well, isn't it funny that my friends in Italy thought exactly the same as me, and now I find you snooping around the warehouse.'

'I've told you once, I'm not snooping.'

'I don't believe you.' With that, he came up and punched me in the stomach. I was more than ready and, having given myself a couple of seconds to recover, the months of training back in Kenya came to my rescue. Two sweet moves and then he was on the floor with a broken jaw.

'Don't you fucking threaten me again, you shit,' I said, running towards the door. As I rushed down the corridor two more warehouse men were coming towards me. One grabbed me and as he did I ruined the other's chances of fathering children. The first one landed on top of the second, out cold.

My cover was blown and I had to get away. I dashed down the stairs and through reception, and that's the last thing I remembered.

Chapter 17

I don't know how long I was unconscious but as I came round I was in darkness, my head was splitting and I felt sick. After a second or two I realised I couldn't move. My arms and legs were tied together and I was gagged. I found myself lying on my back with my hands attached to something above my head. As my senses returned I realised I was moving. It was pitch black and I couldn't see a thing. I felt muddled and sick as I tried to work out how long I had been like this. I was at a loss to know where I was. After a few minutes things began to fall into place. I was in a container on the back of a lorry. I could move my legs and felt wooden pallets surrounding me. Two questions came to mind, where were they taking me and why hadn't they killed me? My one salvation was that they hadn't removed my watch. I remembered Frank's words from what seemed like a lifetime ago.

'This is the watch you'll use from now on, it's a clever little bugger and there's a tracker built in. If ever you're in trouble, press the knob on the right-hand side and you'll see the date change. That tells you the tracker is operational and we can come and find you. The thing is, the baddies would never suspect that an old Seiko watch is anything more than an old Seiko watch.'

Although my hands were tied with what felt like gaffer tape, I had enough movement to twist the fingers of my right hand towards the watch on my left wrist. The trouble was I couldn't reach it. The watch had slipped down my arm and was just out of reach. I shook my wrist and after what seemed like an eternity it freed itself and slid towards my hand. With immense effort, while holding the watch strap with the thumb of my right hand, I was able to press the knob using my index finger. I had no idea if the tracker became operational as I couldn't see if the date had changed. I also wondered if the signal may have been blocked by the container. I just prayed that it would be picked up.

As I lay there my head began to clear and I was aware that I needed a pee, while at the same time having a tremendous thirst. I could tell we were travelling at a reasonable speed as we weren't stopping and starting, suggesting we were on a motorway. My body ached. I was in an extremely uncomfortable position with my hands tied above my head and any pothole in the road seemed to jar every bone in my body. I realised it was dark outside as I occasionally saw the reflection of a car headlight above me. If light can get into the container, I surmised, hopefully the signal from my watch could get out.

After a period of time the lorry came to a halt. I could hear voices and then the vehicle moved forward slowly before the air brakes kicked in and the engine was turned off. In the sudden quiet I also heard seagulls crying above me and a fog horn in the distance. It didn't take much working out, I was in Dover or one of the Kent ports heading for the continent. I assumed we'd just been through passport control. Obviously the authorities weren't concerned about illegal immigrants being exported.

Twenty minutes later the engine restarted and we rolled forward. I heard several clunks, convincing me we were driving onto a ferry. The engine was killed again shortly after, followed by the cabin door being slammed. *The driver would now be heading up to the passenger decks,* I thought, leaving me in the darkness. I could hear other vehicles being driven onto the ship and conversations just yards from me. Being gagged and bound, I couldn't raise the alarm. I was helpless.

I felt drowsy and drifted in and out of consciousness, aware that the ship was moving in the gentle sway of the sea. The feeling was quite therapeutic and a strange feeling of peace came over me. I didn't feel scared anymore. If I'm honest, I didn't feel anything. The calm before the storm, I surmised. With the lorry in a stationary position I felt quite comfortable.

I realised there was no way the tracker signal could be picked up from the hold of a ship so for the time being I was isolated from the outside world. I tried to work out where we were heading. Bologna was an obvious bet and I shuddered at the thought of Signore Aggressor getting his hands on me while I was tied up.

Eventually I heard the ship's engines revving as we came into port. Lorry doors were being opened and slammed as drivers came back to their vehicles to disembark. I heard the ship's gate being lowered as my driver climbed in and the engine started. We chugged forward off the ferry, moving slowly through the port. After a few minutes the speed picked up and I assumed we were probably on the French autoroute.

Time became somewhat meaningless. Gustavo and Fabio had told me lorry drivers could legally drive for about nine hours in a twenty four hour period. I estimated that driving from Slough to Dover would have taken about three hours, giving the driver six on the road before he stopped for the night. I was assuming there was only one driver as I hadn't heard any conversation and only one door opening and closing. I was quite surprised with the amount of detail I had put together while being gagged and bound in the back of a container. I then had another thought – why should the driver worry about driving limits given what he is carrying? Having said that, I wondered whether he knew I was in here. My mind bounced from the best scenario to the worst. One minute I imagined being saved by Zan and the two of us going to live on an island in the Pacific Ocean. The next I imagined Signore Aggressor knocking hell out of me, leaving my body to rot, buried in a Tuscan forest.

I could hold on no longer. I'm afraid pissing and shitting in your pants is the most degrading thing that could happen and lying in it makes you feel worse. I wanted to cry. I don't think I've ever felt so humiliated. I was being stupid, there was nobody around and did I care what my prison wardens thought? Yet I felt I was spinning downwards into an abyss of worthlessness. With the truck travelling across Europe, I found myself getting more distressed and scared. I felt cold, bruised and thirsty. My body ached and for the first time ever I thought dying would be preferable to what I was going through. I was beginning to give up, the value of life becoming meaningless.

I found myself hallucinating and vivid dreams were replacing reality. I saw John in bed with Caroline and Zan laughing, calling me a weak and useless fool. Then I saw Jasmine, naked, beckoning me towards her. Everything seemed so real, tears were streaming down my face and I started to shake involuntarily. I was a mess and couldn't shake off the feeling of being totally useless.

I had no idea how long we had been travelling but I suddenly realised we had come to a stop. For the first time in many hours I was able to focus on reality. The stench was enough to make me feel physically sick.

Bugger that, I thought. Interestingly the reek of urine and faeces helped me focus on the present rather than feeling sorry for myself. I heard the cabin door slam and then silence. I couldn't even hear any birds singing, there was no sense of reality for me to hang onto.

I was drifting back into a semi-conscious state when I heard the back of the container being opened. Daylight created dull shadows above me and the outline of my pallet jail loomed out. I could see a torch and somebody clambered across the pallets caging me in. I didn't feel scared, I was numb but alert. A torch shone in my face.

'Hiya, good buddy.' The words that gave me my life back and hope 'You look fucking awful.' It was John, sounding as calm and measured as ever I'd known him. Within seconds he'd clambered down to my cell, removed the gag and loosened the gaffer tape so that I could free my hands and feet.

'John,' I whispered, my throat so dry I could hardly speak, 'thank God.'

'Have some water, but drink it slowly.' He handed me a bottle. It tasted better than anything I had ever drank in my life. I was aware of somebody else scrambling across the pallets.

'Someone's coming,' I blurted out, trying to get up and collapsing immediately.

'Easy, fella, it's a friend of yours.'

'Jonathan, are you OK?'

Once again tears started streaming down my face. I knew I was far from OK but at least I was now with friends and safe, for the time being.

Zan grabbed me and squeezed tight.

'What about the driver?' I asked.

'He'll be busy for a few hours,' replied John. 'A lady friend of ours is entertaining him. After that he'll sleep like a baby, having drunk a little cocktail we created. He'll wake none the wiser.'

'The tracker worked,' I said.

'With difficulty, the signal was very weak with the container blocking it. You weren't discovered until Dover. MI5 have a tracking station at the port and we put them on alert. They were more than happy to help us with one of their own. We flew across to France in a helicopter and we've been following you ever since in a van loaded with goodies.'

'Where did that come from?' I croaked.

'The Organisation, need you ask. Have some more water.'

'We need to clean you up,' said Zan. 'Take those clothes off, we'll have them washed and dried.'

I was confused. 'Can't we just go?'

'No,' replied Zan. 'We need to find out where they are taking you. With the information we have, we now have a clear understanding as to who is doing what in Orlanda. It makes for fascinating reading. However, we haven't tracked down the people at the top yet. Frank has a hunch that you'll be taken somewhere which may implicate those in charge. It could be pretty explosive stuff, we believe some high-powered dignitaries may be involved. Don't worry we'll be with you every step of the way. Give me your watch and put this one on, it's the next generation and has a stronger transmitter, you'll be easier to find. If things get bad, press the knob on the right-hand side as before and an emergency signal will be sent.'

A third person clambered down to my pallet cell. 'This is Dr Stayton,' said Zan.

It was getting crowded so John climbed out while Zan helped me undress. With the aid of wet wipes, she cleaned me up and some fresh clothes were thrown down. The doctor examined me.

'That crack on the head is relatively minor. You seem pretty alert so I'd imagine you're over the worst of it. You may suffer from headaches, vomiting or being confused and if you do we'll have to take another look at you. In the meantime, take these.' He handed me a couple of tablets.

'What are they?'

'Oh, nothing special, just a couple of paracetamol. Apart from the head you seem pretty fit.'

Zan handed me a sandwich. She was playing the role of mother hen, faffing around to make sure I was okay. I wasn't complaining, just grateful to have help.

'How did you get here?' I asked her.

'I was with John when you disappeared. We were looking at the video footage of the warehouse in Slough. You'd left the phone on and we heard the conversation when you were caught. I felt so helpless,' she said, holding me tight. 'We heard two fights and you running and then a conversation that I will never forget.'

'Go on,' I said, intrigued.

'I heard a crash and then "What shall we do with him?"

'"Get him into the back room and search him."

'"Do we kill him?"

'"Not yet, await orders." I could hear you being carried by two grunting men. After a couple of minutes one of them said, "Put him on the floor over there and search him." The first thing they found was the phone, I got a lovely shot of one of them looking down the camera. I vowed that if anything happened to you I would track him down and kill him.' I squeezed her hand as she went on, 'Amazingly, he didn't twig the phone was on and just put it on a table. I heard keys and money being thrown onto the table and then, "Where's his wallet?"

'"Maybe it's up in the office."

'"Go and have a look."'

'It was in my jacket pocket,' I said.

'I know, because things went silent for a couple of minutes and then I heard, "It's here." The conversation went on, "What's in it?"

'"Credit cards, driving licence, a couple of receipts, that's it."

'"Are you sure this guy's not legit?"

'"No fucking way."

'"But you've got nothing on him, his flat was clean. Maybe he is just a clerk getting copy paper."

'"I tell you, he's been snooping around both here and in Bologna."

'"I hope you're right, otherwise we are in mega shit."

'"Oh I'm right, believe me." I heard another mobile at that point. An explanation ensued about what had happened. I then heard,

"We're taking him to Italy for interrogation. He's to be put in one of the containers going back tonight."

"'They're all single drivers tonight."

"'So it'll take a bit longer, but we're not leaving him here. He may be uncomfortable for a couple of days." Then I heard scuffling as you were carried out of the room. After that, silence. We didn't get the call from Dover for about four hours. I've never been so scared in my life.'

John whispered from the top of the pallet cage, 'There's a car trawling up and down the truck park. Zan, we're out of here just in case. Jonathan, I've left the gaffer tape so that you can slip your arms and legs back into position.'

'My gag,' I said. Zan handed it to me as she cleared up any mess they had made. John clambered back down again.

'Take this pill, it'll make you look bloody awful but you'll be fine. Good luck, my friend.'

'These clothes are different,' I said.

'White shirt, dark trousers, I doubt they'll pick up on it.'

Zan looked at me, and even in the torchlight she was gorgeous. 'I love you, Jonathan,' she said. 'We're right behind you, don't worry.' And with that she and John climbed out and I heard the door lock.

Chapter 18

The clothes were too clean so I rolled around on the floor and rubbed as much dirt into them as I could. I pissed myself again for good measure. Having been horrified before, this time I was amused.

I practiced putting my hands and feet back into the gaffer tape straps. If anybody came I would be ready. A few minutes later I heard banging on the cabin door.

'He's not here.'

'Where the fuck is he?'

'Probably shagging some prostitute.'

'Get the container opened, now.'

They were speaking in Italian. Seconds later I heard an almighty crash and the grinding of metal. This lot weren't being subtle with their entry plans so any trace from my friends in the Organisation was lost.

I put the gag on my face and slipped into the straps. Once again a torch shone in my face and somebody climbed down.

'Well, well, what have we got here?' I heard as my gag was ripped off.

'Who are you?' I croaked.

'You'll find out soon enough.'

'Water,' I said, 'I need water.'

'Let's get him out of here.' A second person clambered down and cut the gaffer tape. I rubbed my hands and feet.

'Oh Christ, he's pissed himself.'

'What the fuck do you expect?' I said.

'On your feet,' came the terse response. I tried to get up and immediately collapsed. *A good bit of acting,* I thought.

'Help him.'

The two of them manhandled me up the pallets, across to the back of the container and out into the bright daylight.

'I need a shit,' I said as I squinted and shook my head.

'We'll sort you out in a few minutes, now get in the back of the car.'

Seconds later we were speeding out of the lorry park and on to the autoroute. I saw a sign saying Strasbourg, thirty kilometres. I'd obviously bounced through Germany and Luxembourg to get there.

I looked at the two men. The one who was driving looked a real brute, not the sort of person you would tangle with in a dark alley. His colleague was sitting next to me on the back seat. He was much leaner, well-dressed with an intelligent air, well-spoken. He had a slight southern Italian intonation.

'Don't get any bright ideas,' he said, removing his jacket from his lap and revealing a Walther P99 semi-automatic pistol.

'Where are we going?' I asked, trying to sound naïve.

'You'll find out soon enough.'

'I don't understand what the hell is going on.'

'No idea,' was the response.

We sat in silence for a few minutes.

'I need a crap,' I said.

A few minutes later we pulled into a scruffy aire which looked deserted. *One thing about the European motorway network,* I thought, *if you want a quiet bog in the middle of nowhere you'll soon find one.* These aires, with nothing more than a toilet block and a car park, were every five miles or so.

'No funny business,' said Signore Intelligente, as I had christened him.

The driver opened my door and followed me towards the toilet block.

'In there,' he said, pointing towards a cubicle with a hole in the ground. Even with my Italian upbringing I still hated those things. Having performed magnificently in the truck earlier I didn't really need one but I had to create a level of authenticity. I shut the door. There was no window so the possibility of escape was zero. The driver seemed quite relaxed.

Back on the road I was offered water and a dry bread roll.

'Very civilized,' I said.

'For the time being,' came the response.

'I don't think Jeff Andrews will be very impressed.' There was no comment, so we sat in silence heading down to Basel and the Swiss border. I'd done similar trips across Europe several times and knew there were no border guards so we drove into Switzerland without stopping, following a sign for Lucerne and Milan.

'What time will we get to Bologna?' I asked.

'Don't be a clever bastard.'

At least the car was warm and my trousers had nearly dried from the soaking I had given them. They stank but I really didn't care. *These little shits deserve to enjoy the discomfort*, I thought.

I reckoned Bologna was about three hundred and fifty miles from Basel which meant I had five hours with these two, assuming that's where we were going. Knowing Zan and John were behind me, I felt quite relaxed and was almost beginning to enjoy the ride. It was lunchtime and we pulled in at a service station. The driver came back with an assortment of sandwiches, complaining about the prices on Swiss motorways. I wasn't in the mood to discuss the economic opportunities in Switzerland so I just ate.

After half an hour or so I was getting bored so I decided to wind things up.

'I can't believe what is happening, could you please tell me what is going on?' I deliberately made myself sound quite forceful yet scared.

'Look, cut the innocent boy crap, we know you've been snooping so just shut up.'

'I don't want to worry you,' I responded, 'but everything I have done has been under the auspices of Jeff Andrews, financial director of Orlanda Marble in Slough. Speak to him, he was extremely pissed off when I was set on in Bologna.'

'It's not us you need to convince. We're just the messenger boys, so keep quiet and enjoy the ride.'

I sat in silence, wondering how far behind us Zan and John were. Eventually I dozed off. Having been up all night and concussed, I was done in. Apart from anything else it killed time on what was a very boring trek across Europe. I woke as we were nearing Milan. By now the autostrada was busy with Italians weaving and darting through the traffic. The driver reverted to type and started waving his hands around and swearing at every move the other cars made.

'Shut up,' screamed Signore Intelligente. It was obvious there was no real relationship between these two.

I decided to have another go at playing the innocent.

'Could I phone Jeff Andrews, please? I'm sure he'll sort this out.'

'Do you not think Jeff Andrews is aware of what's going on?' Signore Intelligente screamed. 'Now if you don't shut up, I'll put the fucking gag back on you.' He was a bag of nerves, and there was obviously something wrong.

I relaxed back into the chair and stared ahead. If nothing else, I had rattled these two and maybe made them feel just a little uncomfortable.

Signore Intelligente's phone rang.

'Si.' There was silence and I couldn't hear what was being said from the other end. 'OK, arrivederci.' He turned to me. 'You will stay in a nice place tonight. Be honest and you will be well treated.'

I turned to him. 'I don't know who you are or what you're doing, but this is all well beyond my level of comprehension. A few weeks ago I joined Orlanda to help with the bad debt problem. And you know what pisses me off, I achieved that and this is how you repay me. Pissed off, you bet the hell I am. I wish to God I'd never got the job.'

'We will see,' came the tart reply.

'For Christ's sake, this is beyond me!' I exclaimed.

We passed Milan and about an hour later came off the autostrada, The countryside was rather flat and uninteresting   the houses and villages looked run-down and drab.

A poor man's Tuscany, I surmised. 'So the clever bastard was right, we are going to Bologna.'

'No, we're not, so shut up.'

'Oh, excuse me, we're all of eighty fucking kilometres away.'

Signore Intelligente grabbed me by the throat. 'I've just about had enough of you for one day. Now shut your mouth before I do something I may regret.'

He then pushed me towards the door. I was delighted to have wound him up, even though my neck felt a bit sore. After about fifteen minutes we turned down a side road into a long driveway and drove up to a large Italian villa. Faded elegance was again the best description, and somehow it reminded me of the training centre in

Kenya. Paint was peeling from the walls and the place had a look of decay and dereliction about it. The gardens were overgrown and outhouses had broken windows with rotten doors left half open.

The drive swept round to the front door where we skidded to a halt on the gravel.

'Get out,' commanded Signore Intelligente.

I climbed out of the car and was pushed up the steps. An old lady in a maid's uniform opened the door.

'Signore Farlow, you are most welcome, do come in.'

I followed, with Signore Intelligente behind me. I noticed he had his jacket over his right hand, no doubt covering the semi-automatic.

'I'll take you to your room where you can shower and change. After a long journey I'm sure you need it. You are to join Signore Chinetti at seven o'clock for drinks and dinner.'

'And who is Signore Chinetti?' I asked.

'All in good time,' came the reply.

She took me up a large spiral staircase, along a corridor and opened a door.

'You'll find everything you need in there. See you at seven.'

The bedroom was very Italian, furnished with heavy baroque oak furniture. The headboard on the king-sized bed had elaborate carvings which matched a varnished chest at its base. A large ornate wardrobe and desk completed the collection. There was a musty smell and the room felt damp, obviously not used too often. A door led into a basic en suite with a bath, toilet and shower which looked as though they hadn't been replaced since 1936. Still the water was hot and I luxuriated under the shower for a few minutes, trying to get a grip on reality. Having shaved with a cut throat razor, I was beginning to feel human again.

Clothes and undergarments had been left on the bed. The attention to detail didn't exactly live up to the Organisation. The shirt and trousers were about three sizes too big, but they sufficed.

I looked at my watch. It was ten to six. Smiling, I realised this was UK time, just another detail the Organisation had got right. It would have looked rather strange had the watch shown Central European time. I just hoped they had thought through everything else.

Just before seven local time I strolled downstairs into the entrance hall where a man in his mid-fifties was standing. He was quite lithe and trim for his age and I thought he could obviously handle himself.

'Ah, Mr Farlow,' he said in English, smiling and offering his hand. 'Good of you to join me. I am Signore Chinetti.' He had only the slightest trace of an Italian accent which told me he must have spent many years living in the UK.

I had decided to play the part of a belligerent young man who was very upset.

'I'm not going to shake you by the hand. I am very angry and, if I'm honest very scared. Who the hell do you guys think you are?'

'We are just trying to establish the truth.'

'Well, I'll tell you one last time. I joined Orlanda on the basis that it was a growing company and I had good prospects. I've only been with them for a few weeks and I find myself set upon in Bologna, my flat turned over and kidnapped from Slough. It's preposterous. What sort of animals are you?'

'We are not animals, just businessmen.'

'Well, it's a fucking weird way to do business, treating new starts like ardent criminals. It strikes me you've got something to hide.'

He wasn't expecting this. I could see I had caught him off guard. 'And what do you think that is?'

'I've no idea, but any company that can't even get simple debt collection sorted has got to have questions asked about it.'

'Why?'

'Because you don't build a multi-million pound operation without getting the basics right.'

He didn't like what I said. The smooth operator was a little lost for words and his face hardened. 'Just tell us who you work for.'

'Oh, fuck off,' I said angrily. 'I really can't be bothered with this anymore.'

'Do you want to eat?' He was trying to recapture control.

'Not if I'm going to listen to this bollocks all night.'

He was rattled. 'Well, I am trying to be pleasant but you do not respond. You're behaving like a very rude young man.'

'Well, maybe that's because I am a very rude young man who has been severely abused by a bunch of wankers purporting to be businessmen.' I deliberately used an Italian accent for the last word just to rile him further.

'This meeting is concluded. You will go to your room.'

'And if I refuse?' Signore Intelligente and the driver walked in. 'Jesus Christ,' I said in a resigned manner. 'A bunch of sad little muscle men who couldn't organise a piss-up in a brewery.' I translated it into Italian to make sure they could all understand my disdain. The driver moved towards me.

'Enough.' Chinetti raised his hand. 'I will send food to your room and we will talk again in the morning.'

'I wait with bated breath.' With that I turned and climbed back up the stairs. I walked down the corridor, opened my bedroom door and slammed it shut, only with me on the outside. Very quietly, I edged back down the corridor. I could hear them talking.

'You've got this wrong,' Chinetti said. 'This is just a foul-mouthed little boy. He's a nothing.'

'I don't think so,' replied Intelligente. 'Too many coincidences.'

'Like what?'

'Being caught red-handed snooping in Slough and in Bologna.'

'Go on.'

'What do you mean?'

'What has he actually done? From what I can gather he was caught getting some paper in Slough and he went on the piss with a couple of drivers in Bologna. Hardly the actions of a master spy.'

'But he saw the packages in Bologna and the marble being processed in Slough.'

'That means nothing, your guys have totally fucked up. This kid is nothing more than a cretin and now we've got to find a way out.'

'I could dispose of him.' It was the first time the driver had spoken.

'No, there would be too many questions raised in England, and then we'd get the police snooping around. That's the last thing we want. What a ridiculous position to put ourselves in.'

'That's if he's innocent,' said Intelligente.

Chinetti sighed. 'Let me sleep on it. Get some food up to his room. I'll talk to him in the morning.'

With that I darted back and closed the door very quietly, this time with me on the inside. A few minutes later there was a knock. The housekeeper was standing outside with a tray.

'Grazie,' I said as she came in and put it on the desk. She smiled and left. There was a decent bottle of Barola so I poured a large glass and drank it like cordial. I knew it was wrong but I'd had a hell of a day and needed something.

The food was half decent, there was some antipasta, pork and vegetables. I ate quickly. Having only snacked during the day, I was damned hungry. I felt quite amused, they obviously had nothing on me and were at a loss to know what to do. The warehouse man in Slough and Signore Aggressor in Bologna had stirred up a real hornet's nest with nothing more than gut feeling. The fact that they were right was irrelevant. Nothing could be proven.

I drank some more wine and pondered what could happen. I would be questioned, so I went through Dean's life story. My concern was that if they really checked up they would find holes. For example, my parents would not be found in Chelmsford. Having said that, I doubted their address would have been on the initial application form. I couldn't be certain because I didn't fill it in. However there would have been no need as references were supplied by the Organisation. I knew Dean was on the voter's roll at the flat in Slough, having supposedly lived there for two years. His previous address was a hall of residence in Brighton. Frank had trained me well, I knew the name, along with key staff at the university. However, I realised if these guys were any good I would eventually be found out.

I was anxious and had no idea what the following day would bring. Having drunk half the bottle of wine, I decided that was enough. I needed my wits about me, anything could happen. I lay on the bed trying to work out some answers, just in case. I decided the best approach was to be totally uncooperative, an extension of what I had been that evening. That way they could prove nothing.

I suddenly felt a bit guilty. Here I was having had a pleasant meal and half a bottle of splendid wine in a lovely room lying on a comfortable bed. I thought of Zan and John, probably still sitting in the van feeling somewhat pissed off.

Life's a bitch, I thought, and slept.

I woke the following morning at eight o'clock Italian time to a knock on the door. The housekeeper came in with another tray. She picked up the plates and glasses from the night before and said 'Signore Chinetti would like to talk to you at nine o'clock.'

'Thank you,' I responded as she left the room.

I wondered how to play things, and decided that my approach of being belligerent was the best way forward. As long as I had my watch I wasn't too concerned about what they could throw at me. I showered and put on the clothes that had been left out the night before. Breakfast consisted of ham, cheese and a fresh roll together with strong Italian coffee. At nine o'clock there was another knock on the door. It was Signore Intelligente.

'Signore Chinetti is waiting for you.'

'Fuck off,' I said.

'I beg your pardon?'

'You heard, just fuck off.'

'Don't make this difficult. Signore Chinetti will be very upset.'

'Well, that makes two of us.' I eyeballed him and he looked away.

'What do you propose?' he asked in a conciliatory tone.

'A ticket home.'

'That will not be possible without information.'

'Well, I'll give you some information. You're a bunch of arseholes.' I turned and looked out of the window. After a few seconds I heard Intelligente leave the room.

Round one to me, I thought, *the next may be a bit trickier.*

A couple of minutes later the door opened and in walked Chinetti with Intelligente behind him.

'What have you done with the third stooge?' I asked with as much sarcasm as I could muster.

'You have no respect,' replied Chinetti.

I burst out laughing. 'You have to earn respect.'

Chinetti ignored that one. 'I have a few questions I would like to ask you.'

'Oh, piss off,' I responded.

'You don't seem to understand how much trouble you are in.'

'I'd only be in trouble if I'd done something wrong. You're the guys who've ballsed up, not me.'

I glared at Chinetti, but he held my stare.

'Let me talk to Jeff Andrews,' I said, trying to take control.

'Maybe that will help,' responded Chinetti, taking a mobile out of his pocket and dialing.

'Chinetti,' he said. 'I have Farlow with me, he wants to speak to you.' He handed me the phone.

'Jeff, what is this all about?' I asked, keeping my voice well under control.

'Just tell them who you are, then we can get you home.'

'For God's sake, Jeff, you know who I am.' I added a touch of hysteria to add authenticity. 'You took me on, I've done everything you've asked of me, if this wasn't so bloody frightening I'd be laughing. Christ, Jeff, talk some sense to these imbeciles.'

'Dean, Chinetti is not an imbecile, he's a big hitter in Orlanda. Please listen to me, for your own protection.'

With that, Chinetti grabbed the phone and killed the call. 'That's enough, now are you going to be cooperative?'

I looked at him in a resigned manner. 'I don't know what to say. Whoever you are and whatever you are, you have the wrong man.'

'Give him a lesson in respect,' Chinetti said to Intelligente and left the room.

'I've been looking forward to this,' snarled Intelligente as he came towards me. He threw a powerful punch which I sidestepped and, with two jujitsu moves he wasn't expecting, put him on the floor. I pushed his chin up hard cracking his head. As he lay unconscious I wondered what the hell I should do now.

'Don't move.'

I froze. 'Now stand up with your hands in the air and turn around slowly.' It was Chinetti. As I turned I could see another Walther P99, this time pointing at me.

'For an amateur, you handle yourself well.'

'As would any black belt in jujitsu.'

'I think we need to take a closer look at you. Maybe my colleagues were right, perhaps you are not what you appear to be. Out of the door and down the stairs.'

I followed his instructions, not wanting to argue with a semi-automatic pistol. He ordered me to go down to the cellar and into a small unlit room.

'Perhaps a few hours in darkness will loosen your tongue,' he said quietly and the driver appeared.

'Chain him,' muttered Chinetti.

I couldn't argue with the gun so the driver grabbed my right wrist, put a handcuff on it and clipped the other end to a solid ring attached to the wall. He repeated the exercise with my left wrist, leaving me sitting against the wall with my hands in the air.

'Now would you like to tell us who you are?' Chinetti asked.

'I've told you, this is ridiculous.'

Chinetti nodded to the driver who slapped me hard across the face.

'This will only get worse,' Chinetti said. 'Relieve the pain and tell us now.'

'I have nothing to say.' My jaw was throbbing. I couldn't tell whether it was broken but the pain was excruciating. This guy knew what he was doing. He then thumped me in the stomach. We'd been trained to roll with a punch but being chained up made it impossible. I lay dazed and in pain as a third strike hit me on the other cheek.

'Why?' I screamed. 'I've done nothing.'

'Have a think for a few hours and we'll talk again.' Chinetti turned and left the room with his henchman behind him. I heard the lock turn. *A wasted exercise,* I thought. As if I could get out of these chains. The room wasn't pitch black, a streak of sunlight light crept in through a crack in the wall near the top, but escape was impossible and my arms were too far apart for me to activate the watch.

I lay dazed, in a semi-conscious state. I became aware of the cold concrete floor and found myself shivering, my teeth chattering, which only served to increase the discomfort in my jaw. I tried to make sense of it all. The world of academia seemed light years away and the thought of becoming a lawyer suddenly looked very attractive. I knew I wasn't cut out for this, and I vowed that if I came out alive I'd be looking for a complete change of career.

My mind was muddled and I found myself totally disorientated. A couple of times I became alert and tried to find a solution to my predicament. I felt sure that at some point Zan and John would appear. Reflecting on what had been said, I wondered whether we had achieved anything by allowing me to be brought to Italy. Eventually a couple of things slotted in to place. Chinetti was an important player, Jeff Andrews had said as much and it was obvious that he was also up to his neck in this lot. I tried to work out the link between the marble importer and the pub chain and went through everything I could think of. Firstly, Orlanda was a front for exporting drugs to the UK and probably the US as well. Secondly, the drugs would be sold on the streets via dealers and pushers. This would create a cash mountain.

Then it clicked. Even though I felt terrible and in severe pain I had one of those eureka moments.

The packages that were sent to the pubs every day must be the cash received from the sale of drugs. The money would be laundered through the tills of the pub as sales of food and drink. It was incredibly simple and foolproof until the company got too big, and that's when the Organisation started asking questions.

I really admired the simplicity of the operation. However, there were still unanswered questions. Where did the drugs come from? The suppliers would have to be tracked and the chain destroyed. How did the pubs balance the books? Stock levels would have to be accounted for. Who was running this operation? Zan had said that Frank had a hunch I'd be taken somewhere which may implicate those in charge. I hoped I hadn't blown it for him.

In my semi-conscious state, I became aware of the door opening. 'Have you thought things through?' asked Chinetti.

'Nothing to think through,' I mumbled. My face had swollen like a balloon and it was difficult to talk.

'Why are you making things so difficult? Do you want to die?' I just looked at him. 'We have a little machine which will help you tell the truth. At least, I hope so, otherwise it will cause you great distress.'

Chinetti clicked his fingers and the driver brought in what looked like a small generator on wheels. He wrapped wire around the fingers of both my hands. The line disappeared into the machine. 'Now, before the pain commences tell me the truth.'

It was a funny thing but, although I knew I was in a dire situation, I had no intention of spilling the beans about The Organisation. I felt confident that I would be rescued in the not too distant future. I just hoped they wouldn't be too late.

I heard a click and the pain was unbearable. My body was thrown sideways in a convulsive state with only the handcuffs stopping me from being slammed against the wall. I was conscious of being bounced up and down with my head hitting brick one second and mortar joints the next. The torture stopped and I lay in a heap, shaking.

Chinetti spoke. 'We don't want to do this, just tell us what we want to hear.'

I said nothing. 'One more time,' uttered Chinetti.

Now the pain seemed worse. I think the power had been increased and I could feel my heart pounding in a manner which was far from normal. I'd heard somewhere that cardiac arrest could follow an electric shock and for the first time in my life thought death may be imminent. The machine was turned off again and once more I collapsed.

'We'll leave you to think. Next time will be worse.'

I felt nauseated and scared, lying in my semi-upright position in the darkened room. I wanted to cry my eyes out, not the act of a hardened spy, but I didn't feel like one. I was still very much a novice straight out of training school and here I was in an impossible predicament.

I've no idea how long I lay there but I became aware that the room was in total darkness. Again the door opened and Chinetti switched on a light.

'Have you seen sense yet?' he asked.

I just looked at him as he sighed, 'One more time.'

I braced myself for the inevitable and the pain came. I knew I was weakening, I couldn't take much more. The torture stopped within seconds and I heard the words in English, 'I think that's enough, don't you?'

Chapter 19

Chinetti turned. I could see a man, smiling, standing in the frame of the door with some sort of pistol in his hand. 'Hello,' he said, looking at me. 'I'm Peter, one of the support team.'

'Good to see you,' I said, still shaking.

'You stay there for a couple of minutes while we sort out these two.'

'I wasn't planning on going anywhere.'

'Get them upstairs and into the van quickly,' he shouted to someone in the corridor. 'Come on out,' he said in a less than friendly tone. Chinetti turned. 'Bastardo,' he said, quietly but with incredible venom. I just glared at him as he was taken.

Zan appeared and grabbed me. 'Are you OK?' I could see the concern on her face.

'I am now,' I replied.

'Good to see you, old boy.' I turned and there was Frank, grinning.

'How many of you are there?' I asked.

'Seven in the van plus several as backup. We need to leave before things hot up around here.'

Peter reappeared with a key. 'I found this on the big bloke, hopefully it'll fit your handcuffs. Otherwise it's the metal cutters.' Within seconds I was free. I tried to stand but collapsed almost immediately.

Zan grabbed me. 'Take it easy,' she said.

'I seem to be making a habit of this,' I quipped.

John walked in. 'How are you doing, buddy?'

'I've been better.'

'There's a body upstairs,' he said. 'Anything we should know about?'

'Self-defense,' I replied.

'I believe you but it's probably wise to disappear before the authorities start asking questions.'

'What about Chinetti?'

'We'll be taking him. We've also got a big fella and an old woman.'

'Is he coming with us?' I asked.

'No, he'll be in a support truck with the others,' replied Frank. 'He'll be more comfortable that way.'

I chuckled, hoping he would get some of his own medicine. 'Let's get out of here.'

I was helped upstairs by Zan and John and one outside I saw a large Mercedes panel van parked along together with a smaller Fiat Ducato. I was ushered into the Mercedes through a side door as the Ducato moved off.

There were two banks of seats in the Mercedes, along with a bench seat towards the back. I could see all kinds of electronic gizmos, listening equipment, laptops, trackers, headphones, cameras and much more that I didn't begin to recognize.

'Gives us a certain element of control,' said Frank, climbing into the front next to Peter, who was already in the driver's seat. Zan and the doctor got in beside me and he gave me a quick once over as we set off.

'You'll live,' he said. 'And normally I'd say take things easy for a few days, your body has been through a hell of a lot. Concussion, beatings, electrocution, it's not good news. But I don't suppose you'll listen.'

'We'll look after him, old boy,' piped up Frank, 'have no worries.'

'That's why I do worry,' responded the doctor.

'What about John?' I asked.

'He's having a little look around the house with a couple of others,' Frank replied. 'We'll see him later. We've also got teams looking at Chinetti's flat, along with that poor fellow's who's no longer with us. We've been watching them for twenty four hours, and hopefully something will turn up on the back of it. If John has time he'll dispose of the body, it's tidier that way.'

I could tell Frank was in his element. As we drove away Zan held my hand and squeezed it tight. I wanted to tell her how much I loved her, but this wasn't the moment.

'You took your time,' I said to no one in particular.

'I knew there was something wrong,' said Zan tearfully. 'I crawled up to the house but couldn't see anything apart from Chinetti and the other man talking in one of the rooms. '

'Yes, sorry,' responded Frank. 'We were listening in as best we could but lost you for a while. We eventually picked up a conversation Chinetti had on his mobile saying that he was going to give you some more electric therapy and that's when we decided to go in.'

'Where now?' I asked.

'A little place I've rented from a friend of mine,' replied Frank, 'but first we need to swap vehicles to reduce the risk of contagion.'

As we approached Bologna we turned off on a farm track and drove into what looked like a cowshed. An Audi A6 was parked in the corner. Four of us got out, leaving Peter. Frank climbed into the driver's seat of the Audi, with the doctor in front and Zan at my side in the back. He took a set of keys out of his pocket and started the car. As usual, the attention to detail was exemplary.

'We're off to Forli,' said Frank, following the sign for Rimini. 'It's about an hour's drive.'

We drove in the dark past Imola, where Ayrton Senna had been killed at the Grand Prix circuit. I reflected on the day's activities. It all seemed like a nasty dream. I didn't feel ill as such, but very strange. My whole body had a sort of tingling sensation and I felt my heart palpitating. I kept getting muscle spasms and aching throughout my body, as if I had been on a long run.

I could hear the conversation in the car but wasn't really taking anything in. Zan kept talking at me, trying to keep me alert but I just wanted to doze off. I felt exhausted. I was vaguely conscious of arriving at the house and being helped out of the car. I know Zan took me up some stairs and I lay on a bed while she undressed me. I remember thinking that my body had obviously taken a hell of a beating, but beyond that I slept.

Chapter 20

I woke to the sun shining in through a window. Looking round I saw Zan lying by my side, staring at me. 'How are you?' she asked.

'Like a bomb's gone off inside me.'

'Not far off the truth. The doctor says you'll be okay in a couple of days but you've got to take things easy.'

'What happens now?'

'We're having a meeting later this morning to formulate the next stage.'

'I want to be there,' I said.

'You can just lie here and we'll sort everything out. Can I get you anything?'

'I feel incredibly dehydrated, can I have a cup of tea?'

'Certainly, oh master.' She kissed me gently but passionately. 'I was scared yesterday,' she said. 'I thought I was going to lose you.' Tears welled up in her eyes.

'Hey, I'm here and I'm alright.' I put my arms around her and we held each other for several minutes.

Eventually she pulled away. 'I'll get some tea,' she said, climbing out of bed and putting on her dressing gown.

I looked at my watch. It was eight thirty. 'Fat lot of good that thing did yesterday,' I said drily. 'Being chained against a wall made activation impossible.'

'Frank said he's going to ask the boffins to look at another approach, maybe a ring that you could activate with the same hand.' She disappeared through the door, leaving me to reflect once again upon what had happened. Although I felt drained, I knew I was going to be alright and decided to get up.

By the time she returned I had showered and was halfway through a shave. I wasn't surprised to find a full shaving kit by the wash basin. I was by now very used to The Organisation's ability to cover all eventualities.

'What are you doing?' demanded Zan, holding a breakfast tray laden with croissants, cheese, ham, fruit, bread rolls, orange juice and tea.

'I feel okay,' I said. 'Not great but better having had a shower.'

'Get back to bed, mister, or I'll send John up to sort you out.'

'There's an offer I think I'll refuse,' I responded, walking back into the bedroom. We sat on the bed and shared breakfast, saying very little. 'What time does the meeting start?' I asked.

'Eleven thirty, but you're not invited.'

There was knock on the door and Frank walked in with Dr Stayton behind him.

'How's the wounded soldier?' he asked.

'I'm okay. Perhaps I can come along to the opening session of your meeting this morning, just to keep me in the loop.' Zan rolled her eyes in disgust. 'Then I'll come back and rest,' I said, looking at her. 'I promise.'

'See how you feel,' responded Frank. 'The important thing is your health. The Organisation can get along quite happily without you.'

'What happened to Chinetti?' I asked.

'He's being questioned as we speak,' said Frank. 'I don't suppose we'll get much out of him or his sidekick, but the housekeeper probably knows a fair amount in terms of people who come and go. I think she'll be easier to break. We'll talk more later.'

'Let's have a quick look at you,' said the doctor, putting a thermometer in my mouth. He took my pulse blood pressure poked and prodded and gave me the once over with his stethoscope. 'You're coming along nicely. In a couple of days you'll be fine, but give yourself a chance, time is a great healer.'

'Listen to the good doctor,' said Zan, smiling as he and Frank left the room. She kissed me again. I felt myself stirring and she pulled away. 'You obviously are getting better. Maybe later, let's go and get a breath of fresh air, it'll probably do you good.'

She handed me some clothes that were hanging in a wardrobe. Needless to say they were a perfect fit, and the very action of dressing made me feel better.

We went down a stone staircase into a large room which was beautifully furnished. Two large cream sofas dominated, with a couple of armchairs to match. Several occasional tables were scattered and an antique mahogany wall unit stood against a wall facing an ornate fireplace. The sun was streaming in through glass French windows and the whole effect gave an incredible feeling of warmth and grandeur.

As we walked in, I heard the words, 'How are you, Jonathan?'

I turned to see Caterina smiling at me.

I grabbed her and squeezed tight. 'God, it's good to see you.' I said but suddenly felt dizzy. The two girls helped me across to an armchair. 'Maybe I'm not as well as I thought.'

'I'm saying nothing,' responded Zan.

'OK, I'm sorry,' I said, holding her hand. 'When did you get here?' I asked Caterina.

'About half an hour ago. I've spent the last couple of days analysing the info I got from the pub and I'm presenting my findings at this morning meeting.'

'I'll be doing the same with the material I downloaded in Bologna,' said Zan.

'And you expect me to miss that?' I exclaimed. 'Not a hope.' Zan shook her head.

John walked in. 'You're looking better, good buddy.'

'I'll be fine. The old team back together, hey, good times. Have you spoken to Caroline?' I asked Caterina.

'Yes, she's fine. I went to see her and she was a bit surprised to hear of my involvement. I explained the job was over so the following day she engineered an argument with the manager and resigned on the spot.'

'What did she do?'

'She took the daily delivery up to his room and walked in without knocking. That was enough for him to have a real go at her. She threw the delivery at him and said she wasn't going to be spoken to like that and who the hell did he think he was? He said in his inimitable manner, "Well, if you don't like it you can eff off." Caroline said that was fine by her, and walked. End of story. I sorted out her money and she's happy.'

'She's a good girl, I must phone her.'

'That would be nice, but leave it for a day or two. Give yourself a chance, Jonathan, you've been through so much.'

'What is this place?' I asked no one in particular.

'It's an old farm that's been converted into a luxury holiday villa,' replied John. 'There's a pool, jacuzzi, tennis courts and a sauna. Apparently it's often used by the motor racing fraternity.' I remembered Imola was close by.

'Come on you, let's go and have that breath of fresh air.' Zan took me by the hand and we went for a walk in the garden.

'You know,' I said, 'life is weird. Yesterday I thought I might die, and yet now here I am in absolute luxury, with the lady of my dreams.'

'Jonathan, how keen are you about making a career in The Organisation?'

I pondered the question. 'A few months ago I would have given the world for this opportunity. Now, if I'm honest, I'm scared. Not for me but I'm scared of losing you. Next time it may be your turn and you might not be as lucky as me. And I may lose you, and that frightens me.' I paused. 'No, that terrifies me.'

'That's how I feel,' she responded as we sat on a garden bench holding hands.

'So what are we going to do?' I asked.

'Let's finish this operation, take some time out and find a way forward, together.'

'Sounds good to me.' We kissed and held each other tight.

Strolling back into the living room, I noticed the sofas had been rearranged theatre-style and a couple of extra chairs had been brought in. At the top of the room there was a screen and projector together with a flip chart, white board and a laptop on a desk. John, Caterina, Peter, Frank and couple of other men I didn't know were standing talking to each other.

Frank beamed as we walked in. 'Ah, here's our local hero. Can I introduce you to Luigi and Habib?' I shook hands with them both. Luigi was obviously Italian, in his late thirties, and Habib looked Middle Eastern, probably mid-forties. We made polite conversation for a couple of minutes before Frank clapped his hands.

'OK, chaps, let's get started, we've got a lot to get through today. Can we all sit down?' I sat next to Zan on one of the sofas and John and Caterina sat together. Memories of the training room in Kenya came flooding back. 'What I want to do today is to get a clear picture as to where we are currently with Orlanda and plan a way forward. For those who don't know, Luigi is head of our Italian operation and Habib is head of North Africa. Let's start with Zan, perhaps you can give us an overview of your findings?'

Zan got up and picked up a remote. The words *The Orlanda Group* appeared on screen. 'Good morning. You are aware that I was parachuted into KPMG, who are the current auditors of the Orlanda Group. The idea being that I could take a close look at the company from an accountancy perspective. The Organisation was concerned at its rate of growth. Over the past seven years, turnover and profitability have increased tenfold, yet gearing has remained remarkably low. Exporting marble was the core business, but now Orlanda have a chain of coffee shops across Europe, a chain of pubs and hotels in the UK, together with hotels and casinos in the States. Jonathan went undercover as an employee of Orlanda Marble in the UK and soon discovered that there was the possibility of a company hidden within the computer system. I was able to access details of that company while on a field trip to the marble headquarters in Bologna.

'It transpires that the hidden company, Orlanda Imports, is used for drug trafficking and money laundering. Quite simply, heroin is shipped into Italy from Greece and cocaine from Columbia via West Africa. The drugs are then processed in the south and transported to Bologna where they are hidden in hollowed out marble slabs. The marble is exported mainly to the US and UK, two of the major markets for both commodities.

'Heroin is the key product, with the profit levels being eight times higher than that of cocaine. However supply chains can be problematic, as the raw material is sourced from Afghanistan where there are stricter controls than there have been in the past due to the war. Cocaine keeps the supply chains open when heroin shipments are low and continues to supply a healthy but reduced profit centre. Why go to all this bother, why not ship the drugs directly to the UK and US? Well, Italy is seen as an easy entry port and Orlanda has proven marble to be to be a foolproof way to transport the drugs across Europe and to the US.

'Any questions?'

'Why Greece?' asked John.

'Heroin is transported along what is known as the Balkan route, through Pakistan, Iran, Turkey and into Greece. From there it can go on a variety of routes into the European market. This particular line is shipped from Greece into Bari and Brindissi in Italy.'

'So why should cocaine be shipped from South America via Africa and Europe back across the Atlantic to the States?' asked Frank.

'I can answer that.' Everyone turned to look at Habib. 'It's a question of supply and demand. Quite simply, the USA's thirst for this product is unquenchable but as the US authorities close down one import route, another one opens. The Columbian drug barons are getting ever more cunning and this route has proven highly successful. While the cost of export is higher trafficking via Africa and Europe, the level of profitability far exceeds any concerns. Especially when the importation can be tied in with another product, i.e. heroin.'

'Thanks,' said Frank. 'Caterina, can you tell us what you've been up to?'

Zan came and sat back next to me as Caterina stood up. 'While Jonathan was working at Orlanda Marble in the UK he came across a situation in the pub and hotel division of the Orlanda group. A large amount of money had supposedly gone missing and Jonathan's boss was seconded across to the division to help ascertain the losses. Jonathan suggested we put someone in as matter of expediency to find out what was really going on. A friend of his went to work at one of the pubs on our behalf, but there was a risk as she was untrained. Her instructions were to watch and report, nothing else. She discovered that a package was delivered to the pub every day which nobody was allowed to touch. It had to be taken straight to the manager on arrival. He was an absolute pig, sacking anyone who annoyed him. He also spent many hours in his office with the door locked. I was therefore asked to apply for a job at the pub to see what I could find. I successfully gained a position and was eventually able to access the PC of the manager.

'The information I downloaded confirmed our suspicions. The pub chain is being used for money laundering. The package sent daily is cash, which is then put through the pub's books as sales of drinks and food. That is why the manager spends so many hours locked in his office, he's cooking the books and effectively doubling the turnover. With cash sales it's that easy. To balance the books and account for the stock of alcohol not actually sold, there is a separate enterprise selling the stock into the black market. From what I can gather, favoured places seem to be markets and small grocery shops.

'What is this worth? My research shows that the average turnover of a pub in this sort of market is about ten thousand pounds per week, or just over half a million pounds per annum. This pub's turnover is projected to be nearly one point one million pounds this year. Therefore, we can deduce that nearly six hundred thousand pounds will be laundered through this one pub in one year.

'The group owns over eight hundred pubs, so in theory Orlanda could be laundering four hundred and eighty million pounds across the network. Having said that, these figures are based on one pub and I doubt very much that all of them will be involved with this operation. However, it gives us an idea as to the size and scope of the fraud. Any questions?'

'What happens to the cash that's generated from the sale of booze in the separate enterprise, as you call it?' asked Peter.

'Good question, and I haven't got the complete picture. My best guess is that it's channelled back into the pub chain. The problem with that is the company will begin to grow like a pyramid sales operation, so at some point they would have to find another approach. However, with eight hundred pubs in the group, they've got plenty of recourse.'

Frank stood up. 'Ladies, I'd like to thank both of you, and especially Jonathan, for the work you have all put in. You have proved beyond doubt that Orlanda is a corrupt and rotten organisation. We now have to find the most effective way to deal with it. This is not going to be easy as we are talking about a multi-national company. We need to capture every aspect of the operation, and to do that we need to move quickly. This is going to be a major task and detailed planning is essential. Before we go on, I think it's time for a cup of coffee.'

Zan turned to me. 'Are you OK?'

'Yeah, I'm fine,' I responded, feeling like shit.

'Maybe you should go and lie down?'

'Perhaps at lunchtime. I'd like to see some of the planning process.'

Others were standing around chatting amiably but I sat quietly, only talking to people if they came up to me. I knew I was far from my best but I felt alert enough to stay with the meeting. After about twenty minutes Frank tapped the table at the top of the room. 'Ladies and Gentlemen, I'm going to hand you across to Peter now. His background is in risk management and he's going to help us map our plan of attack against Orlanda.'

Peter got up. 'Thanks, Frank. For this exercise we are going to use a tool called process mapping. For those who know nothing about the subject, it can be defined as a workflow diagram to bring forward a clearer understanding of a process. Over the next few hours we will develop a flowchart that will give us an understanding of the Orlanda Group and the most efficient way to attack the operation.

Between Zan, Caterina and Jonathan we have a reasonably clear idea as to the structure of Orlanda, so I want to flesh this out to start with and build a detailed model and flowchart giving a comprehensive process to achieve our objective.'

The management speak immediately began to do my head in.

'We'll be doing a fair amount of brainstorming and all ideas are welcome, no matter how trivial or stupid you might think they are. The thing is, your stupid idea may just spark something in someone else. Perhaps we can start with the obvious, what is our objective?'

John spoke from the back of the room. 'To shut down the drug running and money laundering operations of Orlanda, arrest as many of those involved as possible, especially the senior personnel, and salvage the good parts of the company.'

'That sound pretty good to me,' responded Peter. 'Does anyone want to add anything?' We sat in silence as he transcribed John's comments onto the white board. 'OK, let's map the structure of Orlanda as we know it.'

For the next ninety minutes or so Peter began to put a detailed process map together of Orlanda, its subsidiaries worldwide and how we were going to attack the company. Post-it notes were scattered across walls as aide memoirs and he started drawing a model with arrows, ovals, diamonds and rectangles each having its own significance. By then my mind was in a fog. I tried to contribute, aware that I had been a major player and my input was required. However I was having great difficulty trying to concentrate, so my involvement was minimal.

After what seemed like an eternity, the meeting broke for lunch. I turned to Zan. 'I'm going to take your advice and lie down for a while.'

'Thank goodness,' she responded, 'you look terrible.'

'Thanks sweetheart.'

'Off you go, I'll come and see you later.'

I made my way back up to my room and fell into a deep sleep. The pounding my body had taken over. The last few days had taken it out of me and I was only just beginning to realise how unwell I'd become.

Chapter 21

I awoke to see Zan walking through the door, juggling a cup in one hand and a plate with a couple of sandwiches on in the other.

'How are you feeling?' she asked.

'Weird.'

She lay down on the bed and kissed me tenderly. 'Oh, Jonathan,' she said, 'I want out of this.'

'How's the process mapping' I asked.

'Boring but necessary.' We kissed again and then it happened. We heard gunshots, not just one or two but continuous bursts.

'Fucking hell,' I whispered, clambering out of bed and slipping on my shoes.

'We can't do anything,' said Zan, startled. 'We're not armed.' As she spoke someone came up the stairs, firing at random.

The two of us stood on each side of the door and as it opened I grabbed the gun and Zan launched into the person holding it. With a broken neck, he slid quietly to the ground. I grabbed his Browning machine gun and we crept to the top of the stairs. Looking down we saw an armed man run into the hall. I fired and he fell to the ground almost immediately.

Running down with me covering her, Zan grabbed the second machine gun. I heard firing and the splintering of glass. Turning, I saw a man fall to the ground in the garden. Zan stopped firing. 'How many more?' she mouthed.

I shook my head as we made our way into the living room. It was a scene of carnage. Frank lay dead on a sofa, his body covered in blood. He'd fallen on a cushion and looked as if he'd gone to sleep in an upright position. Luigi lay on the floor next to Frank, his lifeless body lying face up with eyes wide open. Habib was sitting on an armchair, still alive. He beckoned me over. 'Four of them,' he croaked as his eyes glazed over and he slumped into the chair.

'There's one more,' I screamed to Zan, and as I spoke I heard more gunfire. I collapsed to the ground and looking around saw Zan firing as another man fell. 'That's it,' I said, 'they're all dead.'

John was squatting against the wall in an unusual position. 'Nice one,' he whispered. I could tell he was hurt. 'I'm glad you learned something in Kenya.'

'Don't move,' I said, 'we'll get help.'

'Too late for that, good buddy. I'm on my way, but I gotta tell you, Jonathan, that I love you. I know I'm a sad, old gay, but you are everything to me.' He coughed up some blood. 'Take care, my friend,' and then his head dropped and he lay still.

I grabbed him and held tight. 'I love you too, my brother.' I said as tears streamed from my eyes.

Zan screamed bringing the horror of the situation back to me. 'Jonathan, Caterina is still alive.'

I ran across. She was lying face-up, her body and head covered in blood.

'We need help. Zan, where's your phone?'

She looked up blankly, obviously in shock.

'Zan,' I screamed, 'where's your fucking phone?'

She ran across to where she'd been sitting that afternoon, her bag still on the floor. She just stood looking. I followed and emptied the contents. Finding the phone, I rang the Organisation's helpline.

'We've been attacked,' I said, as calmly as I could. 'Frank, John, Habib and Luigi are dead. Caterina is critical. Send help immediately.'

'Twenty minutes,' came the response.

'Make it ten.' I killed the call and looked at Zan. 'Where's Dr Stayton?'.

'I don't know, I haven't seen him since this morning.' I searched the house, finding two more bodies, people I didn't recognise. A man and a woman both in their fifties, probably staff. *Poor devils,* I thought, *they had nothing to do with The Organisation.*

As I came back to the living room I heard a screech of brakes outside. It was Stayton. He ran into the house, bag in hand. 'I just got the call, I came as soon as I could.'

'Caterina,' I said, pointing. 'She's still alive.'

He went across and while he was examining her I asked, 'Where the hell were you?'

'I was spending the day in town. I'm a doctor, not a spy, and I don't do flow charts. We've got an hour to save her, an air ambulance is on its way and that's our best chance. She's been hit three times from what I can see, twice in the chest and once in the head.'

He lifted her head and put a cushion under it. 'This is a clotting agent,' he said, ripping open a package and pouring powder onto the wounds. He put pads on the chest. 'Hold these in place,' he instructed me. I lay down and pressed hard.

Moments later I became aware of the whir of a helicopter. Two of them had landed on the lawn and men were running towards the house, some of them armed. Caterina was immediately transferred onto a stretcher and carried out, with Dr Stayton following.

'You two are coming with us,' said a voice in English with a thick German accent. I wasn't about to argue. I looked at Zan and we followed him onto one of the helicopters. As we took off I slapped myself hard, trying to make sense of it all. What had been an adventure had turned into a living hell. Was it my fault? Could I have done anything to save lives? I didn't have an answer.

I looked heavenwards and pushed my head back into the chair as Zan grabbed my hand and held it tight. 'I don't know what to say,' I shouted over the noise of the engines.

'Nothing,' she replied. 'Just say nothing.'

We landed about ninety minutes later. I'd dozed off and was dreaming about getting pissed with John when I woke with a start as the engine increased its thrust and the helicopter touched down. Zan was staring out of the window, looking like a lost soul. The door opened from the outside as the pilot turned. 'Leave the machine in a crouch,' he said.

Zan climbed out first and I followed. We'd landed in the garden of a large mansion. Looking at the mountains around us, I guessed we were in either the Swiss or Austrian Alps. The house looked like an overgrown chalet with a smaller version to the right. Apart from the two buildings, we appeared to be isolated.

A thickset, balding man in his fifties beckoned us towards the house. When we were far enough away from the engine noise I shouted, 'Where are we?'

'In good time,' came the response.

'After what we've been through I don't need this bullshit, just give me a straight answer.'

'In the interests of security, you will have to wait a little longer.'

'Well, it's a pity you people couldn't sort out some fucking security a few hours ago.' I yelled.

Zan grabbed my arm. 'Calm down,' she said, 'it won't do any good.' We followed the man to the house, through a set of French windows and into what looked like a living room.

'I am Heinrich,' he said. 'Can I offer you a drink?'

'Scotch,' I replied. 'And make it a large one.'

'I'll have the same,' said Zan.

Heinrich headed across the room and opened a walnut cabinet to reveal a well-stocked bar. He handed us a good sized tumbler each, half full with whisky.

'Prost,' he said amiably. I ignored him and drank. Zan did the same. 'You've had a tough time?' he said.

'Who are you?' I replied angrily. 'I really don't need polite conversation at the moment.'

'We need to speak to someone,' interjected Zan. 'We want to know how our friend Caterina is and why this tragedy happened.'

'Somebody will be here in the next half an hour. Until then all I can do is make you comfortable. I'm sorry.'

I shook my head as I sat on a settee. Zan joined me. 'Can I get you something to eat?' He was trying to be as conciliatory as possible but neither of us were in the mood to be pleasant.

I drained my glass. 'No, thanks, just fill this up again.'

'Is that a good idea?' he asked.

'Oh, trust me, it's a fucking good idea. Do you want another?' I turned to Zan. She shook her head. Heinrich took my glass and refilled it. 'John would be proud of me', I said to no one in particular.

'Who's John?' asked Heinrich innocently.

'One of the poor bastards who's just been blown away, thanks to your wonderful fucking security,' I found myself shouting. The whisky was beginning to kick in.

'I'm sorry.'

'Yeah, so am I.'

Zan took my hand. 'Jonathan, this won't do any good.'

'I know, I just feel so fucking helpless and fucking useless.' I wanted to cry.

'You and me both, but we're in this together and we'll find a way forward. For John's sake, for Frank, Caterina and the others.'

I squeezed her hand. 'Thank God you're here. But why them and not me? If I hadn't got myself kidnapped, none of this would have happened. I feel terrible.'

'You can't think like that, this is not your mistake. It's something much bigger, but we don't know what,'

'Oh, I think I can guess,' I said.

'Go on.'

'There's only one organisation in Italy big enough and strong enough to pull a stunt like this.'

'The Mafia?'

I nodded. 'It has to be. We haven't established who owned Orlanda, with the mesh of offshore companies as shareholders it seemed impossible. But maybe we should have been a little more attentive and worked our way through them all rather than going gung ho into this. Then we might have found out what we were up against.'

The door opened and in walked Mark from the training school.

'Zan, Jonathan, what can I say?' He came over and gave Zan a big hug, then shook me by the hand.

'If it's any consolation, I've known and worked with Frank for the past twenty years. He was my mentor, my counsellor and my best friend.'

'How's Caterina?' I asked.

'Critical, I'm not going to pretend otherwise. The bullets to the body have been removed but she's not strong enough to have the one removed from her head. It requires major surgery and she's very weak, having lost a lot of blood. The bullet is embedded in the brain. If it moves it could be fatal.'

'When can they operate?'

'It'll have to be in the next forty eight hours. If she's not strong enough by then, she won't make it, I'm afraid.'

Tears started streaming down Zan's face. 'Why, Mark?' she said. 'Why did this happen?'

'I don't know yet, we don't know. It's pretty obvious we were careless, somebody somewhere was watching and this is the result.'

'What happened to Chinetti?' I asked.

'We're still questioning him.'

'So the trail wasn't followed to him.'

'Or they lost him.'

I told him my thoughts on Mafia involvement. 'It's not unlikely,' I said, 'that we were set up.'

'Go on,' responded Mark, intrigued at my suggestion.

'Okay think about it. They've kidnapped me and are convinced I'm not who I appear to be. Do we know if they had people watching who came and went from the house?'

'Good question.'

'So once we set off from the house, we were followed, and probably Chinetti as well. We swap the van for a car but they see this and continue to follow. The net result, they know where we're staying, so they send in the boys with semi-automatics. It's blindingly obvious and we were arrogant enough to believe we had contagion licked.'

'So why just wipe out those in the house?'

'To frighten us off, it's typical Mafia, they show how much muscle they have. The one thing they won't know is that they're dealing with the Organisation, who have a lot more resources than they'll ever have. They probably think we are just another drug cartel.'

'So what do we do now?' asked Mark.

'It's time to press the panic button,' I said, warming to the theme. 'We have more than enough information to bring in the national agencies from every country Orlanda operates in. They should raid the company simultaneously. We bring in MI5 in the UK together with the National Crime Agency and HM Revenue and Customs. In the States we use the CIA, FBI and the IRS. In Italy the AISI, the AISE and the Agenzia delle Entrate. My best guess is that in all three countries the tax authorities will be the ones really wanting to drive this.'

'Sorry,' said Zan, 'who are the Italian agencies?'

AISI is the Italian equivalent of MI5. AISE is the equivalent of MI6 and Agenzia delle Entrate is the Italian tax authority. We need to move quickly to reduce the risk of contagion.' For obvious reasons I put a slight level of sarcasm on the word contagion.

'You're right,' said Mark, 'and I can organise a video conference with the relevant parties later tonight. However, it's not going to bring in the big boys who are running this operation.'

'Correct,' I said. 'And that's where Zan and I come in. To do something we should have done right at the beginning of this exercise. As I've already said, we need to establish who really owns Orlanda. We need to sift through the mesh of offshore companies and the shareholders to see what comes up. Secondly Frank said he had people going through Chinetti's flat to see what they could find. Let's see what they turned up. We also need to look at as many bank accounts within the group as we can to see if they reveal anything.'

'You'll need support,' interjected Mark. 'I'll get half a dozen of my best operators here tomorrow morning at eight am. If you need more, you'll get them.'

'I'll need to bring you up to speed,' I said.

'I'm there already. There's a management approach we've adapted called the Four Eyes Principle. To ensure all projects continue seamlessly no matter what the circumstances, a second manager is always involved. I've talked to Frank most days since the start of this mission. Believe me, I'm well up to speed.'

'Where are we?' asked Zan.

Mark smiled. 'Just outside Geneva, and I promise you will be safe here. Now I've got to get on, if you'll excuse me. I'll ask Heinrich to show you to your room and organise food.'

'I don't really feel like eating,' I replied.

'I understand, but you need to build yourself up. You've been through more than most people in a lifetime over the last couple of days, and out of respect for your colleagues you need to be fit.'

He got up, patted me on the shoulder and put his other hand gently around Zan's neck. 'We owe it to them,' he said as he left the room.

I looked at Zan. 'You were wonderful,' she said. 'The way you took control.'

'That's what half a bottle of whisky does,' I replied.

Heinrich came back in, 'I'll take you to your room. I've put some food in there, should you want it.'

'Thanks,' I said, 'and apologies for my approach earlier.'

'Don't worry, I do understand. I was in the army for many years. I know what it's like to lose good friends, believe me.' I shook his hand. It seemed the only thing to do.

The room was five star opulence and enough food for half a dozen people had been placed on a small table. Rolls, chicken legs, cold meats and salads stared at me. The thought of eating made me feel sick but a small bar had been set up at the far end so I went and poured two glasses of whisky. Zan gulped down half of hers and spluttered. 'I don't normally drink it neat.'

'At least we can drink, unlike our friends.' We lay on the bed silently for several minutes, both of us trying to deal with our grief. Zan put down her drink and kissed me passionately.

'Make love to me,' she sobbed. 'I want to feel alive, I want to feel human.'

Several hours later I woke and Zan was lying on top of me. Her head was on my chest and she was crying. I caressed her hair.

'Don't leave me Jonathan,' she sobbed, 'please.'

Chapter 22

The phone rang. I looked at my watch. Seven thirty. 'How are you feeling?' Mark's New England accent was quite therapeutic.

'OK.'

'I'm having an update meeting at eight o'clock. Are you fit enough to make it?'

'I'll be there.'

'What about Zan?'

'I should think so. Any news on Caterina?' Zan's eyes opened.

'No change, I'm afraid.'

'I suppose you can argue no change is positive.' There was silence from the other end. 'See you in half an hour,' I said and hung up. 'We're having an update meeting at eight, do you want to go?'

Zan nodded. 'I'll take a shower.'

As always clothes were waiting for us and just before eight we made our way downstairs. Heinrich was hovering. 'I'll take you to the meeting room. There are croissants and coffee waiting.'

We walked in and Mark was holding council with four men and two women. They all looked European, aged between mid-twenties and late thirties. 'Ah, good morning, thank you for joining us. Ladies and gentlemen, may I introduce you to Zan and Jonathan?'

The feeling was surreal. The environment so similar to where we had been yesterday, and yet so much had happened. I felt resentful that these people were just being slotted in to replace our friends. I wanted to scream, 'What are we, just fucking pawns that can be changed at a moment's notice?' Sadly, I knew the answer would be, 'Yes, that's precisely what you are.'

I shook hands dutifully. Their names went in one ear and out of the other. I was a million miles away. 'Before we start,' said Mark, bringing the meeting to order, 'you are all aware that we have lost some of our own. I'd like to have a minute's silence as a mark of respect for our fallen friends and colleagues, John, Frank, Luigi and Habib. If you have a God, pray for Caterina, who lies critically ill in hospital.' I bowed my head, aware of Zan crying next to me. 'OK, guys, we have a job to do, and given the circumstances it won't be easy. For the sake of those who have died, let's do it for them.'

'Excuse me,' said Zan as she rushed out of the room.

'Do you want to go with her?' asked Mark, looking at me.

'No,' I responded wearily 'give her a bit of space. Let's get on.'

'Alright,' said Mark. 'Let's sit down and talk.' I helped myself to a cup of coffee and sat at the back.

Mark started. 'I'll be quite honest, I didn't get much sleep last night. I had to pull a video conference together with some pretty high-powered people from around the world. However, due to the power and influence of The Organisation, I was able to do just that at three o'clock this morning. To cut a long story short, tomorrow we will be closing down Orlanda and all its operations. Relevant authorities will raid the Head Office in Zurich, the marble headquarters in Bologna, the processing plant near Bovalino in Southern Italy, the marble headquarters in Slough, a selection of the pubs across the UK, the coffee shop chains in Europe, the US headquarters in New York and the hotels and casinos in the US. The relevant banking authorities are also helping us with as much information as they can supply.

'Make no mistake, this is a major operation, one of the biggest the Organisation has ever pulled together. Normally we would plan such an action in minute detail over a period of weeks. Sadly we do not have that luxury. It is quite likely that there is a leakage factor from within the Organisation, so we have to move quickly.' I looked up. Mark had come up with something I hadn't thought of, a spy in the camp.

'Shouldn't we therefore move more quickly?' asked one of the women sitting in front of me.

'Yes,' replied Mark, 'but logistically that's not possible. We're asking for the impossible as it is, putting this thing together in little more than twenty four hours. If they are onto us, we have enough information to charge those who are implicated. They can't all disappear and even those who try will be found eventually. Believe me, Orlanda is finished. Now the problem is getting to the big boys and that's where you come in.

'As Jonathan said to me last night, we need to establish who really owns Orlanda, We'll have to sift through the mesh of offshore companies, to see what comes up. We need to look at as many bank accounts within the group as possible to see if that gives us anything. We need to find names to see if they match anything we have on file for subversive organisations.

'We also have a couple of people under arrest, Signores Chinetti and Manzoni. They are currently being questioned and information found at their homes analysed. Anything that stems from this will be fed back to you. Jonathan will be heading up the operation, so you report to him. We have four offices at your disposal with full internet access, phones, printers, etc. Any questions? Jonathan, would you like to give an overview of Orlanda?'

As I stood up, Zan walked back in. She'd composed herself and I could see the detached, professional air she'd used at KPMG. 'Mark, could I ask you to bring Zan up to speed?' I said, immediately taking control.

'Indeed. Zan, let's find another room.'

As the two left I began to outline the activities of the last few weeks. Like Zan, I somehow distanced myself from the horror of yesterday. I put myself into training mode and even managed a few attempts at humour. Mark was right about one thing, these people were bright and asked many searching questions. I was able to fend them off and acquitted myself quite well.

Zan rejoined us as the questions came to an end.

'There are eight of us here,' I said. 'I'm good at counting. Now I would suggest we split ourselves into four couples and look at different areas of the group. America, the UK, Italy and Zurich, together with the shareholders. There will be crossover, so don't get precious. Look at the banks and see what, if anything, they reveal, tax returns, accounts, basically anything you can think of. I'll take the UK, I'd like Zan to look at Zurich and the shareholders. Perhaps the rest of you can decide where your skills can be optimized. Let's grab a coffee and work out who's working with whom.'

I suddenly went cold as I thought of Frank doing a similar thing yesterday. Looking at Zan I could tell she was thinking along similar lines. As the others helped themselves to coffee, I went over to her. 'You seem to be enjoying yourself,' she whispered sarcastically. I could feel the anger rising from deep within.

'What the hell am I supposed to do?'

Realizing she had struck a very raw nerve, she responded quickly, 'I don't know. I'm sorry,' and squeezed my hand.

'We're in this together,' I replied, trying to stay calm, 'and as soon as possible we're out of here. We'll find that little south sea island and rusticate, together.'

She looked at me and nodded. 'The sooner, the better. Let's go and join the others.'

A weedy-looking guy who looked about twelve came up to me. 'Jonathan, I'm Ben. I'd like to work with you on the UK. I'm a chartered accountant by training and over the years have done a fair amount of management consultancy in large companies. I think I know what to look for.'

'You're obviously English,' I replied. 'Where are you from?'

'Leicester, originally. I read Classics at Cambridge and joined Deloittes soon after.'

'Excellent, we'll get the others set up and then we can talk.'

Zan was in deep conversation with one of the girls and the other four seemed to be having a healthy debate. I went across. 'How are you getting on?'

'It's a question of who takes what,' responded a Latin-looking man with a French accent.

'Why don't you take Italy, and then you can look at the European coffee chain as well?' He nodded.

'It would make sense if I took the States,' suggested another. 'At least I know the geography.'

'I'd like to work with you, Tom,' responded the other girl. 'With my background in law, I may be some use.'

'You're obviously both from that side of the pond,' I said.

'Canada,' replied the girl.

'California,' said the man.

'That leaves you in Italy,' I said, turning to a six foot four, athletic-looking type.

'No worries,' was the response. I didn't ask what part of Australia he was from, I had no real interest.

'OK, people,' I said, 'let's see what we can find. We'll come together again at five this afternoon but call me if you find anything significant before then. Anyone know where these offices are?'

Heinrich appeared. 'Follow me, please.' He deposited the various pairs in different rooms around the building. Ben and I were ushered into a modern looking room with couple of desks, each with a laptop, phone, writing pads and pens.

I gave Ben as much information as I could on the UK operation. Starting with Orlanda Marble, its address, bank details and, staff names, but truth be told I didn't have that much to go on. From the "O" Cloud we retrieved Caterina's report on the pub division, which was far more impressive. She had accessed staff records, full banking details, suppliers, distributors, building leases, vehicles, insurance, etc.

I stressed to Ben that we were looking for clues to tie in the big hitters. We decided to split, with Ben focusing on the pubs and me on Orlanda Marble. I started looking at the bank details. The Kenyan training kicked in once again. Within a couple of minutes I had full access to the company bank accounts.

'Thank God for internet banking,' I quipped. Ben looked up and smiled.

The main signatories on the account were Jeff Andrews and Roland Peterson, the MD. Others included Julie McDermott, my boss. I couldn't believe she was involved but after what had happened I was prepared for anything. The name that made me go cold was Emilio Chinetti. I told Ben.

'He's the key to this. You keep working on Caterina's report, I need to speak to Mark.'

I went back to the main living room, where a cleaner was polishing a table. 'Is Mark around?' I asked in French.

'I'm sorry, I don't know him.'

'What about Heinrich?'

'I'll go and get him,' she responded and left the room. Seconds later he appeared.

'I'm looking for Mark?'

'Follow me please.'

Mark was on the phone in a small room, only big enough for a desk and two chairs. He beckoned me to sit and killed the call.

I told him about Chinetti. 'He's the link,' I said. 'He's obviously well involved at Orlanda and we were followed after he questioned me. Have we got anything out of him?'

'No, he's a true pro, this one.'

'What was found at his flat?'

'Not much, it was just an accommodation address.'

'His mobile?'

'Good question, I'm waiting on the report.'

'Can you chivvy them along a bit?'

Mark picked up the phone and much to my surprise started speaking in rapid German.

'Anything on Chinetti's phone?' He smiled as he looked at me, awaiting a response.

'Impressive,' I said.

'German father,' he responded.

'I won't ask.'

'Let's just say he was helpful to the Allied forces towards the end of World War Two. Ja,' he barked and started scribbling on a pad. 'Danke.' He slammed down the phone.

'We've checked the last two hundred and fifty calls, and there's a couple to Rome that look interesting. We've tracked them down to an area called Parioli, it's an upmarket suburb.'

'His family?' I asked.

'We think so. With them helping enquiries Chinetti may be more cooperative.'

I breathed in sharply.

'As you were told before you joined, we fight using fair means or foul. After what happened to our friends, we are now quite prepared to use the foul approach.'

I nodded.

'I'll let you know if anything comes of it. Meanwhile, keep on sifting through the info you have and see if you can find anything more.'

I left the room and walked down a corridor. Heinrich approached me. 'What would you like to do for lunch, Jonathan?'

'Sandwich at my desk, please.'

'Is that the same for everyone?'

'Yes, we're beyond playtime now.' I went back to the office I'd been allocated and Ben was glued to his screen. 'Anything?' I asked.

'I'm not sure. It may be nothing, but I've been looking at the car fleet.'

'Go on,' I said, intrigued.

'For whatever reason, they have a Mercedes Benz S500, long wheel base. It costs about eighty thousand pounds new. Now you might say that's the sort of car the CEO would drive, but I've checked the London congestion payment system and it doesn't really go outside of London. The fuel receipts confirm this. The only place it seems to go is Heathrow. The cameras show it's there half a dozen times a week, with an occasional trip to Gatwick.'

'Meaning?' I asked.

'It's an upmarket taxi, ferrying people to and from the airport. Why should a company in the pub industry be picking people up from Heathrow so regularly? It doesn't make sense.'

'Where is it now?'

'According to the car's tracker, in Belgravia.'

'I think we need to pick up the driver and ask a few questions.'

'Absolutely, I'll get onto it straight away.' I began to like Ben, he was extremely proactive with an enquiring mind. I could see why The Organisation employed him.

'Good man,' I said, 'keep up the good work. I'm going to see how the others are getting on.'

I went into another office. 'How's the Canadian-Californian confederation?' I asked because I didn't know their names and hoped they'd be forthcoming.

'Bob's been trawling through the banks and I've been looking through company profiles.'

'Anything?'

'Michelle's found something.'

'Go on.'

'Well, the holding company in the Bahamas has links to companies in Liechtenstein and the Cayman Islands. There's a web of companies, some trading, some not, and it's a nightmare trying to link anything. Now, more by luck than judgement I found that one of the companies in the Cayman Islands also owns a transport company in Italy, and guess what? They have the contract to transport marble for Orlanda across Europe. Now you wouldn't necessarily have found this, as the vehicles are all using the Orlanda livery with lease back arrangements. The connection at that end is at best muddled. However, the CEO is a man called Antonio Suraci, the son of one of the supposed top men in the Ndrangheta.'

'So that's who we're dealing with?' I exclaimed. 'One of the most powerful criminal organisations in the world. They make the mafia look like amateurs.'

The two of them nodded.

'I don't know about you two, but I think I'm a bit out of my depth here. We need to tell Mark. Come with me.' They followed me to Mark's office.

'Apologies for bringing you information in dribs and drabs,' I said, 'but Michelle has found something you need to know about.' She repeated her story.

'There's no need to apologise with a story like that. The Ndrangheta have been on our radar for a long time but until now we've never got close. It's reckoned their drug trafficking, extortion and money laundering businesses account for over four percent of Italy's GDP, with a turnover of seventy to eighty billion dollars a year. Worldwide they employ in excess of ten thousand people. It's run by a loose confederation of families based in Calabria, southern Italy, all linked via the Crimine O Provincia. That's a kind of head office where the various families or strands of the group try to hold the operation together. They are ruthless, corrupt and extremely powerful.'

'So where do we go from here?' I asked.

'That's the billion dollar question,' responded Mark.

His phone rang. 'Ja,' he barked into the receiver. His face looked passive, revealing nothing. *He'd make a great poker player,* I thought.

'OK, danke.' He ended the call. 'We're playing hard ball. Chinetti's family have just been picked up. Bob, Michelle, great work, keep at it. Jonathan, you're coming with me.'

As we left the room he said, 'I thought you may like to see Chinetti being questioned.'

'Where is he?'

'Next door.' We walked out of the main house, down a path, and through a lovely garden. It was rather pleasant to get some fresh air. 'You'll be observing through a glass screen. You've moved up a level, Jonathan, well done.'

'It doesn't feel like well done after yesterday.'

'I know, but we'll get them, trust me on that one.'

We walked into the smaller villa next door, down a flight of steps, along a musty corridor and into a small room. At the far end I could see Chinetti, looking smug through a glass screen. He was sitting at a desk with a bearded man in his early forties on the other side. There was silence, the two of them glaring at each other like gladiators waiting to pounce.

'Now watch and learn,' said Mark as he left the room. Seconds later he appeared in front of Chinetti on the other side of the screen. 'Mr Chinetti.' His voice could be heard amplified through a speaker. 'A pleasure to meet you. My name is Mark.' He offered his hand. Chinetti ignored him.

Mark sat next to the bearded man. 'There seems to be no point in pleasantries, Richard's tried all that and you've not been forthcoming. So we'll have to take another approach. We've never found electrocution particularly effective, it's very messy and time consuming, but we do have other methods. Out of common decency, I will ask you once more. I want names.'

The room fell silent for about thirty seconds. At that point Mark took a mobile out of his pocket, pressed a couple of buttons and laid it on the table. He'd programmed the loudspeaker so the ringing tone could be heard clearly. After a second the call was answered. 'Put her on,' Mark said in German.

A little girl's voice was heard speaking in Italian. 'Papa, quello che sta succedendo?' *Daddy, what's happening?*

A look of horror could be seen on Chinetti's face as he threw his hands down onto the desk while trying to stand. It was only then that I realised he was chained.

'Giovana, va utto bene?' *Are you alright?*

'Papa, ho paura.' *I'm frightened.*

At that point Mark cut the call. He sat eyeballing Chinetti.

After a few seconds he said, 'Your daughters are Giovana, Alessandra and Donna, your sons Enrico and Lorenz. Not forgetting your dear wife Eleonora. We have them all. I suggest you start talking.'

'And if I don't?' He sounded scared.

In a matter of fact tone which was quite terrifying, Mark replied, 'They will die, one by one, and you will see each body.'

Chinetti tried to stand again and could well have broken his wrists as he forced himself forward. He collapsed back on to his chair, his face distorted in pain. 'Who are you?' he screamed.

'We ask the questions. Don't worry, you'll get a new identity, in a country of your choice, where the Ndrangheta will never find you.'

'They always find you.' Now we had confirmation, it was the Ndrangheta behind Orlanda.

'I'll leave you to think things through for half an hour. Do excuse me.' Mark got up and left the room. I met him in the corridor.

'Will he talk?' I asked.

'He'll talk.'

'What about Manzoni?'

'He's light-weight, we'll get nothing of importance there.'

'Maybe a link with one of the Ndrangheta families?'

'Check him out, see what you come up with. Let me know if you find anything. Otherwise I'll see you at the five o'clock catch up.'

I was getting my marching orders so I walked briskly back to the main house. I went into Zan's office to see how she was getting on. The walls were covered with sheets of paper taken from a flip chart. Several packets of Blu-Tack lay on a table and what looked like a family tree had been built going from one side of the room to the other. Closer inspection revealed the names of companies handwritten in green felt tip pen. Shareholding details were in blue, the links between one company and another in red and directors' names in black. A very simple approach, but it looked impressive.

'Brilliant,' I said. 'Have you found anything?'

'Not yet, but we'll match something eventually,' replied Zan. 'It was Heidi's idea.'

'Years of management training,' beamed Heidi.

I brought them up to speed and they seemed somewhat disgruntled that Michelle had found something within their terrain.

'Ladies, this isn't a competition,' I said. 'We're in it together and as I said, inevitably there will be crossover. At five we'll compare notes and names and see if that fleshes out anything else.'

I left them to it and went to look at the Franco-Australian alliance. 'How are we getting on, chaps?' I nearly bit my tongue as I realised I was emulating Frank.

'Good,' replied the Australian. 'We drilled into the programme Zan downloaded in Bologna and came up with some interesting stuff. The first is the payroll for the processing plant in Bovalino. We're back to the alcohol link because its front is a brewery - Birra Calabria. The company's fully legit, producing first rate lager shipped all over the world. Bloody clever really, because the beers go out and the drugs come in.'

'We think,' I interjected.

'A bottle shop to a butcher,' he replied. I didn't understand the Australian slang but got the gist of what he was saying.

'Anyway,' continued the Frenchman, 'one of the directors of the brewery is also a director of the coffee shop chain, showing a direct link between the two. Also many of the people working in the brewery have common surnames, like a family.'

I told them about the Ndrangheta connection. 'You're obviously onto something here, guys, keep digging. I'll see you at five but if something important comes up before then, come and find me.'

I went back to what had become my office and sat down. I suddenly felt knackered. 'Are you alright?' asked Bob.

'Yeah,' I responded. 'The last few days have taken it out of me.'

'Here,' he said, handing me a cup of coffee and a ham roll.

'Found anything more?' I asked with my mouth full of food.

'You'd better believe it.'

'Don't keep me in suspense.'

'The driver was picked up and he's innocent.'

'Oh,' I said, slightly disappointed.

'But he's got a list of pick-ups from Heathrow and Gatwick for the next few weeks. There's going to be a conference at the

Dorchester in London at the end of the month and he's supposed to be ferrying delegates from the airport.' He handed me piece of paper with a list of names. 'Those that are highlighted are the ones he's responsible for, the others are being picked up by coach or another driver.'

I looked at the list. Twenty four names, mainly Italian, with people flying in from New York, Peking, Paris, Sidney, Rome, Zurich and Bologna. A couple of the names looked familiar. Chinetti was one, Antonio Suraci another, with several other Suracis and three Manzonis for good measure. Several cogs turned in my brain. It was another eureka moment.

'Jesus Christ,' I said. 'Have you any idea what you've found? A pound to a penny, this is the Crimine O Provincia of the Ndrangheta responsible for Orlanda. These are the people directing the operation. The Suracis and the Manzonis will be the families heading up this strand of the Ndrangheta. You've fucking cracked it.' We just looked at each other, stunned.

'OK,' I said. 'We need to know if there are any other delegates. Get hold of the Dorchester and see what you can find, also the airlines. I want addresses. I want that driver squeezed for any other info he may have, and check the Orlanda systems both hidden and legit to see if you can find any more on this conference. Apologies for sounding so prescriptive. I'm off to find Mark.'

Chapter 23

I darted out of the office and nearly collided with Heinrich.

'Where's Mark?' I blurted out.

'He's gone back to the other house.'

I ran and soon realised I wasn't in as good a condition as I had been recently. Mark opened the door as I arrived, panting.

'You need some exercise,' he said, smiling. 'And I have a list of names.' He waved a piece of paper at me.

'We need to compare it with this list,' I said, catching my breath and explaining what had happened. We held them side by side. There were a similar number of names on each but apart from most of the names being Italian there was no correlation. Mark pursed his lips.

'Oh dear, he's been telling lies.'

'You realise who's on his list?' I said.

'Go on.'

'It'll be another strand of families from the Ndrangheta. Think about it, we wipe them out, leaving Chinetti's strand in a much stronger position. We put him into hiding and he comes out at some point a hero. But the wonderful thing is we can now wipe out at least two strands and severely weaken one of the most powerful criminal organisations in the world.'

Mark nodded sagely. 'Jonathan, this is fantastic work. I think we need to talk to Chinetti one last time. Come and enjoy the moment.'

'Too many lost friends for that.'

'They haven't died in vain, Jonathan. We are taking out an important supply chain from the revolting world of drugs trafficking. We're also taking out some very senior members of a nasty and immoral enterprise. We won't beat the drug barons, not yet, but it's the old story, how do you eat an elephant?' I looked at him quizzically. 'In small bites. Follow me.'

We went back down to the cellar. Richard was standing in the anteroom, looking at Chinetti through the screen.

'Shall I unchain him?' he asked.

'No,' responded Mark. 'I have a couple more questions to ask.' He handed Richard my list of names and told him what I'd found. The two of them returned to Chinetti. Through the screen, I saw him look up as they entered. Mark sat opposite and said, 'We have a problem.'

Chinetti sat impassively, almost smugly before he spoke. 'And what is that?'

'You've lied to me, and I don't like people who lie.'

'What are you talking about?' responded Chinetti aggressively.

Richard looked down at my list. 'Antonio Suraci, Marco Suraci, Geraldo Manzoni. Do you want me to go on?'

Chinetti sank back into his chair once again.

You obviously have no respect or love for your family,' continued Mark. After a few seconds he spoke again. 'One call, and your family is dead.' He took his 'O' phone from his pocket and held it. Chinetti bowed his head and started mumbling names. 'Louder,' Mark boomed. Richard ticked them off the list as he spoke, adding a couple we'd obviously missed. 'That's better,' said Mark as Chinetti stopped talking.

'What happens now?'

'We'll take your family to a nice place where you can join them.' Mark glared at Chinetti, who looked away, a beaten man.

Walking back to the main house, Mark turned to me. 'Let me have addresses for all the men on this list as quickly as you can. We need to move on them tomorrow while the authorities are raiding Orlanda. By the time I've finished, it'll look like a turf war between the two factions.'

'You have the manpower?' I asked, somewhat incredulously.

'It won't be easy, with everything else going on, but I'll find it somehow,' responded Mark coolly. 'By the way, the four eyes are now you and me. You've proven to be a great addition to the Organisation.'

'Can we find out how Caterina is?'

Mark made the call immediately. 'She's gained enough strength for them to operate this afternoon. It's still very much touch and go.'

I went to find Zan and gave her the news. 'I pray to God that she pulls through.'

'Are you religious?' I asked, realising that there was so much I didn't know about this girl.

'A lapsed Catholic,' she said.

'Likewise,' I responded, kissing her.

'Excuse me,' said Heidi with mock indignity.

Pulling away I said, 'I need everyone to assemble in the meeting room to give an update. Heidi, can you let, er–' I stammered. 'There's so much going on, the Frenchman and the Australian.'

'Serge and Charlie,' she interjected.

'Yes, thank you, can you ask them to join us? Zan, the same with Tom and Michelle. I'll get Ben and photocopy these names.'

When everyone was together I went through the findings of each group, together with a report on Chinetti.

'This has been great work so far,' I said, 'but now we have fifty names and before we call it a day we need addresses and as much information as we can find on each one. Let's split again into our groups and work on a dozen people each. See what we come up with. Zan there's a couple of Chinese names, it would make sense for you to look at them. Just to remind people, the Anagrafe in Italy is the Civil Registry Authority. They maintain the national population records. The majority of people on this list will be found through them. Use the same principal as a starting point for those from other countries. Let's meet back here in two hours and see how we've got on.'

I handed out the names and we split them four ways. I kept Jeff Andrews, feeling very saddened that what appeared to be a very ordinary man had got hooked up with this bunch of degenerates. The name Grimaldi also appeared. I assumed that was my HR friend so I decided to trace him as well.

It was frighteningly easy to find them. Where several possibilities came up we compared the names with the Orlanda records and found a number of matches. The banks revealed other addresses often with links to Orlanda. Where there weren't employment matches we found dividend payments on Orlanda share issues. Other names were confirmed by area, for example people living around Calabria in Southern Italy, the stronghold of the Ndrangheta. By the time we reconvened we'd matched forty two of the fifty names.

Zan was looking concerned. She'd traced the Chinese couple Fei Wai and Sam Chuen. They were leading members of Shui Fong, one of the main Triad groups in southern China.

'These guys are dangerous,' she said. 'The Shui Fong are the Ndrangheta of southern China. They run extortion operations, loan sharking, narcotics and prostitution. They also control nightclubs and gambling dens.'

'I'll give Mark the good news.'

'How are you feeling?' I could see the concern on her face.

'If I slowed down,' I said, 'I'd probably collapse, but I've got to keep going. I owe it to too many people.'

'Take care,' she responded, holding my hand.

'OK, guys,' I said, standing. 'Let's see what we can find on the other eight people. The drinks are on me once we've cracked it. Work as a team to see if any of us have missed anything.'

I found Mark in the office he'd been using and updated him on our findings. He breathed out heavily, pursing his lips again.

'The Triads,' he exclaimed. 'What do you think?'

'It's probable their connection is on the periphery. If there's any trouble my best guess is they will back away and disappear into the sunset, if you'll excuse the mixed metaphor.'

'Go on.'

'If they see a fight between two strands of the Ndrangheta and the Orlanda operation wound up, they'll write off any investment and eliminate all connections.'

'I think you're right. We're back to small bites ,and today is not the day to take on the Chinese Triads.'

He looked at me for a second. 'I can't stress how important it is that our actions against the Ndrangheta look as if they've come from a turf war, similar to one in 1975 when over three hundred people were killed. Their own 'Code of Silence' helps us in this respect. So what I suggest is that we start by taking out half a dozen from the list that Chinetti supplied. It looks to me as if they are from the Condello strand. We do this just after the raid on the brewery. The fact that the families don't communicate helps us no end. However it's important they know the Suraci clan are responsible for the murders. My best guess is the leaders will learn very quickly that Orlanda and associate companies have been struck and put two and two together. Just to add to the confusion I think we should take a few of the De Stefano clan out as well. It will help create a 'Fog of War.' Judging by history, retribution will come quickly and part two of the plan kicks in. We then take out all those on your list based in Italy. We can mop the others up later. By then there should be enough mayhem for a real turf war to start. We'll finish off the rest of the Condello tribe but, having said that, I think the families themselves will be well on the way to helping us in that respect. We disappear and let them get on with it.'

I sat back in my chair, thinking the plan through. After a few seconds I asked, 'Where does our manpower come from?'

'One of our finest anti-terrorist soldiers is putting together a team for me. He's ex-SAS and the best we have for this sort of caper, the sort who'll relish the challenge. He'll have a squad of thirty men in situ by tomorrow afternoon. Once he gets the signal that the brewery has been raided, he'll swing into action.'

'What happens if any of his men are hit?'

'They won't be carrying ID, and they'll be using powerful motorcycles with registrations leading to a little old lady in Venice. In other words, no trace. Pick-up points will be arranged and the men and machines will disappear into the backs of lorries. They'll be halfway to Rome before anyone realises what's happened. Just like *The Italian Job,* but nobody will get smashed and take the truck off the road.' He smiled. 'I'll have to take Serge and Charlie away from you I'm afraid, they'll be joining the action in Calabria. They're rather good at that sort of thing. Have I missed anything?'

'No, but why don't we run the plan past Zan? She's incredibly detail-conscious, it may just help.'

'I like that, go and get her and see if we've found any others on the list.'

I paced back to the meeting room. There was a hive of activity but only four people visible. Serge and Charlie had already gone. *Christ, this is moving fast,* I thought.

'We've got another four,' shouted Heidi.

'Great work,' I said. 'Keep it going. Zan, can I borrow you?' She followed me out of the room and I told her briefly about the plan. 'We'll go through it in detail and I want you to find any flaws.' By the time we got back to Mark's office, he had a map of southern Italy up on a large screen behind the desk.

'Let's start,' he said, 'by marking all the addresses on the screen, colour-coded by family.' He was using a derivative of 'Bing Maps', so was soon able to build a picture of the addresses. At the same time he updated Zan with details of the plan.

'We don't have details of any of the De Stefano family yet,' Zan said.

'Good point,' replied Mark. 'Ask Heidi and the team to come up with half a dozen names and addresses.'

Zan disappeared, returning five minutes later. 'They've tracked all those on the lists and are now working on the De Stefanos.'

The phone rang and Mark picked it up. 'Thank God.' he said. I could see relief in his expression. 'They've successfully removed the bullet from Caterina. The next twenty four hours are crucial, but her odds of recovery have improved dramatically.'

We sat quietly for few a seconds. 'Come on, let's get on,' said Mark. 'We owe it to her. Let's test this plan.'

Zan spoke, 'We need a flip chart, so I can map the detail.'

Again Mark picked up the phone and spoke in rapid German. Two minutes later Heinrich appeared, manhandling the requisite piece of equipment. He pulled out some marker pens from his top pocket. 'I've taken the liberty of ordering coffee,' he said, disappearing out of the room.

'Seems like a good man,' I said.

'I'll tell you about him one day,' responded Mark. 'He's had an interesting life.'

'I'll begin the mapping,' piped up Zan. She started writing, *Thirty men.*

'Question mark,' said Mark. 'I'm still awaiting confirmation.'

'Transport?' She added trucks and bikes.

'Same.'

'Weaponry.'

'Same.'

'Let's talk to the guy who's heading up the field op.' He pressed three buttons on the phone.

'Gerard, you're on loudspeaker so no swearing, there's a beautiful lady here. How are we doing?'

'We'll all be in Naples by eight tomorrow morning.' The intonation was northern English. He was precise and clipped. 'It's a four hour drive down to Calabria.'

Zan started scribbling furiously.

'Equipment?' she asked.

'Thirty bikes sourced and fuelled, five lorries sourced and fuelled, different logos on each lorry, two back-up cars sourced and fuelled, all have sat nav, weaponry in place, "O" phones in place, food ordered, clothing in place including bulletproof jackets and helmets. All we need are target details, together with photographs where possible.'

Mark looked across at me. 'We can get pictures from the Carta D'Identita, the Italian ID card, along with driving licences and passports.'

'Also security photos for Orlanda and the brewery workers,' interjected Zan. 'I can't guarantee one hundred per cent, but we won't be far off.'

'Do what you can, love.'

Zan grimaced, she hated being called 'love'. 'What happens after the event?' she asked.

'Five meeting places arranged. These are subject to review dependent on the density of target areas. Back-up cars centrally placed to pick up on any stragglers or unfinished business. Lorries head in different directions, Naples, Brindisi, Sicily, etc. Operators disappear in a variety of ways, using the back-up cars, trains, planes, buses, etc. All in place.'

'Passports?' I asked.

'Agents in place at relevant airports, ports, train stations and bus stations to hand over documentation. Five hundred euros per man emergency expenditure fund. Standard procedure.'

In other words, stop asking stupid questions, I'm a pro so leave it to me.

'Thanks, Gerard, we'll put target details on the "O" Cloud asap under "Op Calabria". I'll let you know when it's all in place. Good luck.'

'Speak soon.' With that he was gone.

'I have no concerns about Gerard,' said Mark. 'He's as good as you get.'

'It's astonishing how quickly he's put all this together,' I remarked.

'That's why I chose him. He bullies and cajoles until the job is done and he's a man with tremendous vision and experience. Right, let's focus on target details. The more information we have, the safer our men will be.'

Zan and I headed back to the meeting room. For the next four hours the six of us worked at checking and rechecking name and address details. Photographs were accessed from the various agencies and in total we found full information on forty seven of the fifty people.

Mark came to see how we were doing. 'Fantastic effort,' he said, looking genuinely pleased. 'If you'd have asked me, I would have guessed you'd find about thirty five, so well done.'

We loaded the information on to the "O" cloud in alphabetical order and geographically. Our work was done.

'We're rather like the directors of a theatre show,' mused Mark. 'We've chosen the play, the theatre, we've cast it, rehearsed it, the set's up and it's opening night tomorrow.'

'Let's hope the actors have learned their lines,' quipped Michelle.

'That's not the concern,' replied Mark. 'It's expecting the unexpected. Anything could happen and probably will. All we can do by planning in meticulous detail is minimise the risk. Let me buy you all a drink, you deserve it.'

We trooped into the living room where Heinrich was hovering. I collapsed onto a settee, suddenly feeling drained. It was just after nine, and we'd been at this for over thirteen hours non-stop. I ordered another whisky. The effect was almost immediate as I swallowed, having only had a ham roll all day.

'I'm buggered,' I said to no one in particular.

'You've not given yourself a chance to recover from your own ordeal,' responded Zan, coming to sit next to me.

'There'll be plenty of time for that after tomorrow. I wonder how Caterina's getting on?'

I looked across at Mark, who was chatting to Michelle and Ben. He again took out his phone and put it to his ear. The room fell silent. Although the others didn't know Caterina, they still cared. She was one of our own and had become a symbol of what this was all about.

'She's doing fine,' said Mark. 'She's in a controlled coma. which allows the body to switch off and focus on the healing process. If she remains stable then they'll start reducing the drug dosage in a couple of days. She's not through it yet. Cognitive impairment may follow recovery from the coma.'

'Brain damage,' said Zan, shaking her head.

'Too early to tell,' replied Mark. 'We've just got to keep hoping and praying for her.'

'Dinner is served in the dining room,' announced Heinrich. I really didn't feel like making polite conversation.

Mark was looking at me. 'I think you need to lie down. I'll have something sent up to you.'

'Do I look that bad?' I asked.

'Clear off' he said.

Chapter 24

I went up to my room, lay on the bed and fell immediately into a deep sleep. Later I became aware of Zan taking my clothes off. 'I think this is rape,' I murmured.

'Not tonight, my darling, just hold me.' The next thing I became aware of was an alarm going off. I looked at my watch. Seven o'clock. I'd slept for nearly ten hours.

Like Caterina's drug induced coma, the sleep had done me the world of good. For the first time since being kidnapped I felt something like my old self. Slapping Zan on the bottom, I said, 'Come on, things to do.'

'I take it you're feeling better,' she replied sleepily.

'Yup. I'm ready for action and need something to eat. Let's go.'

'What exactly will we be doing today?'

'No idea, but I don't want to miss it. Come on, into the shower.'

We caressed and held each other under the hot soapy water. Given what we had been through it was a beautiful experience and for the first time in days I felt life was worth living. We got down to the dining room just before eight and most of the others were already assembled. Breakfast was a buffet so I helped myself to bacon, scrambled eggs, English sausage and toast.

'You seem remarkably perky this morning,' said Michelle in her soft Canadian drawl.

'It's amazing what a good night's sleep does for you.'

Mark appeared. 'Where's Roger?' I asked.

'He's taken Chinetti and Manzoni to a safe house and then went down to Naples. He's part of that team.'

'What are we doing today?' asked Zan.

'You're all to stay here, helping me to oversee the operations we have under way. Anything could happen and we need to be able to move fast. That could mean offering support in the US, France, England, Switzerland or Italy. Heinrich has set up an ops room and we'll take things as they come. Be prepared for anything, from boredom to mass slaughter.'

I went cold as the image of John, Frank, Luigi, Habib and Caterina covered in blood came to mind.

'Alright,' said Mark. 'Follow me and let's get to work.'

He took us upstairs into a large room with a dozen desks. A laptop stood on each with telephone headsets, scrap pads, pens and pencils. It looked like a call centre I'd once worked at during a university vacation. There was a large TV screen on each wall, together with white boards, maps of the UK, Europe and the USA, and three clocks showing US, UK and Central European time. There were two coffeepots in the corner along with cups, milk, sugar and teaspoons. Heinrich was standing by one of the desks.

'Good morning,' he said. 'May I first show you how the phones work? Please sit down at one of the workstations and put on your headsets.'

Heinrich went through the system. It wasn't rocket science but we needed to be totally comfortable with the process. The phones were linked into the "O" system via the laptops. If any of the field operators used the video cameras on their 'O' phones, we could watch and listen to the action.

Mark walked to the front of the room. 'Each of you are the communications manager for a specific area. Jonathan, I want you to work with Gerard in Calabria. Heidi, you are responsible for the raid on Orlanda in Bologna, working with Hector. Tom, the UK, working with Thomas. Michelle, the US with Bruce. Heidi, France with Alain. Zan, Switzerland with Ferdi and the brewery raid in Calabria with Enrico. You'll find contact short codes on the "O" cloud.

'The raids across the Orlanda Group are to take place simultaneously at fifteen hundred hours Central European Time. That is nine hundred hours Eastern Standard Time in the States and fourteen hundred hours in the UK. Our people are working undercover as employees of the IRS in the States, National Crime Agency in the UK, Ministère de l'Économie et des Finances in France, the AISI in Italy and the Swiss Federal Tax Administration. The Guardia di Finanza, that's the Italian Customs Police, are also in place to raid a couple of ships in Brindisi and Bari, together with the brewery and Orlanda lorries. Gerard and his team will commence activities one hour later in Calabria. Their actions are to look like reprisals for the raids on Orlanda.

'Apart from the US, I'd ask you to touch base with your colleagues now. Michelle, can you speak to Bruce at about twelve thirty? Remember, you're not working in isolation. We are a team and if need be pull on each other, Heinrich or me. Any snippet of news, I need to know immediately. Zan and Jonathan, inevitably there will be interaction between the brewery raid and Gerard's op, so keep your eyes on any crossovers. Good luck and remember communication is key.'

I slipped the headphones over my ears and pressed the relevant buttons on the laptop. 'Morning, Gerard,' I said. 'It's Jonathan. I gather I'm your communications manager for the day.'

'Good. I gather you're quite useful,' came the terse response.

'One tries, sir, one tries. Can you give me an update as to where you are?'

'Yep. All five lorries are on the road, along with the cars, and we should be in situ by twelve thirty. The equipment and people are in place, it's now just a matter of waiting until we arrive, at which time all equipment will be rechecked. I've also sourced two further bikes as back up.'

'Is there anything I can do at this stage?'

'Just check all the target info on the "O" Cloud one more time. Ensure addresses are correct and match with photo ID and sat nav details. I'll phone if we need anything and keep you updated as the day progresses.'

'Will do, and good luck.'

'Thanks.' The line went dead.

I spent the next hour and a half checking and rechecking the target information on the system. Thank God I did, two of the pictures had been transposed. Again I realised the importance of being detail conscious. It was one slip like this that had cost Frank and John their lives.

I was somewhat frustrated at not being close to the action. Having been an integral part of the operation for so long, I felt almost cheated. It was as if Mark read my thoughts.

'No matter what op you're involved in,' he said, 'you can't be the hero all the time. Knowing when to delegate and to whom is more important than anything else you've been trained to do.'

He was right of course but I couldn't help feeling surplus to requirements.

'How are you getting on?' I asked Zan.

'I've spoken to Ferdi and Enrico, who seem well on top of things. There's very little more I can do at this stage.'

I poured coffee for everyone in the room. 'So much for being the master spy,' I joked.

I spent the rest of the morning going over the day's activities. I wrote in longhand every aspect of the plan that I could think of to see if we had missed anything. When I couldn't think of anything more I said to the others, 'I'd like to run through this just to see if there are any glaring omissions.'

For the next hour we looked at every strand we could think of to see if there were any facets we'd missed. Amazingly, only a couple of minor points came up.

'We're as ready as we're going to be,' I said. 'Good luck to us all.'

Heinrich appeared with a buffet lunch, sandwiches, quiche and chicken legs. I was too wound and ignored it.

'Here,' said Zan. 'You've got to eat, give yourself a chance.'

'Thanks, Mum,' I said.

She mouthed something derogatory, I half smiled.

Just after two, Gerard called. 'Right, we're in position and everything is in place. Unless we hear otherwise, it's go for sixteen hundred hours.' The others had similar calls from their field agents. Everyone was ready.

At three o'clock we sat in silence, staring at our laptops, waiting for news. The raids would now be happening and beyond our control. To use Mark's analogy, the actors were on stage and there was nothing we as directors could do. By half past three my nerves had been torn to shreds, we'd heard nothing and you could have heard a pin drop in the room.

'Can we get TV news on one of these screens?' I asked Heinrich.

He found a remote and Sky News UK appeared. I'd been out of touch for so long, it was quite interesting catching up. At about three forty five the newscaster said, 'We have some breaking news. We're hearing that the head office of the Orlanda Marble Group, based in Slough, together with the offices of their pub and hotel division have been raided by the National Crime Agency and HM Revenue and Customs. More news on that story when we get it.'

I turned to Mark, and he was smiling. 'We got the story out to the media to help the cause down in Calibria,' he said. 'It will give the ramifications more credibility.'

'Can we switch to Sky News Italia?' I asked.

The Orlanda logo appeared on screen together with that of the brewery. 'We are hearing that the Orlanda Marble head office in Bologna, together with the brewery company Birra Calabria, have been raided by the AISI and the Guardia di Finanza. We'll keep you up to date on that story.'

I translated for all to hear. 'Excellent,' said Mark. 'Update Gerard.'

I phoned immediately. 'Give it fifteen minutes for the news to sink in and we'll be off,' he said.

Calls started coming in, confirming the raids were taking place. The authorities in each country had taken charge and were confiscating computer systems, arresting senior management and interviewing everyone from the security guard upwards.

Zan looked up. 'Enrico confirms that a large amount of what is suspected to be heroin has been found at the brewery and on lorries waiting to depart.'

Everybody clapped. We were winning.

Tom piped up, 'It's the same thing in Slough, many arrests, apparently the area is in gridlock due to road closures by the police.'

'No change there then,' I said, laughing.

Bruce confirmed large amounts of what was suspected to be heroin had been found at the Orlanda buildings in New York and the US authorities had raided a ship being unloaded at the New York port, where marble slabs had been seized containing heroin and cocaine.

I put my head in my hands and then slowly looked up. Zan was staring at me. 'We've done it,' I said. 'We've bloody done it.'

She half smiled but there was sorrow in her eyes. 'Was it worth it?' she asked sadly.

The headphone bleeped in my ear. 'Gerard,' I said.

'Nine down, forty one to go.'

'Do you need anything?'

'No. I'll be in touch.' The line went dead as I relayed the news.

'How many do you expect them to get?' I asked Mark.

'Twenty will suffice, thirty would be superb. There isn't a hope in hell we'll get them all and that wasn't the plan, the plan is to rattle a few cages, they'll do the rest.'

Every half hour Gerard phoned with an update.

'Fifteen.'

'Twenty six.'

'Thirty one.'

'Thirty three.'

'It's slowing down, tell them to get out,' said Mark. 'That's an order, they've done their job.'

I relayed the information. 'Will do,' responded Gerard.

'Will he act the hero?' I asked.

'No,' responded Mark. 'He's too much of a pro. What they're doing is extremely dangerous, and he knows we've got the bigger picture back here. If we say get out, he'll get out.'

We sat pretty well in silence for the next hour or so. The suspense was dreadful, and we were powerless to do anything except wait.

Eventually the call came. 'Thirty eight is the final tally. All the team are back safely and we're out.' I relayed the news and the room erupted. Mark grabbed my headset. For the first time I heard real emotion in his voice.

'Gerard, superb news. Well done, my man, I knew I could rely on you.' He turned to us all. 'That's it, we've done it. This has been the biggest operation the Organisation has ever pulled off, and we've been incredibly successful. My dear friend Frank, as you knew him, would be so proud. Thank you, thank you, thank you, and a special thank you again to our fallen colleagues. Heinrich, a case of champagne please, my man. We deserve it.'

'Follow me, please,' Heinrich said and we all went back into the living room. Everyone was laughing and joking apart from Zan. She looked so sad.

'I can't do this anymore,' she whispered to me.

'We don't have to,' I said. 'It's job done and we can get out.'

She kissed me passionately. 'I hope so,' she said. 'I hope so.'

The champagne flowed that night but neither Zan nor I were up for a party. We chatted amiably but were looking for the first opportunity to leave. Mark came up to us. 'I realise this is bittersweet for you both but for what it's worth, you have done an incredible job. To have come straight out of training college and manage an operation like that is a great feat. Well done. We'll talk again in the morning.'

We nodded, made our excuses and went up to our room. I sat on the bed. I can't say I was tired, just numb. I certainly didn't have a feeling of euphoria over a job well done. I just felt a great deal of grief for losing John and Frank. I was in mourning, it was as simple as that. I said as much to Zan.

'We both are,' she replied, 'and there's nothing we can do. They say time is a great healer. I hope so, because at the moment I feel pretty raw.'

Chapter 25

We went to bed and I slept through to six forty five. I felt wide awake but Zan was still asleep. I got up, showered and dressed.

'You're early,' Zan said sleepily.

'I woke up. You have a lie in, I'm going for a walk.'

'Love you,' she said.

'I love you too. See you later.'

I went downstairs and as I was walking past Mark's office I heard him talking on the phone. He beckoned me in, so I sat opposite while he finished the call.

'Don't you ever sleep?' I asked as he hung up.

He smiled. 'Four hours does me, rather like your old Prime Minister, Margaret Thatcher.'

'What's happening?'

'The best news is that Caterina is responding well. Everything being even, she will recover. However it's too early to tell whether she'll suffer any brain damage.

'Thank God,' I said, shaking my head. 'Can we see her?'

'Could be difficult, best not. Hope you understand.' I didn't really, but I was prepared to let it go for the moment.

Mark went on. 'There's been absolute mayhem down in Calabria. War has broken out between the various strands of the Ndrangheta. From police reports, we believe well over two hundred people have been killed. Each side blaming the other. We lit the blue touch paper and they did the rest. Perfect.' He smiled. 'Your friend Jeff Andrews has agreed to help police with their enquiries, as the saying goes. He's a weak little louse who's now spilling the beans on all his compatriots. He'll get a reduced sentence but I doubt he'll live through it. The Ndrangheta will see to that. KPMG have been appointed as liquidators to the group. They hope to sell quite a few of the assets as going concerns. They're working on a vastly reduced fee as they're rather embarrassed about their involvement. Hopefully many of the jobs will be saved.' He paused. 'How do you feel?'

'I don't know. I'm not sure if this life is for me,' I responded. 'And I'm not talking out of turn when I say Zan feels the same way.'

'I expected that and do understand. If it's any consolation, I went through a similar thing just after I joined the Organisation. I felt very bitter at the time and thought that was it. However, I had a wonderful boss. You knew him as Frank. He said to me, "Take a break, dear boy. Have six months off, see the world. I'll keep you on full salary and then we can talk again. If you still want to leave, that's fine, no hard feelings. But if you decide to stay, I'd be delighted." I'm making the same offer to both you and Zan. I'll be quite honest, I don't want to lose either of you.'

'That's very generous, Mark, thank you. I'll talk it over with Zan and get back to you. Out of interest, what have you done with Chinetti and Manzoni?'

'I'm afraid they got caught up in the Calabrian war. And something else that will interest you, the bodies of Messrs Fei Wai and Sam Chuen have been found outside the building where the Italian Consulate is based in Hong Kong. Their hands and feet have been chopped off and a meat cleaver found between them. Triad experts tell us it's a message to say they are severing all ties with the Ndrangheta.'

'Are the Triads the next on the list?' I asked.

'No, it'll never happen. Even the Chinese government couldn't put them down when they were a communist regime. We can bruise them from time to time but nothing more. The world will never be perfect, Jonathan, all we can do is try to make it better than it currently is.'

'I take it you haven't got a problem if I phone Caroline?'

Mark thought for a second. 'No, that's fine. Tell her Caterina's been hurt but she should be OK and leave it at that. Don't mention Frank. She'll obviously know about Orlanda, it's the biggest news story of the year, but keep things vague.'

I chuckled. 'With everything that's been going on I haven't got a mobile.'

Mark smiled, taking one from a drawer. 'Here, use this. We'll sort out some ID for you as well. Stay here as long as you want and then go and have a holiday.'

I left him and went for a walk. The mountain air felt cool and refreshing. I found a track to stroll down, accessed the "O" Cloud on the phone and found Caroline's number. 'Hi,' I said.

'Oh my goodness,' she replied sleepily, 'the return of the prodigal. What time of day do you call this?'

'Sorry,' I said, realising it was seven o'clock UK time. 'How are you?'

'I'm fine. You've obviously been busy, judging by the news.'

'You could say that.'

'Are you OK?'

'Yeah, just a bit stressed. Josephina had an accident and was nearly killed, but it looks as if she's going to pull through.'

'Thank God! What happened?'

'I'd rather not go into it at the moment, but she'll be fine.'

'Can I see you?'

'That could be difficult for the time being, but I just wanted to make sure you're OK. The next time I'm in England I promise to take you somewhere special, and it won't be a grotty Italian in Slough.'

'A Big Mac would be nice.'

I laughed. 'You're a lovely person, speak soon.' I walked back to the house and up to the bedroom. Zan was sitting at the dressing table putting on makeup. I updated her on all the news.

'So what do you think?' she asked.

'We may as well take the six months' money,' I replied. 'It would be stupid not to.'

She nodded. 'Where do we go?'

'A south sea island, as we said. We'll become beach bums for a few months, take stock and find our own way forward.'

'Sounds fun.'

'You better believe it, baby.' I gave her a hug. 'Come on, let's go and find some breakfast. I'm starving.'

By the time we got downstairs only Tom was still around. The others had departed to who knows where and all he said was, 'I've got a flight booked for two o'clock this afternoon.' We wished him well and went into the dining room.

'There doesn't seem much point in hanging around here,' said Zan.

'No,' I responded. 'I suggest we say to Mark we'll take the sabbatical and clear off.'

Zan nodded. 'Free.'

'As a bird.'

A few minutes later Mark appeared and we told him the news.

'Good, I'm pleased you're not doing anything rash. I'll organise documentation. Where are you heading?'

'The south seas,' I responded.

'Excellent. Could I ask you to travel under separate cover and meet in Sydney? As usual, to reduce contagion. Zan, perhaps you could go overland to Paris and on to London. There's a direct train leaving Geneva at sixteen twenty nine this afternoon. Jonathan, perhaps you could fly from Dijon to Bordeaux and then train to Paris. It's a two and a half hour drive to Dijon and there's a flight at sixteen thirty. Heinrich will take you.'

Zan and I looked at each other and nodded.

'I'll be disappearing myself in a few minutes, so good luck. I'll keep in touch if I may, and update you on Caterina's progress.' With that, Mark shook me by the hand, gave Zan a hug and waved as he left the room. We sat back down and I sipped on a coffee.

'It's all broken up so quickly,' I said.

Zan nodded and stared out of the window. 'Was it worth it?' she said again.

'I don't know,' I responded. 'I don't know.'

After breakfast we went upstairs. A small travel bag had been packed for each of us.

'How much do you reckon they spend on clothes?' I asked.

Several newspapers had been put out. I spent half an hour flicking through them. Most of the stories on Orlanda were wildly inaccurate. Everything from the company going bust to it being another Polly Peck. They were looking for the Asil Nadir of the organisation. The misinformation department had done a great job. Slowly the truth would be revealed, without any mention of the Organisation's involvement.

At about twelve my phone rang. 'Jonathan, it's Heinrich. Can I go through the documentation I have for you?' We went downstairs to what had been Mark's office. Heinrich was sitting there with two piles of paper in front of him.

'Zan, you first,' he said. 'Passport and train tickets to London. You'll be met at St Pancras. Text this number when you're on the train from Paris. You'll be given another passport and flight ticket for Australia and taken to a hotel. Here's two thousand euros to keep you afloat, plus a couple of credit cards to add authenticity. You can use them in emergencies with your usual pin code.

'Jonathan, similar thing. French national ID card will take you to Paris. You'll be met at the Gare Montparnasse, transferred to a hotel and given another passport and flight ticket to Australia. Again, text this number when you're on the train at Bordeaux. Two thousand euros for you, as well as credit cards.

'You'll both be met in Sydney and taken to the same hotel, where for the final time you'll be given new ID. Then you're on your own. Do you think you can cope?' he asked, smiling.

'Just about,' I said.

'Jonathan, we leave at thirteen hundred hours. Zan, you'll be taken to the airport at fourteen fifteen.'

'As always, superb organisation,' remarked Zan.

Heinrich smiled, 'Would you like some lunch before you leave?' We both shook our heads, just wanting to get away to start our lives again. I stuffed the tickets and passport into a side compartment of the travel bag and slipped the money and cards into my trouser pocket.

'See you in a couple of days.'

'You know,' said Zan, 'a few weeks ago I'd have said all this changing of passports and contagion is nonsense. After what's happened, I wonder if it's enough.'

We sat chatting about where we could go and what we should do over the next few months. I got quite elated at the thought of island hopping and living in little shacks on the beach. It was like a dream coming true, but there was a tremendous feeling of guilt regarding the friends we were leaving behind. I actually got quite emotional and could feel tears yet again welling up in my eyes.

'Time,' said Zan. 'We have to give it time.' There was knock on the door.

'Jonathan, we need to go.' Heinrich took my case. 'The car is at the front of the house. I'll see you in a couple of minutes.'

The two of us stood up, the end of one chapter and the start of another. 'Safe journey,' I said. 'See you in Oz.' We held each other and kissed fervently.

As I walked to the door I heard, 'I love you Jonathan.' Zan ran to me and we kissed again.

'Come on,' I said. 'We'll be together again soon, forever.' She smiled through the tears as I left the room.

Chapter 26

I walked outside and Heinrich was sitting behind the wheel of an old BMW 5 series. Climbing in, I looked back at the house. Zan was nowhere to be seen.

'Don't worry,' said Heinrich. 'We'll look after her.'

'Will this old bus get us there?' I half joked.

'It's comfortable, reliable and doesn't attract attention,' came the simple response.

As we set off I became aware of the spectacular countryside. Vineyards dominated the area, with a backdrop of imposing mountain ranges. Beautiful castles and eye-catching farmhouses completed the idyllic setting. It seemed so incongruous after what we'd been through. We jumped on the A40 motorway, heading west towards Bourg-en-Bresse.

'Long way round,' I said.

'It's half an hour quicker staying with the autobahns,' replied Heinrich. 'Also I don't have to tackle the hairpin bends. I want to keep you safe.'

The engineering of the road astounded me. We climbed the mountain range and descended, frequently travelling over countless bridges and through numerous tunnels. Heinrich kept to the speed limit at all times. 'We don't want to raise attention by getting tickets,' he said.

At Bourg-en-Bresse I saw the Dijon sign and we headed north on the A40. Heinrich chatted amiably, but I wasn't really in the mood for conversation so I kept it to a minimum. By now the mountains had softened and we drove past picturesque vineyards stretching into the distance. As we approached the airport I could see a lot of building work being carried out.

'It's actually still a French air force base as well as a civil airport. They're expanding the passenger terminals and upgrading the runways,' explained Heinrich. He pulled into a car park, got out and took my suitcase from the boot. 'Good luck, my friend,' he said, shaking my hand.

I walked across to the main concourse feeling like a lost soul. *This should really be an exciting day*, I thought, *six months paid leave with the girl of my dreams*. Yet somehow I couldn't raise any enthusiasm. As I checked in there was little more than a cursory glance at my ID and I drifted through security, following signs for the gate. I felt jaded and began to realise just how much this experience had taken out of me, both physically and mentally.

We flew in a little Jetstream aircraft across to Bordeaux. The flight was busy and I was squeezed in a window seat next to an overweight middle-aged businessman. His sole intention appeared to be to knock back as much brandy as he could on the ninety minute flight. Rather than make conversation I closed my eyes for about half an hour and spent the rest of the trip gazing through the porthole. Fortunately the flight was on time and we were off the plane in a matter of minutes. Having no luggage to collect, I made my way to the taxi rank.

'How much to the train station?' I asked a guy beckoning taxis forward and putting luggage in the boot.

'About thirty euros.'

Half an hour later the taxi pulled up outside the train station. The driver said, 'Soixante euros.'

I threw thirty at him, saying, '*Va te faire foutre, ne prevez pas la pisse.*' *Fuck off, don't take the piss.* He sped away in high dudgeon, wheels squealing. *Another one who lost his tip, taxi drivers are the same the world over*, I thought!

By now it was just after seven and the next train was leaving at eighteen minutes past. The station had an old Victorian charm and there was a celebration of Gustav Eiffel as I walked through. He'd designed part of the station as well as the Eiffel Tower. Having never been to Bordeaux, I would have loved to look around the city. Instead I made my way to the platform where the train was waiting. It was a bright modern TGV which sped through the French countryside at over two hundred miles per hour. *A stark contrast to the garbage in my own country*, I thought. I sent the text as requested and sat gazing out of the window, taking little in. I felt content just to let the world pass me by. It was if my body was saying, 'Payback time. I'm now in relaxed mode and rebuilding my stamina.'

Just over three hours and three hundred and fifty miles later I was conscious of the lights of the Paris suburbs as we started to slow down. I climbed down from the train and sauntered up the platform, waiting for a contact.

'Jonathan,' I heard, 'follow me, please.'

I turned to see a serious looking man, probably in his mid-forties, wearing a trilby hat and looking a little nervous. We walked to the taxi rank, saying nothing. He said to the driver at the front of the line, 'Sheraton, Charles De Gaulle,' and we drove off. Handing me an envelope with the name Andrew Harrison typed on it, he whispered, 'French ID and credit cards.' I exchanged one for the other and slipped the envelope into my top pocket. No attempt at conversation was made and I didn't encourage it. At half past ten at night Paris was still busy but at least the traffic was flowing. The driver battled his way onto the route périphérique and we arrived at the hotel fifty minutes later. The contact shook me by the hand. 'Bon chance,' he said and disappeared into the airport complex.

I walked up to the reception. 'Good evening. I have a reservation in the name of Andrew Harrison.'

'Certainly, sir. Could I have a credit card for sundries and your passport?' I pulled out the envelope, praying there hadn't been a balls up. Sure enough, there was the passport and two credit cards. *How do they produce these things?* I asked myself for the umpteenth time, keying in my pin code.

'Could you send up a ham sandwich and fries please, as soon as possible?'

'No problem, sir, and to drink?'

'Just a beer would be fine.'

The hotel was clinically luxurious but I wasn't really concerned about the decor. I went straight to my room and phoned Zan. She picked up immediately. 'How are you?' I asked.

'Tired, but I think the question should be who are you? I'm losing track.'

'Thirty six hours and counting,' I said. 'And then we're together, forever. Love you and night night, whoever you are.'

'I love you too.'

I ate my sandwich drank the beer and then decided to raid the minibar. *Sod it,* I thought, *after what I've been through the Organisation owe me more than a couple of drinks in a hotel bedroom.* The prices were ludicrous and I grinned like a silly schoolboy as I helped myself to a half bottle of Cote du Plonk and a whisky miniature.

I looked at my flight details. Departure was at midday, with a three hour stopover in Singapore. I wasn't really looking forward to a twenty three hour journey, but at least the end was in sight and I could be with Zan. That was all I wanted.

Feeling slightly merry, I hit the sack and slept almost immediately. It was a deep sleep and when I woke the following morning I had a slight sense of panic. For one moment I thought I'd overslept and missed my flight. I relaxed. It was only eight thirty.

I knew I was recovering and felt like doing some exercise for the first time since I'd been kidnapped. The clever people at the Organisation had thoughtfully packed some shorts and a T-shirt so I went down to the fitness centre, did a few weights and jogged on a treadmill. Panting heavily within a matter of minutes, I was appalled at my lack of fitness and vowed to straighten myself out in the very near future. In the meantime I showered, dressed and had a cooked breakfast. *Training tomorrow,* I thought.

As the hotel was in the airport I checked out just before ten and made my way across to departures. I was flying Singapore Airlines, which pleased me. I'd been told they were the colour when other airlines were black and white so I was looking forward to trying them out.

I had the boarding pass and grimaced as I hit the security queue. Arriving airside forty minutes later, I felt pissed off as usual about the ridiculousness of it all. I'd done too much flying recently and promised myself that I would stay as far away from airports as possible once I reached the south seas.

The flight was great when compared to other airlines. I was escorted upstairs to business class which by most people's standards was better than first class. The food was to die for, from Eurasian cuisine at its absolute best to a magnificent English cream tea served on bone china, not the standard plastic container you get in cattle class. More quality films than I knew existed appeared on the screen in front of me and the service was impeccable. Beautifully dressed Asian girls looked after me in a manner I'd never really experienced. By the time we arrived at Singapore I was almost sorry to be getting off.

The flight had really lifted my spirits and I was beginning to feel positive about life again. During the three hour stopover at Changi I went to a diamond boutique and bought a magnificent ring, twelve diamonds surrounded a deep blue sapphire and costing more than anything I'd ever bought in my life. She was worth every penny, and I intended for it to last a long time.

For much of the second leg, I slept. The seat folded down to reveal a proper bed and since I'd been up for nineteen hours, sleep came easily. I was woken to a delightful breakfast of eggs, ham, cheese and coffee. The fact that it was evening in Australia seemed totally irrelevant. I felt remarkably refreshed and incredibly excited about seeing Zan again. Very shortly we'd be starting our life together.

The flight landed just before seven in the evening local time and much to my delight I soared through immigration. The staff were actually pleasant and I couldn't decide whether it was the mood I was in or their natural demeanour. At last I was in Australia and as the double doors opened to the outside world I saw the name Andrew Harrison being held up by a pretty brunette about my age. 'Hello,' I said, shaking her by the hand.

'Welcome to Australia.' As usual, no name was given.

'Thanks.'

'You must be bushed after that long flight?'

'Well, actually, no.' I explained about the sleep from Singapore. We walked to the taxi rank, where the queue stretched for about fifty yards.

'It's always like this, I'm afraid.'

'I'd hate to be here when it's busy.' Fortunately I felt quite relaxed. It was now eight o'clock local time and warm. I was beginning to feel as if I was on holiday. I knew Zan's flight was due to touch down at ten past so the chances of bumping into each other at the airport were minimal. I was prepared to play the contagion game through to the last moment. After what had happened there was no point being stupid about it. Twenty minutes later we clambered into a taxi.

'The Four Seasons,' my chaperone said to the driver.

'How far?' I asked.

'About half an hour. Here's your envelope.' This time it was addressed to Richard Harris.

'Shall we do swapsies?' She laughed as I gave her the passport and credit cards I'd been using since France.

'I bought rather a large item using the company's plastic I'm afraid, ask them to invoice me.'

'No probs. Anything nice?'

'Oh, yes,' I said, 'very nice indeed.'

She didn't pry, bless her. Something to do with being part of the Organisation, I assumed.

'You're booked in for three nights.'

'That's fine.' I didn't intend to stay that long, wanting out of civilisation as soon as possible. Seeing signs for Beaconsfield and the Surrey Hills made me smile. Although fiercely independent, Australia had so many strong links with the UK and could never escape its past. As we approached the city centre, skyscrapers came into view, giving a feel of Manhattan. Although it was dark, I was struck by the sense of wealth and grandeur. Initial impressions were of a very bright, vibrant and modern city.

We drew up in front of the hotel as a Rolls Royce pulled away. A doorman opened the car door and took my case. The Organisation were pampering us and we deserved it.

'Thanks for your help,' I said, shaking the hand of the unnamed lady.

'Enjoy your stay,' she shouted as the taxi drove away. At check-in, a sour-looking woman in a grey, sexless uniform gave me my room key.

'Can I help with your luggage sir?' asked a porter.

'I think I can manage.' We both chuckled, looking at the small travel bag sitting next to me. The room was delightful, overlooking the Opera House and the Harbour Bridge. I phoned Zan. 'Where are you?'

'Waiting for a taxi.' She sounded fed up. 'There's a queue half a mile long and we've been here ten minutes already.'

'Yep, been there.' I gave her my room number. 'See you in an hour or so.'

I had a shower and shave, changed and was admiring the view when there was knock on the door. Opening it was one of the happiest moments of my life. There stood Zan, suitcase in hand and smiling. Oh, that smile. It's something I'll never forget.

'Would you like to come in?' I asked formally, with a silly grin on my face.

'That would be nice,' she said, walking straight past me. I grabbed her and we kissed for several minutes. Our life together was finally complete.

'Let's have a shower,' she said. 'I feel dirty after travelling halfway around the world.'

'I've only just had one,' I teased.

'Well, you'd better have another, mister.' She ripped off my shirt.

A couple of hours later we lay naked on the bed, touching, caressing and kissing each other.

'Shall we go out?' I asked. 'I'm wide awake, in body time it's still morning.'

'What, you don't want me anymore?' she asked, wide-eyed with mock innocence.

'Oh yes, more than anything.' We kissed again.

'Where can we go?'

'I don't know. Let's have a stroll and a drink somewhere.'

'Sounds fun,' she said, jumping up. 'Let's go.'

'I've got something for you.'

She looked at me as I fished in my jacket pocket. Opening the little case I said, 'Zan, would you do me the honour of marrying me?'

Tears streamed down her face. 'Oh my darling, Jonathan, yes, yes, and yes again. I love you so much.' I put the ring on her finger, and she looked more beautiful than ever.

Chapter 27

We dressed quickly and headed down to reception where I changed some euros into Australian dollars. The exchange rate was lousy but I couldn't be bothered to argue. Zan was looking at the ring and smiling as I went across to the concierge. 'Is there anywhere nearby where we can go for a drink?'

'The Three Wise Monkeys is just down the road, sir. It's a pub on the ground floor, a bit more sophisticated on the next level and live music above that.'

'Sounds perfect.'

'Have a great night.'

We strolled in the warm evening air, holding each other tight.

'How do you feel?' I asked.

'Wonderful, but full of guilt. It's so incredible to be here, in the warmth with you, but I keep thinking…'

'I know,' I said. 'I feel exactly the same.'

We had a fantastic evening. Beer was the order of the day and we worked our way from bar to bar. The band was fantastic, playing every request thrown at them. We danced and drank and danced again. The place was packed and the atmosphere electric. We were almost disappointed when the music stopped and the place closed at four am.

'You're drunk,' Zan said in an accusing manner as we staggered back to the hotel.

'And you're not?' I slurred, holding onto her more for balance than anything else. My body clock was all over the place but we both slept that night. Truth be told, it was more of a drunken slumber than real sleep and I woke at about nine with my head throbbing. Zan was in the bathroom, throwing up.

'Have I got to face this every morning?' I growled.

'Shut up,' came the response. She stumbled back into the room looking awful.

'I take it a fry up is out of the question?'

A towel was thrown at me.

'Come on,' I said. 'Let's go and get some fresh air and look at Sydney.'

We spent the day seeing the sights, touring on an open-air double decker bus. In many ways it felt like our visit to Shanghai, which seemed an eternity ago. We saw Darling Harbour with its restaurants, bars and museums, the Rocks with its quaint buildings on the shore of the harbour, Chinatown, the Opera House, the Royal Botanic Gardens, Hyde Park, Kings Cross and Woolloomooloo. By the end of the day we were punch drunk but happy.

'That's Sydney,' I said.

'It'll do me,' replied Zan. 'Can we get out as soon as possible and find our south sea island?'

'Wonderful idea. Fiji?'

'Why not?'

We caught a cab back to the hotel and I went online looking for flights. After half an hour of surfing I turned to Zan. 'We can fly to Nadi in Fiji tomorrow at either six thirty or twelve fifty five.'

'Twelve fifty five,' replied Zan. 'Don't fancy getting up at four am. How long's the flight?'

'Three hours and fifty minutes.' She nodded so I pressed the relevant buttons on the keyboard, inputted my credit card details and scribbled down the booking reference.

'Here we go again,' I said. 'Another bloody aeroplane.'

'Last one for a while,' beamed Zan, kissing me on the neck.

'Where shall we go from Nadi?' I asked.

'Who cares? We'll book a small hotel and find out what's what.'

That night we went for a stroll and found a small but charming Italian restaurant. Chatting to the owner, it transpired that he was second generation Australian who'd never been to Italy and had no intention of doing so.

'What do I want to go there for?' he joked. 'There's plenty of us over here.'

We ate beautiful prawns and home-made pasta, as good as any I'd ever had. After the night before we drank water but the two of us were relaxing down. I felt fully fit again and Zan seemed much more at ease than she had been in recent days.

On the way back to the hotel, Mark phoned. 'Caterina is pulling through. She's regained consciousness but has a little paralysis on her right side. The doctors are hopeful that with therapy she will make a full recovery. She'll be flown home when she's fit enough, hopefully within a couple of weeks.'

'Can we see her?' I asked.

'In good time, but I'll send her your best wishes.'

I didn't sleep well that night. Something to do with jetlag and the events of the last few weeks. At one point I woke in a cold sweat, having dreamed about the shooting in Italy. This time I saw Zan falling in a trail of bullets.

'It's okay,' she said, 'I'm here,' and held me as I drifted off.

The following morning we got a cab to the airport. Check-in, security and walking to the gate was as interesting as ever.

'I don't want to fly again for a long time,' I said, strapping myself in. 'I seem to have spent my whole damn life queuing for security and sitting on planes.'

'Let's find that shack on the beach and chill.'

I picked up the in-house magazine and idly flicked through it. 'Well, well,' I said. 'Look at this.' There was an advert for Bounty Island, one of the Mamanuca group just off the coast of Fiji. The blurb read, 'Thirty minutes by ferry from Port Denarau Marina, an island paradise where you can stay in a beautiful bure, twenty feet from the clear blue sea and watch glorious sunsets.' There was a picture of a beach chalet by the ocean.

'This is too good to be true,' said Zan. 'They're probably full.'

I kept looking at the advert, hardly believing my eyes. I felt as if we had really found our island paradise. I was so excited I could hardly contain myself during the flight and kept walking up and down the aisle to control my fidgeting.

'Is this for real?' I asked a stewardess as she walked past.

'Oh yes, we have quite a few of those scattered across the islands.'

As we landed I was phoning the number. 'You're supposed to wait until the plane stops,' said Zan, grinning. I put my tongue out at her.

'Do you have a bure available for two people tonight?'

'For how long, sir?'

'Let's say a week for starters.'

'One second... No problem, one hundred Fijian dollars per person per night for bed, breakfast and evening meal.'

'That's fine.' About seventy five pounds, a hell of a lot less than I was expecting to pay.

'Where are you now?'

'Nadi Airport.'

'Get a cab down to Port Denarau Marina. It should take about twenty five minutes, and don't pay more than thirty dollars. We'll meet you there.'

I gave my name and card details as we disembarked. The airport was bigger than I expected, single storey, busy and efficient. The immigration officers smiled as we passed through welcoming us to Fiji. I found a cashpoint for local currency just beyond customs and walked up to the taxi rank.

'How much to Port Denarau Marina?'

'Sixty dollars, sir.'

'Twenty five.'

'Forty.'

'We'll catch the bus, don't worry.'

'Thirty.' We climbed in.

'Is there a bus?' asked Zan.

'No idea,' I responded.

'You're a hard man.'

'I need all the money I have for a very expensive woman who's going to become my wife.' She laughed and put her arm around me as we drove off. I could see a large mountain range to the east but we headed west, passing sugar cane plantations and the inevitable palm trees. Already I felt as if we were in a tropical paradise.

Port Denarau Marina had a laid-back feel to it, with shops, bars and restaurants scattered around the quay. A market seemed to be doing good business with a mixture of locals and tourists. The port was larger than it appeared in the brochures and a cruise ship dominated the view, lying at anchor in the middle of the harbour. Boats of all shapes and sizes bobbed up and down in the water, parked cheek by jowl around the marina. As we got out of the taxi, an Asian-looking man came up to us.

'Mr Harris?' I nodded. 'Welcome to Bounty Island. I am Abdul. Let me take your bags and follow me, please.'

We were taken along the jetty to an old boat with a dozen seats and a rickety canopy. Climbing aboard, a young lad steered as Abdul cast off. The sway of the boat felt very therapeutic and with the sun shining I began to feel rather good.

'We're really in the south seas,' I said disbelievingly. Zan kissed me. 'You can do that again,' I said, feeling a slight stirring.

'Later.'

In less than half an hour we waded ashore onto the island with trousers rolled up. Abdul followed with our socks, shoes and suitcases. The sea was so warm and the sand a brilliant white. We just smiled. We were simply in heaven. Several single storey buildings, each with a high green roof, housed the bar, restaurant and reception. There were no doors or windows, just a gentle breeze blowing gently across the tables and chairs. This was a million miles from the glitz of Sydney, and there was real sense of simplicity. Everybody smiled and life looked effortless. All the locals wore brightly coloured shirts and shorts, which looked particularly stupid on the American tourists who tried to emulate them.

We walked up to the reception building and while signing in were handed a delicious tropical orange drink. I was in love with this place already and knew it could only get better. A little Fijian boy took us to our bure. Tears started rolling down my face as I looked at it. We were in paradise. The bure was a simple beach chalet, with a bed, fridge, dressing table, hanging space and bathroom. That was it, and ten paces on, past the hammock, there was the sea, deep blue with a slight whisper as the gentlest of waves rolled onto the shoreline. I gave the boy an Australian five dollar bill.

'Thank you very much, sir,' he said, smiling from ear to ear.

'You look after us, OK?'

'Yes, sir, thank you, sir.' And with that he ran off.

'What are you?' asked Zan. 'The last of the Raj?'

'Of course,' I replied. 'That's why I must have my little Chinese courtesan!'

She put her middle finger up, and I blew a kiss.

We changed and ran into the sea, spending most of the afternoon swimming, sunbathing and just having fun. That's how it was for the next week. We'd eat at the restaurant, on a table with bench seats. Often we'd share it with others, mainly backpackers or retired people. There were no tablecloths and the food was at best basic, but we didn't care about that. Every night the waiters and bar staff formed a band and sang. We spent the days snorkeling, walking or jogging around the island. In the evening we'd read trashy novels borrowed from a library in the reception. There was something magical about lying on a hammock with the sea lapping at your feet, reading a well-leafed paperback.

We'd gotten to day six and as I woke Zan was looking at me. 'Shall we stay a little longer?'

'How about a lifetime?' I replied sleepily.

'I'll go and book another couple of weeks.'

I loved the way she took control. She got up, put on shorts and T-shirt and disappeared through the door. I climbed out of bed and was just getting dressed when I heard in Italian, 'Well, well, if it isn't Dean Farlow.'

I turned and froze. Signore Aggressor stood at the door, holding a pistol. I remembered Chinetti's words. 'They always find you.'

'You look surprised to see me,' he snarled. 'Been having a good time?' At that moment Zan returned, looking ashen. She was followed by the warehouse man from Slough, also holding a pistol. 'Well, this is nice,' said Signore Aggressor in English. 'It's taken a while, but here we all are together. Now, what are we going to do with you two?'

Zan and I looked at each other, saying nothing.

'Cat got your tongue?' sneered the English warehouse man. 'Sit down on the bed, the two of you.'

We obeyed. 'How did you find us?' I asked, trying to give myself thinking time.

'It was just a matter of piecing things together,' replied the warehouse man, clearly proud of what they had achieved. 'You were obviously involved,' he said, looking at me, 'but we thought we'd got rid of you in Forlì. You gave us the clue,' he said, turning to Zan. 'We checked the security tapes of the house where Chinetti interviewed your boyfriend and guess what? A little Chinese girl was seen crawling around the garden. That triggered bells in Luigi's mind.' He looked over at Signore Aggressor, who continued.

'I remembered a Chinese girl being with the accountants who came to look at our books in Bologna. Again, we checked the CCTV and, goodness me, a perfect match.'

'I'll be quite honest,' said the warehouse man, 'we had no idea who you were or where you were from. The only pieces of the jigsaw that matched were you two. Knowing that our people in Forli had been wiped out I asked the question, could Dean Farlow still be alive? Then the longshot, we asked our people around the world to keep their eyes open for a pretty Chinese girl travelling with an Englishman who speaks Italian. You have to remember the Ndrangheta is a large organisation, with fingers in many pies and contacts globally. We pay well for information from many different sources. That's what keeps us ahead of the game.'

'Most of the time,' I interjected.

'Don't be a smart ass,' the warehouse man retorted viciously. He went on. 'We were lucky. Did you enjoy your Italian in Sydney?'

I just glared at him, shaking my head. 'It was so kind of you to say you were flying to Fiji, you made our lives very easy. Once here, it's amazing what information twenty US dollars will buy.'

'So now what?' I asked.

'We could kill you,' said Signore Aggressor.

'But we don't want to do that,' the warehouse man continued smugly. 'One simple question and you'll live.' He paused. 'Who are you working for?'

I didn't have a clue what to do. With two pistols pointing at us, I just sat looking dumbly at the two of them. After what seemed like forever but in truth just a few seconds the warehouse man spoke again.

'Maybe it's time to loosen your tongue. I'll ask you once more, who are you working for?' With no reply, I heard the gun fire and an excruciating pain shot up my leg. I'd been hit in the foot and as the blood spurted I collapsed onto the floor, screaming in agony.

'The next bullet is for the young lady,' said Signore Aggressor, smirking. 'Now answer the question.'

'You are way out of your depth,' replied Zan, quietly but with full control.

'What the fuck are you talking about?' screamed the warehouse man. Zan stared at me with a strange look in her eyes.

'It's over,' she said simply. Glancing across at the warehouse man she said, 'I suggest you contact De Felice at the Crimine O Provincia, he'll vouch for us.'

They just stood staring at her. My leg was throbbing like hell as I tried to make sense of what was going on. I held it tight, the grip acting like a tourniquet.

'Do it now, because if I die you stand no chance.'

'Don't give me shit,' said the warehouse man. He started to raise his pistol. Everything then happened so quickly. Zan sprang at him and pushed his gun to one side. The weapon fell to the floor and skittlled across the room towards me. Rolling over, I grabbed it and heard a shot. I fired at Signore Aggressor first and then the warehouse man. Zan was on her knees with her back to me.

I crawled over. Her T-shirt was covered in blood. As I put my arms around her I asked, 'Who are you?'

'I'm sorry,' she croaked. 'But I do love you, and that's why I wanted so desperately to get out.'

'But who are you?' I screamed.

She looked at me with terror in her eyes. 'The Triads aren't all bad people,' she said. 'We have kept many communities alive during the communist regime in China and were instrumental in turning it back into a capitalist state. We had to finance our existence. That's where the exportation of narcotics came in. I joined the Organisation to ensure our survival, we needed to know whether you had any designs on us. As long as I was fighting battles that didn't impinge on my people, I was to give the Organisation full commitment, and I did. But I fell in love. Bad mistake.'

She looked at me and half smiled. 'It might sound strange,' she said, 'but we have been on the same side, I promise you. Whatever has happened, be it Frank and John's death, Caterina, your kidnapping, they were nothing to do with me.'

'But the drugs and the money laundering,' I said. 'You knew all about them from the start.'

'Not all. I knew we shipped them across to Europe, but I knew nothing about Orlanda.'

'Where does De Felice fit in?' I asked.

'He's now director of operations for the Ndrangheta.'

'The top man,' I muttered.

'After the Calabrian war, the operation was in turmoil. We took control last week and put De Felice in charge. He's our man.'

'How?'

'Money talks.' She was getting weaker. I was losing her.

'Why are you telling me this?'

'Because I love you.' By now she was speaking in barely a whisper, but she went on. 'I hoped that we could spend a lifetime together. Don't hate me, please.'

Squeezing my arm, blood trickled from her mouth. She went limp and her eyes glazed over. She was dead.

I remembered her words. 'Was it worth it?'

Holding her, I just cried, and cried, and cried.

Printed in Great Britain
by Amazon